THE WIDOW GINGER

Meet again the colourful characters from Not All Tarts Are Apple...

It is 1954, and Rosie and her beloved Auntie Maggie are opening up their café in Old Compton Street when the Widow Ginger comes to call. An ex-GI with ice-cold eyes, the Widow Ginger has unfinished business with Uncle Bert – business which involves a lorry-load of guns and explosives 'liberated' during the war. Meanwhile, the lovely Luigi is suffering from unrequited lust, Bert and the local Mafioso Maltese Joe have an acrimonious falling-out and, most worrying of all, Rosie's best friend Jenny has begun to keel over in the school playground.

THE WIDOW GINGER

THE WIDOW GINGER

by

Pip Granger

Magna Large Print Books
Long Preston, North Yorkshire,
BD23 4ND, England.

British Library Cataloguing in Publication Data.

Granger, Pip
    The Widow Ginger.

    A catalogue record of this book is
    available from the British Library

    ISBN   0-7505-2095-7

First published in Great Britain in 2003 by Corgi

Copyright © Pip Granger 2003

Cover illustration © Gordon Crabb by arrangement with
Alison Eldred

The right of Pip Granger to be identified as the author of this
work has been asserted in accordance with sections 77 and 78 of
the Copyright, Designs and Patents Act, 1988

Published in Large Print 2003 by arrangement with
Transworld Publishers

F LP
1510450

Magna Large Print is an imprint of Library Magna Books Ltd.

Printed and bound in Great Britain by
T.J. (International) Ltd., Cornwall, PL28 8RW

In loving memory of my father, 'Cliff'
and our beloved Sally

Acknowledgements

Many thanks to
Ray, for his help and support
Selina Walker for a wonderful edit
The late Fred Potter for the phrase
'The Widow Ginger'
Jane Conway-Gordon for being my agent
Linda, Judith, Lizzy, Deborah, Kate, Prue,
Helen and all the behind the sceners at
Transworld who make books happen.

1

It wasn't my fault, honest; none of it. According to my uncle Bert, keeping your gob shut is the very best thing, but failing that, sticking to your story is the next best. Of course, that's the advice he doled out to the punters who found themselves in trouble with the coppers or the military police. Me, I was supposed to own up, tell the truth and take the consequences like his 'brave little soldier'. Which I mostly did. But what are you supposed to do when you're not sure what the truth is? Or when you do know, but telling it could get someone you love into lots and lots of trouble?

And there's another thing: why is there one set of rules for grown-ups and a completely different set for the nippers? I really would like to know because it never felt fair to me and still doesn't. But all Auntie Maggie and Uncle Bert would say when I asked them is that life isn't fair. Now what kind of answer is that? Still, I'd better start right at the beginning and not get stuck in to what is and isn't fair. I could go on for ever about that.

It started one Saturday morning in March, 1954, with a thundering on the cafe door. It must have been really early, because even Auntie Maggie and Uncle Bert weren't up yet and the work in our cafe starts about six. Usually, banging on the door at strange times of day or night meant that my mum had been on a bender with one of her blokes and was in need of more money to carry on, or was in trouble, or simply felt like visiting and was too Brahms and Liszt to realize that sparrowfart was not the time to do it. But my mum was safely tucked up in a clinic again, where they lock 'em in, so I knew it couldn't have been her — unless she'd escaped.

The thought that she might have legged it was what got me across my bedroom with my lug to the door in the first place. I was there almost before I heard Uncle Bert's muttered curses as he creaked down the stairs. I heard him say, 'Bleeding 'ell, Sugar Plum, what time do you call this?' and then, 'Hang on a tick while I get this door open.' By this time, my auntie Maggie had heaved herself out of bed and was trundling down the stairs herself. That meant it would soon be safe to take up my usual listening post just behind the door that shut the cafe off from our private bit. It was a good spot because I could usually get out of the way and back to my room in very swift order and

I could see and hear almost everything from there.

Anyway, it was Sugar Plum all right. He must have come straight from work because he was twinkling like a Christmas tree as the lights across the road reflected off the three million sequins on his floor-length dress. I knew it was three million because he'd told me that he and Alma Cogan's mum had spent weeks sewing them on. He was holding his silver high heels in his hand and I could see that his stockings were in tatters and his feet were grubby from the wet pavements. He obviously hadn't even had time to remove his make-up and false eyelashes, but he had got rid of the lovely blonde wig that made him look a bit like Marilyn Monroe. His long, dangly diamond earrings looked funny with his short back and sides. He parked his glinting buttocks on the edge of one of the tables and fought to get enough breath to speak.

'It's Bandy, Bert. She says to come to the club straight away. The Widow Ginger's just blown in and is being what you might call quietly menacing.'

Now, I don't think I had ever seen my uncle Bert stuck for words or even surprised before. Let's face it, if you were born and bred in the very heart of Soho, it's difficult to think of anything that would come as a shock, but the words 'Widow Ginger' obviously did, because he and Auntie Maggie couldn't have looked more stunned if Sugar Plum had sprouted wings and started whizzing around the cafe, dive-bombing them as he went.

Uncle Bert finally found his voice. 'I thought we were shot of him when he was incarcerated by the Yanks. What's brought him back?'

'I dunno, Bert. He says they slung him out of the military when he'd done his bird. Must've been something a bit weighty if even that bunch wouldn't keep him. I mean he *wanted* to stay and, normally, having a heartbeat is the only requirement. He's not saying a lot, just sitting there looking around like he's totting up what fixtures and fittings might fetch down the auctions. It's best you get round there and see what's what. Bandy says I can stay here and help Maggie get started, if you want. Truth to tell, I don't like the way that bleeder looks at me, so I'd rather stay if it's all right with you.' He waved a bag about in the air. 'I've brought me mufti, so's not to excite the punters. Can I nip upstairs and wash and change?'

That was my cue to get back to my room, so I went. The next time I saw Sugar he was eating a bit of toast in our kitchen and was dressed in sensible shoes, neatly pressed trousers, immaculate white shirt and a perfectly knotted, striped tie. You'd never

16

guess that the vision in sequins and this soberly dressed man were the same person, and in a way I suppose they weren't. Sugar explained to me once that he felt like two people living in the one skin, and that's why he liked to wear dresses sometimes.

It was lucky that he lived and worked with Bandy at the club, because neither she nor the punters cared what he wore. I didn't like to tell him that I did care, but I always thought he looked better when he sparkled. I didn't want to hurt his feelings because I had decided to marry Sugar when I grew up, so he could make me some lovely dresses.

2

I suppose I'd better explain a bit about our set-up. I had lived with my auntie Maggie and uncle Bert in a cafe in Old Compton Street since I was a dot small enough to fit comfortably into a sideboard drawer. They're not my real aunt and uncle, but that's what I got used to calling them over the years. One story says that my real mum chose them to look after me because she realized that she couldn't do it herself. Another story says she nipped into the cafe one day to borrow a few quid and somehow managed to leave without me. I expect it was a bit of both, as my auntie Maggie always said. Either way, it was all official by then; I was properly adopted with the papers and everything. Which was good, because I loved my auntie Maggie and uncle Bert and I wouldn't have swapped living at the cafe for anything. I was coming up for nine when this Widow Ginger person crashed into our lives.

Bandy Bunyan's drinking club was just round the corner, down an alley that you wouldn't notice unless you were looking for it. According to my auntie Maggie – and she should have known because she knew everything and everybody in our patch of Soho, and every other patch come to that – Bandy and Sugar had been a team for years.

The pair of them had shared the flat above the club ever since it opened up for business right after the war. Sugar served the drinks and Bandy pulled in the punters by sitting in her favourite spot, drinking Gordon's gin, smoking Passing Clouds and insulting her paying customers in a rich, dark brown voice and ripe language. She always dressed in flowing silk pyjama-type garments, designed and made by Sugar, in an assortment of glowing colours. They hung in just the right way to soften Bandy's bony edges.

How Sugar got the silk from the Chinese

in Gerrard Street nobody knew, because hardly anyone could get even a nod and a wink off them in the normal way. The Chinese preferred to stick to themselves mostly, except for Mrs Wong who helped out at the cafe. Even she hardly ever said anything to anyone, and she rarely smiled either, although I swear she twinkled at me sometimes.

Nobody knew where Bandy came from, because she wouldn't tell anyone and I mean *anyone*, not even Sugar. She had just turned up one day, the way people do in Soho, and never left. Well, almost never; she did move a couple of miles away in the war to do her bit, whatever that was. You could never be sure with Bandy, or so Auntie Maggie said.

Mind you, being secretive about your life past or present was not at all unusual around our way. Miss Welbeloved (who wasn't) used to tell the kids in her class at school that Soho had been a bolt-hole for the wanted and unwanted of Europe for centuries. Miss Welbeloved, strict, plain and ancient, belonged with the unwanted ones, at least as far as our school was concerned. She had been there *for ever*, terrorizing several generations of local kids, and was still treated with respect by the most hardened of bruisers.

Still, Bandy was a woman of mystery. For

19

instance, I never understood why she was called Bandy, because her legs were as straight as mine, but that's what she answered to. What's more, she didn't pay any protection money to anyone. Uncle Bert said it was because she was well able to look after herself and that it took a brave man or woman to take her on. Everyone knew that she could flay you alive with her tongue and anything else she happened to have about her person. Many's the drunk who found himself lying on the pavement in the early hours with only the haziest of notions as to how he had managed to escape with everything intact. But Auntie Maggie said it was because Bandy did someone an enormous favour once, and she'd never needed any protection since.

Uncle Bert said he thought it was one of the great mysteries of life why anyone would actually *choose* to drink at Bandy's place when she insulted them the way she did, but they seemed to love her being rude to them. People actually begged to be allowed to join her club and carried on begging year after year. Members said it was the way she spoke to them that was so wonderful, but I couldn't really understand that any more than Uncle Bert could. If we treated our punters like that the cafe would be empty toot sweet. He put it down to the fact that Bandy's lot imbibed plenty of strong drink, which addled their brains, whereas ours only got tea, which didn't. Still, as he also said, Bandy and Sugar made a bloody good living out of her foul mouth, so they were obviously doing something right.

Sugar was another mystery person. He said he came from Ireland originally, but his accent was pure London, so he must have been young when he crossed the Irish Sea. He found Soho when he was still at school and ran away from his family to 'come home' as he put it. What I think he meant is that his original home, wherever that was, couldn't or wouldn't get used to his dresses, whereas some of the clubs and theatres of Soho would and did. Nobody ever bothered to search for him. Or if they did, they didn't think to look in the obvious place. Sugar felt it was probably a relief for them to get shot of him but I couldn't see why; Sugar was just lovely and made gorgeous frocks and silk pyjamas.

Anyway, Sugar was in Auntie Maggie's spot behind the counter that morning, and Auntie Maggie was in Uncle Bert's kitchen doing the cooking. According to Uncle Bert, Saturday mornings were always busy in the cafe because on Friday nights the punters came to Soho to spend their wages in the local pubs and clubs, and come the morning they needed a nice cup of tea and a fry-up to help them line up behind their

21

eyes. That's if they had got any money left after the dedicated local professionals had done their very best to relieve them of it.

Still, our customers were a varied lot. The Saturday morning mob were mostly strangers, although some turned up *every* Saturday, regular as clockwork. Then there were our proper regulars who came in every day, at least once, even when we weren't open. Luigi Campanini was one of these.

I was hovering near the corner table, the one reserved for us and anyone else who could be called 'family', when Luigi showed up. Family to us meant anyone we liked enough to include, and Luigi was very definitely one of those. He belonged next door but one in the delicatessen run by Mamma and Papa Campanini and their huge tribe of sons, daughters, grandchildren and in-laws.

Luigi was Mamma's baby, and he came in early most mornings, not having been to bed the night before. Mamma would turn the lock on him in an effort to get him to mend his wicked ways, but it didn't work. He just found somewhere else to sleep and went to Confession on Saturdays. That way, he said, he started his weekend on the tiles with a clean slate. Personally, I couldn't see what slates and tiles had to do with anything except building houses and as far as I knew, Luigi had never built anything, except mashed potato mountains on his dinner plate. Auntie Maggie said he was young and sowing his wild oats but I was pretty sure oats had nothing to do with it either and that he was just hanging about with his mates in the spielers, or canoodling with one of his many girlfriends. He did a lot of that on account of being gorgeous. He had flashing brown eyes, sparkling white teeth and a glossy black barnet all set off by a lovely olive skin free of even a single pimple. Anyway, Luigi was the first of our regulars in that morning.

'Morning, Shoog. How's the angle of your dangle?'

'Perfect, thanks, Luigi. What's your pleasure, young sir?'

'I don't think I'll say in front of young Shorty here' – that was me – 'but a cuppa will do nicely for now, ta. What are you doing here all dolled up in a tie and everything? Bandy slung you out, has she?'

Sugar looked carefully around, checking out the punters to see who was earwigging – besides me, that is; everybody knew my lugs were always flapping up a storm. He inclined his head, inviting Luigi to lean in a little closer, and mouthed in his ear, 'It's the Widow Ginger. He's back, and round at the club. Bandy sent for Bert to help her decide what to do. You never know, we may get shot of him before anything really nasty happens.

But I doubt it somehow. Something tells me that the brown stuff's about to hit the proverbial. The Widow's bad enough on his own, but mix him with Maltese Joe and you've got all the makings of World War III. I reckon that round about now would be a bloody good time to take a holiday, but of course we can't leave the club–'

'Hang about, Shoog. Who is this Widow Ginger? A bloke, is it?'

'Sorry, Luigi. I s'pose you're a bit young to remember him. His name's Stanley something or other – he has one of those foreign-type surnames full of js and zs that I can't get me mouth round. He was in business with Bandy, Maltese Joe and Bert during the war. Army surplus you might call it, only it wasn't quite surplus when they got their mitts on it, if you catch my drift. He's a Yank, came over with their military. According to Bandy, he can be a merciless sod, which is why everyone's underwear's in a bit of a tangle now he's resurfaced. Mind you, I don't s'pose I know the half of it. Bandy's not exactly forthcoming when it comes to the gory details, as you well know.'

Sugar paused for breath and I noticed the cup rattled loudly against its saucer as he handed Luigi his tea across the counter. Sugar was seriously worried, I could tell, and he deliberately changed the subject. 'Now, did I hear you'd got yourself a job, or was I dreaming? Sit down, why don't you, and I'll join you while it's quiet.'

I sort of slid into a seat at the table with Sugar and Luigi, which is how I came to hear that Luigi was finally working after a time of what Uncle Bert called 'creative lolling'. Normally, a Campanini would wind up working in the deli, but Luigi had never been keen and there was no shortage of labour among their mob. He took a gulp of his tea, leaned back in his seat and smacked his lips appreciatively. 'Your tea's almost as good as Maggie's, Shoog, and that's saying something. As it happens, I am a working man nowadays, yes. I'm running for Tic-Tac and doing very nicely so far, thanks very much. As my old papa always says, "Thees ees when you see the Italian at his best, when he is rrronning!"' Luigi's impression of Papa included full eye rolling and arm waving, as well as his thick accent. 'And of course, he ain't wrong, 'specially if the running is away from the men in blue and towards a thumping good wodge of dosh. With my mates and contacts, I'm not short of punters, and Tic-Tac's passed on his regulars an' all. He's given me a cut of the takings, so it's turned out sweet.'

'That would explain why you've not been to our place in a while. I s'pose you're hanging about at Running Jack's.'

Running Jack's was a drinking club

handily situated near the post office, which had a row of telephone boxes right outside. The runners, armed with a ton and a half of pennies, would be in and out of those boxes 'like farts in a colander', as Madame Zelda kept saying, despite Auntie Maggie's pleas that she shouldn't say it in front of me. The runners telephoned the bets through to their bookies before the race and then would call up again to get the results. Of course, in those days there was no such thing as a betting shop; people had to go to the track to put a bet on a horse. As only the rich and idle could make a regular habit of going to the races, the rest had to rely on bookies' runners to place their bets for them and sometimes to dole out their winnings when they got lucky.

To be a successful runner, you needed four things: a good memory, good legs, good contacts on the street and in the cop shop and plenty of pockets for stuffing betting slips, coins and crumpled notes into. Luckily, our Luigi was well qualified on all counts.

The large figure of Auntie Maggie came out of the kitchen at that point and stopped just long enough behind the counter to pour another cuppa before joining us at the corner table. The cafe wouldn't get really lively again until dinner time. The chicken and ham pies were made and only needed cooking, and the beef and carrot casserole was already in the oven waiting for the rush. She lowered herself carefully on to a seat, on account of not being built for flinging herself about in an unladylike fashion.

Auntie Maggie's lap was as soft and comforting as a large armchair, and despite being far too old I climbed into it. To be honest, talk of this Widow Ginger bloke had put the wind up me, especially after what had happened to me the year before. I really needed Auntie Maggie's reassuring cuddle. Her plump arms wrapped themselves around me and I snuggled for all I was worth into her mighty bosom. She smelt of soap, Yardley's face powder and just a dab of 4711 cologne behind each ear and down her cleavage, so that when she got warm the scent sort of wafted upwards and she got a whiff. She said it made a nice change from the smell of fry-up. She took a sip of tea, being careful not to tip it on my head, which was in the way.

'You look half dead, Sugar. Even the bags under your eyes have got luggage. Surely there's only so much daylight you can stand? Hadn't you better get your head down for a bit before you turn into something?' Auntie Maggie had given Sugar the once-over as she came across to our table.

'She's right, Shoog. You look as if the cat's had you on the landing two or three times in

27

the night,' Luigi observed.

'That's just how it feels, Luigi, only we haven't got a mog. No, it's wondering what that Stanley's up to and how Bandy and Bert are faring, that's what's doing me in. I'm better off keeping busy.'

I didn't dare move. I didn't dare *breathe* in case I was sent away, just as things looked as if they might get interesting. Whenever the grown-up talk looked like turning really juicy, my beloved auntie Maggie would shoot the talker her 'stop right there' look, which made them act like goldfish at feeding time, mouths wide open but not a word coming out, until she'd dealt with me. She'd send me to do something like muck out my bedroom or fiddle with the jigsaw puzzle that lurked beneath the plush tablecloth in the front room. It was kept there for those moments when I was whining that I was bored and by some miracle my bedroom had passed muster. 'How about that jigsaw?' she'd say, and I'd know I was about to miss all the really tasty bits of gossip yet again. But not this time. I was like a statue willing the talk to continue, and it did.

Sugar's voice grew quieter as he spoke and I had to strain to hear him, what with one ear being stuffed with bosom, but it was worth it in a very scary kind of way. I learned that the Widow Ginger had been quiet, but really threatening as he told Bandy and Sugar that he was back to wind up some unfinished business. 'He's the coldest bugger I've ever met. Brass monkeys had better keep a good grip on their best bits when he's around, I'm telling you. He thinks Joe, Bandy and Bert cheated him in the war. It had something to do with "getting him out of the way of the gravy train just before it got into the station".' He didn't like the sound of it, he continued. It wasn't so much what the Widow said that put a ferret up his jacksie, apparently, as the way he said it.

My bum was numb, my lugs were flapped almost to tatters and my goosepimples had goosepimples by the time Sugar had finished giving us his impressions of the Widow Ginger. It reminded me of the Ghastly Godfrey, my mum's stepfather and a really nasty piece of work. He was the one who had been behind me being snatched out of the school playground, belted in the mush and shoved into a cupboard the previous summer. I closed my eyes and there, like it was yesterday, were Godfrey's dead-looking yellow eyes glaring at me across the snowy white tablecloth at the Marble Arch Lyon's Corner House. I shuddered and opened my eyes quick to get rid of the awful picture. Sugar was talking again.

'He may be a runt next to me, but then

29

most blokes are. But he gives off this feeling that although he's in control and all quiet-like, if he threw a wobbly then he would be a right beserker. A stop-at-nothing sort that'd be very happy to inflict all kinds of damage on a body.' Sugar gave a sickly grin before carrying on. 'He's enough to give Bandy a sudden attack of charm, and you know what that means. She either wants to bed him or she's afraid of him, and knowing Band as I do I'd say she was afraid. I always know that when she stops insulting 'em something's up, and if she pours on the old oil she thinks the situation is serious.'

Everyone sat around with worried looks on their faces until Auntie Maggie remembered me when I sort of squeaked in fright. She gave me a tight squeeze and came over all hearty. 'What? Nothing better to do than earwig, young miss? All right then, how about giving your auntie Maggie a hand in the kitchen while I'm doing the veg? You can make pastry flowers for the pies, if you like. I've got some pastry left over in the larder.' She tipped me gently off her lap and heaved herself to her feet.

I thought that being in the warm, fragrant kitchen with Auntie Maggie until my uncle Bert got home was the very best place on earth to be. I liked being with one or other or both of them when there was trouble; it made me feel safer. By now, I knew that the

30

Widow Ginger was a threat to us, but what made it really frightening was that I didn't know what kind.

3

I was waiting on tables when Madame Zelda breezed in with a very tall, red-headed woman none of us had ever seen before. Although I say 'waiting on tables', I was only allowed to carry the non-sloppy food and the cold drinks, in case of spillage. Sugar was still behind the counter, Auntie Maggie was in the kitchen and Luigi had been in and out all morning. Mrs Wong was in as usual. She was always there in the middle of the day when things got busy. Auntie Maggie and Uncle Bert did a fine line in home-cooked dinners, which meant we were always heaving with punters then. We offered a soup, a couple of main dishes and ice cream or a pie or tart with custard for afters, to keep it simple. A lot of the preparation was done the night before or early in the morning, before I turned the 'Closed' sign round to 'Open' and unbolted and unlocked the cafe door.

Things that cooked slowly in the oven or on the hotplate in a saucepan were preferred, because they took the rush and bustle out of it. Winter was the best time for that, because then there were lots of stews and casseroles and soups that tasted all the better for hanging about on a low heat. Auntie Maggie was a dab hand at suet puddings, sweet or savoury, and was famed round and about for her spotted dick, Christmas pud and my own favourite, lemon syrup pudding. Her steak and kidney puddings were the best in the world, everybody said so. The way that the time-honoured routine of the cafe and the seasons, the menu and the shopping rolled on was comforting, like my liberty bodice in winter.

That day, the menu was Scotch broth, chicken and ham pie or beef and carrot casserole, and apple pie and custard. The kitchen was still running along its usual well-oiled lines, despite Sugar's early morning bombshell. As Auntie Maggie said, if Hitler couldn't close our cafe with his rotten war, she was blowed if she'd let that damned Yank do it.

Chicken and ham pies meant making pastry, and Auntie Maggie had whipped up loads the night before, and made the apple pies for pudding while she was at it. Chicken carcasses turned into stock and various soups, starting with cock-a-leekie or maybe cream of chicken. Ham bones also turned into stock and the next day's soup would almost certainly be split pea and ham. The bones would be simmering gently on the back burner with odds and ends of vegetables, peppercorns and bay leaves floating about in the pan.

The stockpots were bubbling away and Auntie Maggie was keeping me busy with laying the tables for the dinner trade. Routine, she said, was a good way to keep troublesome thoughts away. She was right, too. First, I went round all the empty tables wiping up spilt tea, sugar, bits of egg and dustings of fag ash. Then I went round with a bucket and emptied all the ashtrays into it – yuk! The ashtrays got a lick and a promise with a damp cloth and any empty salt and pepper shakers were filled while I was at it. Then I laid each place carefully with a knife, fork and two spoons, a round one for soup and an egg-shaped one for afters. Auntie Maggie reckoned that supplying the hardware to scoff with encouraged people to go the whole hog at dinner time, and try for three courses. Being chief-in-charge of table laying meant I learned left from right in double-quick time, and, as Auntie Maggie said, that was a bonus.

Sugar rationing was finally over, which meant the precious stuff was no longer doled out grain by grain by Auntie Maggie behind the counter. Each table now had its own chunky glass bowl, complete with spoon. Some ignorant so-and-sos used the bowl spoon for stirring their tea instead of the one provided in their saucers, which meant that when they dumped it back in the bowl, still wet, it soon got crusty and brown and had to be replaced with a fresh one. What's more, the sugar in the bowl formed hard brown lumps as well, and it was my job to pick them out with a pair of tongs and then replace them with fresh sugar poured from a large, thick paper sack of Tate and Lyle's finest. The still recent memory of sugar shortages made us resent those wasteful claggy spoons and little brown lumps and sometimes, I must confess, I shoved a few in my gob. My cheeks were bulging lumpily and I was just thinking that Sugar was probably called Sugar Plum because he was so sweet when the beautiful Betty Potts walked into Luigi's life and ours.

You could tell Luigi was stunned the minute he clapped eyes on Betty. She certainly was a stunner. Six feet if she was an inch, and most of that legs, she had the most gorgeous red hair, skin the colour of rich cream with no freckles, and eyes that were green with brown flecks, like birds' eggs. She really stood out, even round our way where the showbusiness hopefuls congregate and there is a lot of talk about beauty and glamour. Betty was already beautiful, and before long you just knew she'd be drop-dead glamorous as well. Working in the Soho clubs would see to that, but it didn't change her nature. She'd stay the Betty we would come to know and like, a real sweetheart as Uncle Bert and Auntie Maggie always said, but my, didn't she cause trouble?

Anyway, I'm getting ahead of myself. But I can still see her now, walking into our cafe, alongside Madame Zelda. Betty didn't seem to have a care in the world and simply glowed with health and vitality. Madame Zelda, on the other hand, was a bit red in the kisser, having had to scurry to keep up with her; her little legs were a good foot shorter than Betty's *and* she was a martyr to her feet. Madame Zelda is the 'Clairvoyant to the Stars' who lives next door with Paulette above the offices occupied by Sharky Finn, who Uncle Bert describes as 'Lawyer to the Bent'. Madame Zelda's sign and Sharky's brass plate nestle grubbily together on the green front door wedged between our cafe and the Campaninis' deli.

'Wotcha, Sugar,' she said cheerily. 'Meet Betty, new client and resident.' Now, I know that Madame Zelda was dying to know why Sugar was behind the counter at our cafe and not grabbing a few million zeds in his bed above Bandy's club, just as we were dying to know more about the lovely Betty, especially Luigi, who was staring, I swear, with his tongue hanging out. But she couldn't ask, in case anyone suspected that she had a duff crystal ball or something. It never does to look surprised in her trade; it's bad for business. And we couldn't ask, because that would have been rude. So they ordered their dinners, the casserole for Betty and chicken and ham pie for Madame Zelda and teas all round, and I cleared a space on our table so that they could settle down.

All Luigi had managed to do was lurch to his feet when they approached and fumble about with chairs a bit before sinking back into his, looking dazed. Pretty soon, the two women were tucking into their food and chatting about nothing in particular while Luigi gulped like a guppy in trouble.

It turned out that Betty had arrived on a train from Brighton that very morning, had dumped her bags with a girl she knew who was in the chorus at the Windmill, and had come straight round to consult Madame Zelda. But she'd arrived at the very moment when Madame Zelda had her coat on to nip down to the cafe to feed 'the inner soothsayer' as Sugar put it, so they'd come together. I wonder if Madame Zelda saw all that was to unfold in her crystal ball?

Madame Zelda and Betty Potts had just got to their afters when my friend Kathy Moon turned up with a memorized message from Uncle Bert. 'Would Luigi please proceed with all haste round to Bandy's place, preferably with a brother or brother-in-law or several in tow? Also to tell Sugar that the coast was well on the way to being clear and he could go home as soon as he liked.' She said this in a single breath, her big brown eyes scrunched up in concentration. Once the message was safely delivered, word for word, her solemn face split into a huge relieved grin and her eyes sparkled with triumph.

Luigi snapped to attention, rolled his tongue back into his cake'ole and left to find a few relatives, as requested, while Sugar decided to stay until the rush was over and Uncle Bert was safely back in his kitchen. I could tell he was in his element. In between taking the money and doling out drinks, he was engaged in a lively conversation about what colours went best with auburn hair and what a good thing it was that Betty Potts had decided to embrace her great height and not to *slouch* because round shoulders did nothing for the *hang* of fabrics. Sugar could talk about clothes for ever, and there was nothing he liked better than meeting what he called 'a decent frame', just begging to be dressed by his own fair hand. Sugar really should have been a proper dress designer, with a salon and everything, but he always said that he preferred to keep it as a hobby among friends.

About an hour after Luigi left, he came back with Uncle Bert and Bandy Bunyan. Seeing Bandy out in daylight was, luckily, a very rare event. She looked less like a horse sitting on a bar stool, glass in one hand and long cigarette holder in the other. The ruby-coloured glass lampshades in her place gave her complexion a soft and rosy glow, whereas sunlight made her look as if she'd recently been dug up. Of course, she'd had no sleep at all on top of what sounded like a very difficult night, so that hadn't helped. Sugar took one look at her and without a word, produced a strong black coffee with a hefty slug of the brandy that Auntie Maggie always kept under the counter for Sharky Finn and emergencies.

The brandy brought a faint blush of red to Bandy's pasty cheeks and tired eyes. Auntie Maggie came out from the kitchen bearing a large cup of tea, the colour of mahogany wood stain, for Uncle Bert, who also looked exhausted. Nobody said anything until the pair had downed their drinks, apart from introducing them to Betty Potts, that is. Then Auntie Maggie made them each a plate of food and we all watched as they wolfed it down. More drinks followed, until Bandy finally found enough energy to speak.

'Thank God we finally managed to rid

ourselves of that deranged fucker,' she said before Auntie Maggie could stop her. She didn't even pick up the loud tut Auntie Maggie managed to squeeze in. 'That Stanley Janulewicz is without doubt the maddest bastard I've ever had the misfortune to witness crawling out of the woodwork and believe me, that's saying something. Our club's more or less cornered the market in mad bastards, being mainly painters, actors and writers, and you know how close to the edge *they* can be. Goes with the territory.'

We all nodded at this. There *were* some very odd types about, and a lot of them belonged to the arty-farty mob. They wore a lot of black clobber with flowing scarves and berets and had dramatic, wine-drenched love-lives. When they weren't getting sloshed around at Bandy's or playing pass-the-partner in their attics, they were in our cafe, sobering up and talking about who was with who that day. They were a source of endless fascination. Funny thing was, only a few of them actually seemed to find the time to paint, act or write anything.

'But Stanley, he's in a league all of his own,' Bandy assured us. 'He makes our mob look positively *overburdened* with marbles and brimming with the milk of human kindness to boot. Mark my words, he'll be back and we'd better be ready for him.' Bandy suddenly seemed to see me, although

I'd been right there all the time, and she gave me a wide, but rather tired and strained, grin.

'Rosie, my honeypot! Come here and give an old bag a hug, there's a dear.' So I did. I never minded a snuggle with Bandy. She liked kids in general and me in particular and the feeling was mutual. Some grown-ups demand kisses and cuddles the first time you ever clap eyes on 'em just because they're grown-ups, or they knew Auntie Maggie's second cousin's cousin forty years ago, or something. I never liked that. I wanted to know if I liked them first, but it's tricky when you're just a kid and they're grown-ups and everyone's taking it for granted that you don't mind. I don't know who's worse, them or the cheek pinchers. Still, Bandy was all right. She was one of the ones who let you make up your own mind and they're the best. She smelt of Turkish tobacco, brandy and sandalwood soap smuggled in from France, and she felt solid and bony, not soft and pillowy like Auntie Maggie.

After a cuddle, satisfactory to both sides, she let me go, sighed and heaved herself to her feet, saying, 'Sugar, let's wend and get some sleep. Bert, I'd try to get hold of Joe if I were you and I'll have a go when I surface tonight. 'Bye, all. See you later, Bert.' And with that, she and Sugar were gone.

40

Uncle Bert yawned and stretched and began fiddling with his beloved pipe. 'Gawd, Maggie my love, that Stanley ain't half hard work. I'd forgotten that about him. He never comes straight out with anything, like what the hell he wants. No, he has to be all mysterious and enigmatic on us, long silences, hints here, veiled threats there. The man's so twisted he makes that Machiavelli geezer look like a bleeding learner. All I managed to get out of him is that he feels he's owed some lolly and he's here to collect. Wants Bandy and me to pass the message to Joe. But you could tell that that wasn't all the bleeder was after.' He paused and began to light his pipe. Once he'd got a decent fug going, he turned to Betty Potts. 'Still, enough of our troubles. What brings you to Soho, Miss Potts?'

Taking the hint, we all switched our attention to the safer topic of Betty Potts. 'Oh, you know,' she said. 'A yen for the bright lights and better money. I had a job in Brighton for a while, but thought I'd try my luck in the Smoke.' A lively discussion followed as Auntie Maggie, Uncle Bert, Luigi and Madame Zelda all came up with suggestions for finding work.

For once in my life, I said nothing. I was far too busy wondering where this Machiavelli bloke came into it, when I wasn't worrying my nut off about this madman, the Widow

Ginger, or Stanley Janulewicz as Bandy called him. I was to worry even more when I found out later that what I had heard was a heavily censored version of events on account of the stranger at our table and my ever-ready lug'oles.

No, the whole truth about the Widow Ginger's past turned out to be a lot more frightening. I wasn't happy. I wasn't happy at all, and neither were my grown-ups.

4

My friend Mr Herbert didn't open up on Sundays because it was against the law for most shops to trade on the sabbath. Mr Herbert sold books in the Charing Cross Road. But we were mates, and there was no harm in taking a quick squint at the books while we were there having our tea, now was there? As long as no actual money changed hands at the same time as borrowing books from a friend, it was no crime. So that's what we did. We borrowed books one Sunday and coughed up for them the next. We went to his place to do the borrowing and he came to ours for his tea and to collect his lolly. What my uncle Bert called 'a very amicable arrangement'. Both the bookshop and the cafe were open at the same time, you see, so proper visiting and getting books had to be done on a Sunday or after hours. Uncle Bert, Mr Herbert and I liked Sundays best, and once a fortnight Auntie Maggie got to spend an afternoon on her big bed, reading, listening to the wireless or having what she called 'forty winks' in peace. I watched her more than once and I reckon there was a load more than forty of those winks. Forty thousand, more like. Auntie Maggie liked a snooze. She said it was much more peaceful when we weren't there, so everyone was happy.

I loved Mr Herbert's shop. The old books had a smell all of their own and that, together with the beeswax that Mr Herbert lovingly rubbed into the beautiful, gleaming wooden bookshelves, created a scent I have never forgotten. It was a mixture of dust, leather, polish and the special glues and inks used by different generations of printers. One whiff and I was, and still am, in heaven. The Charing Cross Road was almost an enchanted place for me, because it meant a dose of Mr Herbert combined with a trip out with my uncle Bert, just him and me, and we both loved that. Funnily enough, it was my mum who first took me to Mr Herbert's, so I also associated the shop with happy times with her, when she wasn't drunk and there were no snakes crawling out of the walls that only she could see. It was my mum who taught me to love books, helped a lot by Mr Herbert.

Then, of course, there was Great-aunt Dodie, who was also a good friend of Mr Herbert's because they grew up together. I'd been mad about her since we'd met the year before, and we often saw her at the shop when she was in town. So you see, going to Mr Herbert's was a jolly good thing all round. This time, though, Great-aunt Dodie was terrorizing the people of Kathmandu, and nowhere near the Charing Cross Road, and a couple of really creepy things happened that scared all of the joy out of this particular visit.

It started on the way out of the cafe. I was prancing ahead as usual. Uncle Bert always said that I'd never just walk when a hop, skip, jump or jitterbug would do. Anyway, Uncle Bert had stopped, with his back to the street, to lock the cafe door, so he never saw the man come round the corner from Greek Street and stop dead as if he'd just seen someone he didn't want to see. I looked around, but there was no one in our bit of the street but us. Sundays were dead quiet round our way. When I turned back, the man had disappeared back round the corner. I don't know why, but when Uncle Bert turned towards Greek Street to take the Soho Square route to Mr Herbert's, I grabbed his hand and steered him the other way, towards Cambridge Circus, so that we walked up Charing Cross Road instead. All the way, I kept wanting to look round, almost as if I could feel eyes behind me, but every time I turned there was no one there.

I loved Mr Herbert, who looked like a little Father Christmas. His pink, round face, equally round specs and electric white hair all positively shone with enthusiasm as he showed me a leather book, with gilt-edged pages and a gold, embossed title on the cover telling me it was a special copy of Kenneth Grahame's *The Wind in the Willows*. Mr Herbert opened the book reverently and showed me the marbled endpapers, cream and brown whirls sometimes brightened up with just a touch of coral pink. It was a lovely book, but way, way beyond the threepenny bit and three measly farthings that were left in my piggy bank. I'd recently raided it to buy a miniature sideboard for my doll's house.

I'm not very good at saving. Sadly, I'm much better at spending. I'd have no proper savings at all if Auntie Maggie didn't sometimes snatch some of my birthday or Christmas money off me and squirrel it away into a Post Office Savings Account. The savings book had my name on it all right, but it was out of my reach because she hid it in 'the family vault', a scruffy Typhoo

Tea tin on top of her wardrobe. It was pushed right to the back, so that I couldn't reach it, even with a chair. That battered old tin held all the important bits and pieces in our lives, including insurance books kept up to date by 'the man from the Pru', who had called every week for as long as I could remember, Auntie Maggie's and Uncle Bert's wills, important letters, one of many copies of my adoption papers and all our birth certificates.

Anyway, I had to tell Mr Herbert that I couldn't afford the book, even though he hadn't yet told me how much it was, because it was obvious you didn't get tooled leather and marbling for threepence three-farthings. I'd hung about at Mr Herbert's often enough to know that. But he didn't lose his rosy glow in regret. Instead, he upped the wattage until I thought he must explode with glee. 'That's the beauty of it, Rosie dear. Your dear mother has sent a cheque that more than covers this volume and perhaps a modest second tome, Arthur Ransome perhaps? It's for your Easter present; a tad early, I confess, but I couldn't wait to show you what I'd found. I hope you like it.'

Like it? I loved it! I opened the book, raised it to my hooter and took a deep sniff as my mother had taught me to do. It smelt wonderful and I launched myself at the little

46

man and almost squeezed the life out of him in gratitude, or so Uncle Bert said.

After tea, I whizzed up and down the aisles between the bookcases on the wheeled library steps that were ordinarily used to get books from the very top shelves. But I liked zipping back and forth and screeching to dramatic halts just before I crashed into the furniture. The men chatted for a bit and then it was time to go. I had school the next day and had to have a bath before bed.

The twinkling brass bell at the end of its elegantly curved arm tinkled as we opened the shop door to leave. Outside it was quiet and dark, and I wished the bell had not tinkled quite so loudly as I peered into the shadows. This time, we did turn into Sutton Row, heading towards Soho Square and Greek Street. Once again I skipped ahead, playing invisible hopscotch along the pavement, looking down so I didn't land on the cracks. Invisible hopscotch is like real hopscotch only you don't have the grid, the throwing stone or anyone to play with. What you do is use the paving stones to practise the jumping bit, first on one leg in one square then on two legs on two squares, turn and turn about. I was so busy watching out for cracks that I wasn't looking where I was going. I was just turning left at the end of Sutton Row, by the big left-footers' church there, when a bloke stepped out of nowhere, right into my path. I landed heavily on his right foot, he grunted in pain and I looked up into the coldest pair of eyes I have ever seen.

'Why don't you look where you're going, you little bastard?' he demanded. 'Look what you've done to my shoe.' His voice alone could've given you frostbite.

I looked down and there was a large scuff mark on the toecap of an otherwise gleaming black shoe. Next thing I knew, he had grabbed me by the scruff of the neck and was forcing me to my knees. 'Clean it!' he ordered.

I was just going to ask what with when we both heard Uncle Bert's steady footsteps approaching the corner. I twisted my head and broke the man's grip on my collar and when I turned back he was gone. I was so taken aback that if you'd tortured me two seconds later I couldn't have told you what had happened to him. He'd simply vanished into thin air, and not for the first time that night. I swear it was the same bloke I saw disappear at the start of our jaunt to Mr Herbert's. I scrambled to my feet just in time for Uncle Bert to come up. The whole affair had taken seconds.

'What's the matter with you? You lost a shilling and found a penny or what? You're shaking like a leaf and you're as white as a Sunday hanky.' (Which was very white in our house. Auntie Maggie took a pride in her whites and used a blue bag to make sure.) Uncle Bert looked at me hard and then looked around to see what had frightened me so, but there was nothing in sight and I couldn't speak for fright.

'I tell you what, do you want a piggyback home? You can tell me all about it over a cup of Ovaltine. What do you say?' I nodded, and then I scrambled and he heaved me up on to his shoulders. Even though I was small for my age, I was still getting a bit too big for piggybacks, but I wasn't ready to give 'em up yet.

Once I was aboard, we hurried home.

Auntie Maggie and Uncle Bert were not happy about my tale of the strange man. They were even less happy when they realized I'd seen him twice and they exchanged worried looks when I described just how cold, threatening and frightening he'd been.

Auntie Maggie's voice was gentle as she stroked my hair and asked, 'Can you remember what he looked like, Rosie love? You say he spoke to you. Was there anything about his voice?'

I closed my eyes and tried to drum up a picture of the man as he stood in the shadows. 'He was thin, with a dark overcoat and a black hat. His shoes were very shiny and the creases in his trousers looked ever so sharp, like he pressed them every day the way Luigi does.' I thought some more and saw once again those cold, grey eyes, like chips of ice glinting beneath the dark brim of his hat, but I didn't know how to describe them properly. 'He had iceberg eyes, like they could freeze you to death if he just stared at you long enough, and he sounded like a Yank, but I couldn't be sure. He didn't say much.'

This was the best I could manage, but by the way my uncle and aunt looked at each other, it was good enough. They knew who he was and they didn't like it, they didn't like it at all. Neither did I, because I was pretty sure I knew who it was as well: the mysterious and very scary Widow Ginger!

I was hustled into my bath and got away with the merest hint of a wash before I was out, dried, dressed in my pink winceyette nightie with the blue rosebuds and bundled into bed. Auntie Maggie said I could have a ten-minute read of Arthur Ransome or a gloat over my precious new book if I liked, and then lights out, because it was school tomorrow. I don't know how she expected me to sleep. I had been very rattled by the Widow Ginger. It was all too much, like the year before when that awful Dave creature had stolen me to give me to Ghastly Godfrey and the lady Great-aunt Dodie called 'that vapid half-wit Evelyn', who was my grandmother. I shuddered under my eiderdown, and just for a minute I felt sick.

I must have dropped off, though, because the next thing I knew I was woken up with a terrible start by raised voices. Shouting was about as common as hens' teeth in our house, so you can imagine how it made me jump. 'I don't care what a good friend you say that Maltese Joe is, Bert Featherby; the truth is he's always led you into trouble, ever since you was nippers. I've heard the stories. The Widow's a dangerous man, Bert, you've said so yourself. I'm telling you to keep it quiet, for all our sakes. Can you imagine the kind of trouble those two will stir up once they tangle? You don't want to be in the middle of that; you could wind up dead. And where does that leave Rosie and me, eh? I'm asking you, where does that leave us?'

I couldn't make out Uncle Bert's mumble but Auntie Maggie's reply was loud enough to be heard clearly in Tipperary. 'I'm telling you, Bert Featherby, if you go running to that so-called pal of yours, then me and Rosie will pack our bags and go and stay with my sister, you see if we don't.' And then the bathroom door slammed and there was silence.

The next morning everyone was very quiet. Uncle Bert's face was set like concrete

51

and he kept his pipe clamped in his mouth, even though there was no baccy in it. He barely spoke to anyone but me and then it was just to ask what I wanted for my breakfast and to kiss me goodbye when I set off for school. Auntie Maggie wasn't much better. Her normally jolly kisser couldn't work up a beam for anybody, not even for me. I trailed down Old Compton Street to the corner of Wardour Street and turned left to wait for my best friend Jenny in St Anne's Churchyard. We always walked to school together, and I liked to feed the pigeons and sparrows with bits of left-over bread while I waited. For some reason, I knew it wasn't right to blab about our troubles with this Widow Ginger geezer, even to Jenny – and we normally told each other everything. So when I spotted her coming in the gate, swinging her satchel, I decided it was best to plaster a grin on my chops and try to forget the atmosphere at home and the terrifying stranger who had caused it.

5

Things went very quiet in our house for a while as we all tiptoed around trying to pretend nothing was the matter. However, I did find Bandy, Uncle Bert and Luigi deep in conversation one day shortly after our visit to Mr Herbert. Bandy seemed to be arguing with Uncle Bert about something to do with the Widow Ginger and Maltese Joe and Luigi was backing her up. 'Bert, I'm telling you,' Bandy said angrily, 'he was in last night and asking about Rosie. You can't not tell Joe. That's madness and you know it. I know Maggie's never trusted him, but it makes good sense to me to have him in our corner and you think so too.'

Luigi was nodding so hard I thought his bonce must drop off. But it didn't. He spotted me instead and they all went schtum. All I gathered was that they'd settled on Luigi and his various relatives having a word with the Widow Ginger to get him to see reason, and, if that failed, then to divert his attention from the cafe and Bandy's club, at least for a while. Luigi just said that he and his cousins Mario, Enrico and Fabio could simply help find him 'a better place'. Uncle Bert said that it wouldn't hurt for him to meet a small mob of well-muscled Italians either, to show him that he and Bandy were not without friends, whereas the Widow was.

Now, when the religious say 'a better place', they mean heaven, but when Luigi said it he didn't. He meant a place called Ruby's, where the Widow would be a more than welcome guest. Ruby's wasn't anywhere near us. In fact, it wasn't even on our side of London. Ruby's place catered for 'certain appetites' but nobody ever said what those were. I had visions of the Widow living entirely on fish and chips, treacle tarts and tons of gobstoppers, but our friend Paulette explained it had nothing to do with food, which left me stumped. What other kind of appetite could a person have? When I asked, I was told that I didn't need to understand. What *need* had to do with it I'll never know, because I was simply being nosy as usual.

When that line of inquiry dried up, I decided to ask Paulette about something else that had been bothering me. Everyone else had sort of skated round the question ever since I'd started asking it. Somehow I knew Paulette wouldn't let me down.

'Paulette?' I said.

'Yes, dear?'

'Why's the Widow Ginger called the Widow Ginger when he's not a widow and he certainly isn't ginger? I've seen him and he's got fair hair.'

For a minute I thought that Paulette was going to change the subject to the weather or something boring like that and I was never going to find out but then she changed her mind. 'It's rhyming slang, Rosie love. Widow Twankey – you remember, like in *Aladdin* – means Yankee and ginger beer's, well, queer. So it means the, er, queer American, like he's a bit funny. You've noticed that yourself, I dare say.'

'You bet I have,' I assured her with a shudder. He really was a peculiar man, that was for sure. Frozen and frightening.

Anyway, everyone seemed to agree that whatever Ruby's place was it was likely to keep the Widow busy, happy and, most importantly out of our hair long enough for us to form some sort of plan. According to Luigi, when Ruby and her helpers had finished showing Stanley a good time, it'd take him a week to be able to stand on his own two feet and a month for his liver to recover. Or maybe it was the other way round, I forget now. The point is, what with Ruby and one thing and another, the Widow was gone for quite a while.

The most important thing was it allowed time to break the news to Maltese Joe gently, if at all. Everyone carried on arguing about that one. It was agreed that once Maltese Joe knew that the Widow had resurfaced he was likely to go off half-cocked and that could cause even more trouble, and that it wasn't going to be easy to steer Joe into a less explosive approach. Auntie Maggie blamed what she called 'that hot Latin temperament of Joe's and the deadly bleeding rivalry between the two of 'em'. Everyone agreed with her, but they still thought we should at least try to break it to Joe gently and the sooner the better. Auntie Maggie stuck to her guns, though. One word to Joe, and she and I were off to the seaside, maybe for ever.

Meanwhile, poor Luigi had troubles of his own. Perhaps one trouble would be more accurate, in the form of Betty Potts. Now, I knew something was the matter with him because he'd gone all sort of quiet and droopy. I had never seen a quiet and droopy Luigi before, although I was going to see it again, when I was getting all grown up and what Uncle Bert called 'coming into my clog' and Auntie Maggie called 'turning into a swan', though of course they were biased. But Luigi was not his usual bouncy, happy-go-lucky self and I began to wonder if he was ill. It was Madame Zelda and Paulette who put me straight on that one.

'No, lovey, he's not ill,' Madame Zelda told me. 'He's just suffering from a bit of unrequited lust, that's all.'

I must have looked blank because Paulette explained a bit more. 'He's got a pash on Betty, Rosie, and she ain't playing at the minute, on account she's got other things on her mind. She's got to find a job, for one thing, and her mate Mary's got the needle to her, because she's one of Maltese Joe's bits of sly and he's taken a big shine to our Betty. So what with dodging him, keeping the peace with her mate, trying to find a place of her own and a way of paying for it, she's a busy gel. Too busy to worry about men, anyway. And, of course, our Luigi ain't used to that. He's used to having to beat 'em off with a club, or not as the case may be. He's just not used to having to *work* at it. Not that it'll do him any harm. He can be a cocky little sod when it comes to women.'

Luigi- and Betty-watching became the favourite pastime of the cafe females, and very fascinating it was too. We had never, not once, seen the Campanini charm fail before, and judging by the effect it was having on Luigi he wasn't used to it either. As Auntie Maggie said when she thought I wasn't listening, 'Normally he only has to smile to get 'em flat on their backs with their legs in the air and lending him money *and* feeding him for the privilege.' But not this time, not with the magnificent Betty, who seemed to be immune to his charm and Italian good looks.

After a long, happy afternoon's gossip, when Auntie Maggie, Paulette and Madame Zelda searched their collective memory and I listened with rapt attention, they agreed that it was definitely love and that they had never, ever seen it strike Luigi before.

'As Sugar said the other day,' Madame Zelda said, taking off Sugar's husky voice to a T, '"The lovely Betty seems blissfully unaware of the stir she's causing in the Campanini heart and trousers." She's far too busy dodging Maltese Joe's dishonourable intentions, is what I told him.'

'She told me that she didn't go out with married men, on account of the way her dear old ma suffered because of her dad and his floozies,' Paulette explained. 'He's a fast worker, that Joe. Betty's hardly been here five minutes and he's already breathing down her neck. Do you reckon she'll give in when she realizes just who Maltese Joe is?'

'I think she already knows, Paulette, but she's not daft, that one. She seems to be able to tell him to get stuffed somewhere else without getting up his hooter, if you take my meaning. I've seen her in action. She can brush him off in such a way that he seems to love it.' Madame Zelda leaned forward and instinctively we huddled closer too, forming a confidential little circle. 'He was waving this fur coat at her the other day at Bandy's when she was trying to have a nice quiet drink with Sugar, and she turned it down like she was doing him a favour, and what's more he didn't rant at all. The coat wound up on his missus's back, according to Sharky. Where it should've been in the first place, if you ask me. Betty made him think it was his idea all along and *what* a clever bloke he was to treat Mrs Joe so well. Wound up making everybody happy, except p'raps his bit of sly. Now *that's* clever. I'm telling you, don't underestimate that girl. It'd be a big mistake.'

'You're right, Zelda,' Paulette agreed. 'I've seen her turn Luigi down too, and make him think that what he really wanted to do was go to the jazz club with the lads. It's a treat to watch her working and I'm still blowed if I can see just how she manages it. It's got something to do with that quiet little voice she uses on the blokes. She's always so good-mannered about it, too, and really appreciative that they even thought to ask little old her.'

Auntie Maggie laughed and added her two penn'orth. By this time I was getting dizzy from my bonce turning this way and that as the women gossiped, but I stuck with it. 'Then of course there's that smile. It could melt an iceberg, that smile could. Mind you, looking like that, she must have had plenty of practice in her time, even though she's still only a youngster. It must be a bit of a burden to be that good-looking, with a figure like that. She says she developed really young, too, poor little mite.'

Personally, I thought 'poor little mite' was coming it a bit strong, even for my auntie Maggie, who could turn an all-in wrestler into 'a dear little thing' when she put her mind to it. After all, Betty Potts was the tallest woman I had ever seen.

6

Of course, while all this stuff was going on, I had to go to school. I have to admit, I didn't feel that safe at school because it was hard to forget that I'd been snatched from the playground only the summer before. A person doesn't forget that kind of thing in a hurry, especially when there was another nutter on the loose who didn't seem to like us much either. Normally, though, I didn't mind school because it was a bit of a relief to be among other kids so that we could do the usual kid-type things. There are all sorts of games that are either lonely or hard to play alone, like hide-and-seek, tag, knock-down-ginger, conkers, two balls, five stones and proper hopscotch, to name but a few. Where's the jollies in always playing these games on your tod? You need your friends to get a giggle out of it. So school was all right.

Lessons could be boring sometimes, but most of the time I found learning things quite interesting, although it was more than my playground life was worth to admit that. The worst thing to be at school was a swot, a teacher's pet. Well, actually, the very worst thing to be at school was a smelly sneak who dripped green snot candles all year round, like poor old Enie Smales. The next worse thing was to be too clever. It really was best to hide that particular light under your hat. Even when I knew the answers, I made sure that my hand didn't shoot up too often and I never, ever, allowed anyone to see me reading for fun. Most of my school friends didn't know that I was a secret reader, although Kathy Moon and Jenny Robbins, who were my best mates, did catch on in the end. Of course, they'd seen my bulging bookcases when they came to play, but they just figured that the books were presents from my missing mum, which many were. They didn't think for a moment that I might actually *read* the things. The truth was, I not only read them, but I spent quite a lot of my pocket money at Mr Herbert's lovely shop and I belonged to the library as well. But I never let on. When Kathy and Jenny found out my secret, they kept mum too. I didn't ask them to, they simply understood, as any kid would and any adult wouldn't.

Kathy, Jenny and I were in Miss Welbeloved's class, the top class in our year. Amazingly, so was Enie Smales, she of the damp knickers, hefty honk and green candles. We couldn't stand her then. Now, looking back, I realize that I should have felt sorry for her, but I didn't. She was always creeping around the teachers, telling them that I was on the toilet roof gobbing into the boys' playground in the hope of hitting one. (I know that was disgusting, but they were always doing it to us. They liked to hear the screaming of girls rushing about trying to avoid being caught in the bombardment.) Or that it was me who wrote 'Be alert, your country needs lerts' and 'Enie Smales stinks' in blue crayon all over the new whitewash on the PE cupboard walls. In fact, it was me that wrote about lerts and Jenny who wrote about stinky old Smales. Enie even told Miss Welbeloved that I'd snuck in at playtime and written 'HOT NEWS... Old Welbeloved ain't!!!' on the blackboard. I got caned for that but I got my own back and clocked Smales one after school. She told them that as well.

Anyway, it was that year that Jenny started to clunk out at school. She'd be standing there in assembly, or sitting on the bench next to me or charging about like a mad thing in the playground and suddenly she'd keel over and lie so still she could have been dead.

It had been really frightening at first. Then she began to be away for the odd day or two. Now that really was strange, because Jenny would be sent to school no matter what. Her mum couldn't afford to take time off work, because she didn't get paid if she did. Jenny's dad, known to all as 'Hissing Sid' on account of the way he spoke in a kind of hiss out of the side of his mouth, hadn't paid for her upkeep since he'd legged it with some skinny blonde woman called Mary Cowley. Sadly, they hadn't gone far, and seeing them almost daily made things even harder for Jenny and her mum. Auntie Maggie told Madame Zelda that Mary had told her that Hissing Sid always had to cough up a bit of jewellery whenever they had a row, which was often. No rock, no leg-over, whatever that meant, but it explained why he didn't trouble about his maintenance payments, or so Auntie Maggie said.

'Which is a bit rich if you think about how snotty she is about the working girls round here, as if she was any better. For my money, taking jewellery for a bit of the other is prostitution. What else could you call it?' My auntie Maggie asked the question, and Madame Zelda agreed with her.

I wasn't supposed to have heard all that, but it cheered Jenny up no end when I reported it back to her. We often saw Mary Cowley in the street, and sometimes we'd hang out of my bedroom window and try and hit her with our pea-shooters. In the end, Auntie Maggie reluctantly put a stop to it when too many innocent bystanders copped it by mistake and complained. Still, we got Mary a few times before we were banned from trying.

We hated that Mary Cowley and took to calling her the Mangy Cow instead. Well, Jenny hated her passionately, and loyalty made me dislike her too. That, and the fact that she once threatened to thrash me to within an inch of my life when a well-aimed spitball landed on her head. Nobody besides teachers and other kids had ever hit me, or even threatened to before, on account of the fact that Auntie Maggie and Uncle Bert didn't believe in it. Even the school thought twice about clouting me after Auntie Maggie finished telling them their fortune. When Auntie Maggie gave anyone a tongue-lashing they stayed lashed, and were very, very cautious about sticking their heads above the parapet for a second go.

Jenny had been away from school for two whole weeks when Mrs Robbins came to see us one Saturday morning. She hardly ever came to the cafe, except to collect Jenny when she was playing with me and was late for her tea or something. It hadn't crossed my mind to try and visit Jenny while she'd been away because I had never been inside her flat in all the time I'd known her. We'd never discussed it, but it was somehow understood that going to her place just wasn't on. The most I'd do was ring the bell and wait for a head to pop out of the window to tell me whether Jenny could or could not come out to play. So you can imagine my surprise when Mrs Robbins came looking for me that day and invited me round to visit Jenny on the Sunday. I looked at her tired, strained face and then at my auntie Maggie's round, jolly one and saw her nod very slightly; I was to go, no question. Mrs Robbins tried to smile but it was tight and never reached her eyes, unlike Auntie Maggie's beam which always made her whole face light up and her eyes twinkle like Sugar Plum's sequins.

'What time would you like her there, Mrs Robbins?' Auntie Maggie's question seemed to stump Mrs Robbins for a minute but she finally said that after dinner would be fine.

'Is Jenny laid up in bed, then?' my beloved aunt asked, and when Mrs Robbins nodded she carried on. 'Well, then, how about I pack up a little picnic and Rosie can bring a few games and stuff and they can make a real afternoon of it. That'll cheer them both up. Our Rosie's been hanging about like a wet weekend in Bognor ever since your Jenny's been poorly, so it'll be good for 'em both.'

I realize now that the strange look that flashed across Mrs Robbins face was a complicated mixture of gratitude, relief and a sort of strangled pleading that she couldn't voice. Her eyes filled with tears which she wiped away with an impatient hand. 'I'd better get back. I've left her with my husband and he's useless at the best of times.'

Auntie Maggie had also seen that complicated look and would have none of it. 'Well, then, they'll do all right for a while, I'm sure. Why don't you come upstairs and have a cup of tea with me? I could do with a bit of a rest and you're just the excuse I need.' She didn't wait for Mrs Robbins's reply before yelling into the kitchen, 'Bert, I'm going upstairs for a bit. Keep your eye on things, will you?'

She managed to sweep Mrs Robbins along with her before the poor woman could get a word in edgeways. However, when I went to follow I was told very firmly to stay put and help Uncle Bert. There was no possibility of getting an earful of what they were talking about upstairs. It was much easier to hide behind the door and listen to what was going on in the cafe than it was to do it the other way round, because all anyone had to do was glance down the stairs and they'd see me. I had to wait until Mrs Robbins had left before I got to know anything at all.

It was a good hour before the two women came down again. Some of the strain had left Mrs Robbins's face but my auntie Maggie looked grim behind her kindly smiles as she showed her guest out. I knew the signs. Something Mrs Robbins had told her had made her good and mad, and she was hell bent on doing something about it. Her voice was sharp as she turned to me and told me to nip next door and see if Sharky Finn would be kind enough to pop in at his earliest convenience.

Most solicitors expect you to make an appointment to see them in their offices, I realize that now, but it was never like that when we wanted to see Sharky. Sharky always came to the cafe and it never occurred to anybody to do it any other way. If he came to us, he got free brandy in his coffee and we didn't have to close the cafe, so everyone was happy.

Sharky Finn was out on his own when it came to lawyers. Uncle Bert always said that Sharky was so bent that he could hide behind a corkscrew, no trouble, but Auntie Maggie said he'd be too busy using it to hide behind it. But they both agreed he was as sharp as anything when it came to the law. Which is just as well, because, as he said himself, most of his clients were as guilty as sin and it was his job to keep them out and about and earning so that they could pay him handsomely for his services.

He was never short of clients. He needed plenty of paying customers, he said, because he had more overheads than most people. He had to run a wife, several children and a mother-in-law that no one round our way had ever seen. He had them tucked away somewhere, no one knew exactly where, although Golders Green was most people's favourite guess. Madame Zelda started that rumour when she said she'd seen it in the cards, but Auntie Maggie said he'd muttered something about the place once when he was Brahms and Madame Zelda had heard him.

On top of the mysterious family, he had several mistresses, a thirst for brandy that would knock over several very large horses and a gambling habit that would bankrupt a small nation when he lost and keep one when he won. Sharky needed his wits about him to keep everything ticking over and the bulk of his customers out of the nick. The amount of brandy he sunk never seemed to dull those wits either. On top of that, rumour had it that he kept secret files, stashed well away from his office. 'An insurance policy,' he once told us, 'to ensure prompt payment and limited aggravation from my wayward clientele.'

We had always regarded Sharky as 'family', especially when he pulled off my adoption over the protests of my real mum's rich and snobby family, and I'm pretty sure he felt the same about us. We never seemed to get a bill from him.

Anyway, Sharky came to the cafe almost before the request was out of my mouth. When Auntie Maggie thanked him for his promptness he assured her it was his pleasure, the alternative being a trip home to the wife and kids, something to be avoided at all costs. I sometimes wondered if they really existed, this shadowy family of his; I never did find out for sure. I couldn't think of a reason for inventing them, though, until I was older and realized that they were a handy excuse for not marrying any of his women.

Once a steaming cup of coffee, laced with a hefty slug of the 'medicinal' brandy, had been placed before him and he'd lit his fat cigar, he was ready for a consultation. 'You called, dear lady, and, as you can see, I have arrived. What can I do for you?'

'It's not me, Sharky, it's that poor woman Lizzie Robbins. She's got big trouble.'

By this time, of course, I was out of Auntie Maggie's direct line of sight. I'd nipped behind the counter to get some water just as things were getting interesting, so naturally

I hovered a bit, fiddling about. I wish I hadn't, because what I heard really, really upset me and there seemed to be nothing I could do about it. I couldn't even tell my best friends because I knew this bit of news wasn't meant to be blabbed all over the playground. It was, I realized, even more serious than the Widow Ginger turning up. This was personal. Jenny was one of my best friends and she was very, very poorly. Next to that, the Widow Ginger's squabble with Maltese Joe didn't seem so bad. But then, I didn't know just how bad things were going to get with the Widow or with Jenny. I was going to find out soon enough, though.

As Auntie Maggie always said, there were times when listening to grown-up talk could leave you wishing you hadn't, and this was one of those times all right.

7

Whatever was wrong with Jenny, it was nothing simple like a cold or chickenpox. It had a strange name that involved about a yard of Latin and was very serious; that much was clear from what I remembered of Auntie Maggie's talk with Sharky. I could tell that she was really upset by what Mrs

Robbins had told her, because she was so angry with Hissing Sid and the Mangy Cow that she didn't even notice me. I can hear the edge in her voice now, the one she had when she was fighting back tears with a hefty dose of rage.

'Those two have kept Lizzie and Jenny short ever since they took up with each other. It's been a nightmare for that poor woman to keep their bodies and souls together and now, when it looks as if she could lose the battle, they're *still* keeping 'em short.' Her voice rose to a pitch that could cut through girders. 'Isn't there some way to *make* the devils pay? That trollop Mary Cowley is saying that she can look after Jenny while Lizzie carries on working. Reckons she did a bit of nursing in the war, before she became a blood-sucking leech, that is. I know for a fact that Jenny, poor lamb, can't stand her at any price. Of course, that spineless git Sid Robbins is agreeing with her, says it'd be better for Jenny to live with them and be nursed by a professional. He's even on about their place being more comfortable for an invalid, and' – at this point her voice wobbled dangerously – '*whose* bloody fault is that? It's that hag with her sodding jewellery that keeps Lizzie so skint she's had to pawn or flog almost everything but the bare essentials. Do you know she has to weigh up whether she can afford to buy the poor little soul an orange or an egg?'

Sharky listened quietly without interruption and by the time Auntie Maggie paused to catch her breath she had the attention of everyone in the place. I could tell that by the silence that followed her speech. Then there was an embarrassed cough and the normal cafe noises started up again. But the damage was done; the story flew round Soho quicker than a pigeon with the trots and from that moment on virtually no one would speak to the Mangy Cow or Hissing Sid unless they had to. What's more, mysterious parcels containing fruit, veg, sweets and eggs would be left on the landing outside Jenny's flat at regular intervals. The market traders, led by our friend Ronnie, had heard what was going on and had taken action. They also took to overcharging the Mangy Cow at every opportunity, so in a way she was helping to keep Jenny and Mrs Robbins despite herself.

But all that came later. For the moment, Sharky listened carefully and we waited to see what he had to say. We had a good long wait because Sharky wasn't one to be hurried. His cup was refilled and he puffed thoughtfully on his cigar until he'd made a fine old fug around his head of thinning fair hair. At last he spoke.

'It's tricky, Maggie. If Lizzie were to go for

a formal separation prior to divorcing the little prick, we could probably get a court order ordering him to pay a percentage of his income, but enforcing that court order is another thing entirely. They've only got to move about a bit. Then again, who is to say just how much he earns? I don't suppose, as a trader in dirty books, he keeps strictly accurate accounts, or any accounts at all for that matter.' There was another long pause, accompanied by deep puffs, the odd slurp and the tinkle of cup hitting saucer. 'No, I feel that this situation requires a little more thought and possibly a slightly more original approach than your actual *legal* solution. Leave it with me, dear lady, and I will have a more substantial think on the matter. Meanwhile, I feel it behoves us to consult with T.C. on the beginnings of an idea I have that I feel might just work. I won't elaborate now; too many witnesses. After all, we don't wish the persons in question to get the slightest inkling of our plans, especially before I've had the opportunity to firm them up and get T.C.'s opinion. Can you send a runner to indicate that a visit would be appreciated, at his earliest possible convenience of course?'

Auntie Maggie cast her eye about, looking for me, and spotted me still behind the counter. 'Rosie, love, we need you to nip along to the cop shop and see if T.C.'s around. If not, leave a message with the desk sergeant asking him to come to the cafe as soon as possible.'

Now, policemen or women were not that popular in our bit of London because quite a lot of people earned their money on the wrong side of the law. It was an unwritten rule that nobody got too friendly with them because they were, after all, the official enemy. Most of the time, though, both sides rubbed along together without too much fuss and bother. Still, T.C. was seen to be different. He was a decent bloke, everyone thought so, and he had never been known to take a bribe or fit anyone up. He was also widely believed to be my dad, although no one said this out loud while his wife Pat was still alive, because it would have hurt her and we all liked her a lot as well.

Paulette had once explained it all to me. T.C. couldn't leave his missus for my mum and me, because she was ill and needed him more than my mum or I did. After all, I had Auntie Maggie and Uncle Bert to look after me and love me to bits. And, anyway, no one was *sure* he was my dad. When I pointed out that my mum was ill too, being tucked up in that clinic to prove it, and had been for quite a while, Paulette got a little bit flustered because it was true.

'Yes, but T.C. can't help your mum with her particular trouble. No one can really, but he can help Pat with her wheelchair, getting her in and out of bed and all that sort of thing. Besides, he was married to Pat when he met your mum, so I expect he feels he owes it to her more.

'Anyway, you know your mum. If he left poor Pat for her, how long do you think she'd stick around, eh? She gets itchy feet does your mum, you know she does. Even your mum agrees that T.C.'s more use to his missus than he can be to her. Still, that doesn't mean he doesn't love you both, because I reckon he does. He keeps an eye out for the pair of you, doesn't he?'

And it was true, he did. He was always popping into the cafe to see us all and he never once forgot my birthday or Christmas. He regularly got my mum out of scrapes and he even paid her fines sometimes when she was caught picking up men or being drunk and disorderly. Of course, he did it on the quiet, because policemen weren't supposed to be doing that kind of thing. He usually gave the money to Paulette or Madame Zelda and they handed it over. So T.C. was considered all right by one and all, despite his calling in life.

I know it's big-headed to say so, but I was a favourite down at the cop shop. They always made a fuss of me when I nipped in to see them and I made a small fortune in threepenny bits and shiny silver sixpences. I blame the fact that I looked a lot like Princess Anne at the time, all blonde curls and blue eyes, and I expect they'd also heard the rumour about who my dad might be. On top of that, I made a nice change from all the old lags that passed through their doors, according to Smiley Riley, the usual daytime desk sergeant. He was on duty that Saturday and told me that T.C. wouldn't be available until the following day, but he would pass on the message.

Meanwhile, I made half a crown and a cup of cocoa in the canteen, so it wasn't a wasted trip. I bought copies of *Girl* and *Schoolfriend*, which were Jenny's favourite comics, with my profits, although I did read them from cover to cover before I handed them over the next afternoon. Auntie Maggie said it wasn't polite to cop a read of someone else's present before you gave it to them. Personally, I thought it was an act of nobility buying Jenny's girlie-type comics at all, rather than *Eagle* and the *Topper* which were my own favourites at the time.

Still, Jenny didn't seem to mind when I told her that I'd already read them, so I suppose it was all right despite Auntie Maggie's objections. My auntie Maggie could be a bit strict about what she called 'manners' when the mood was on her.

8

I was very nervous on Sunday by the time I rang Jenny's bell. I always got nervous when I went somewhere new, and anyway, I didn't know how the yard of Latin was going to make her look. I needn't have worried too much. Jenny was Jenny, only paler, and her face was a bit thinner. I couldn't say what the rest of her looked like because she was wearing a nightie that covered her from neck to wrist to ankle; it was a case of once round her and twice round the gasworks, it was so big.

Her bed had been brought into the living room and stuck beside the window so that she could watch the comings and goings in the street. I couldn't help noticing that instead of the plump, rose-pink satin quilt that covered my own bed Jenny had thin khaki army blankets, the colour of horses' poo after they've had a lot of grass. For a London kid I was quite an expert on horse droppings, on account of getting pally with some donkeys in Weston-super-Mare when I was on my holidays visiting Auntie Maggie's sister, Auntie Flo. I'd also been introduced to various horses by Great-aunt Dodie, who took me riding on Hampstead Heath when she was in town. I've always loved everything to do with horses, their smell, their muzzles, their lugs and even their poo, which I knew was a great help when growing veg because Auntie Flo told me so.

The whole room seemed dark in Jenny's flat, like the inside of a dreary old cave. The shabby lino was brown with a deeper brown swirly pattern all over it. The rug was brown, too, and brushed almost bald in places. A pair of tired leatherette armchairs, brown yet again, sagged each side of a small grate that had been fitted with a gas fire that glowed a friendly orange with blue bits where the flames spluttered around the jets. The fire was the only bright spot in the whole room. When I told Auntie Maggie how fond Mrs Robbins seemed to be of brown, she explained that the colour didn't show the dirt and therefore needed replacing less often. I told her I didn't think dirt stood a chance in Mrs Robbins's house. What little they had had been scrubbed, brushed or polished to within an inch of its miserable life.

After a shy start, Jenny and I soon fell into talking and giggling as usual. We had to catch up on all the school gossip to start with. The big news there was that Miss Welbeloved had suddenly sprouted an engagement ring. We spent a happy hour or so trying to imagine the kind of man who would fancy her in the first place and had the nerve to take her on. We were both beside ourselves with laughter and had to make several trips to the bathroom so as not to run the risk of smelling like Enie Smales on a bad day.

Next, we played snakes and ladders, ludo and beat your neighbour out of doors, finishing up with a very loud game of snap, accompanied by lots of shrieking, yells of triumph or 'Rotten cheat!' and much groaning and crowing with delight. 'All good clean fun,' as Uncle Bert would have said if he'd been there, being a great crower himself when he was winning any sort of game. Auntie Maggie always said that crowing was bad form, but we enjoyed it. Where's the fun, clean or otherwise, if you can't have a jolly good crow?

Auntie Maggie had been so determined that our indoor picnic should fill all of our corners, she'd packed enough grub to feed a small army of starving Brownies. She'd also told me that I had to insist that Mrs Robbins joined us when noshing time came. The basket had been so heavy, Luigi had been grabbed off the street to carry it to Jenny's front door for me. I was left to carry the games and the comics I'd bought the day before.

We had a nice afternoon and a fantastic picnic. Auntie Maggie had really gone to town. There were paste sandwiches, a homemade Victoria sponge, a bag of custard creams, a large bowl of strawberry jelly covered with a starched white serviette, three bags of Smith's crisps, a bag of Cox's orange pippins and a large, homemade pork pie. Mrs Robbins had tried hard to argue the toss about joining us, but Jenny wouldn't take no for an answer either, saying that she wouldn't wrap her laughing gear around one scrap unless her mother did too. Naturally, there was tons of food left over and once again I had precise instructions from my aunt. I was to make sure that I left it with Mrs Robbins come hell or high water. My excuse was that I'd needed a bearer to bring it, and having no one to help on the return trip I'd better just take the basket.

'And if she tries to come with you, remind her that it's best not to leave Jenny on her tod. Got that?'

I got it and did as I was told. Mrs Robbins didn't put up that much of a struggle, as it happens. I think it was the sight of the faint pink glow on Jenny's cheeks that swung it; she didn't want to ruin the mood with a squabble. It was agreed that I would come again while Jenny was too poorly to come to school. I was to be a frequent visitor to the little flat during the next few weeks.

When I got home, I found the Campaninis had come to visit and were filling the cafe almost to bursting. There were too many of them to fit into our living room upstairs. Poor Luigi was being teased something rotten by his sisters about his lack of success with Betty Potts. He took it in good heart, but then life would have been misery for him if he hadn't. As the youngest, he got more than his fair share of teasing, and if he'd risen to it it would have been far worse. I knew how merciless those Campanini women could be, especially if they had a good target like their baby brother in their sights.

'So, she's toying with you, huh, Luigi? Like a big red pussycat with her little mouse. Serves you right. If she keeps it up for the next hundred years, it still wouldn't be enough to make up for all those broken hearts you've trampled on over the years.' Gina was enjoying herself hugely.

'What do you mean, a hundred? A thousand, more like. Don't forget what he did to Maria Gambini as was. She was my best friend until Romeo here stole her poor heart and her piggy bank all in the one afternoon. You remember, it was at the Sunday school party the year he turned ten. She was an older woman, too, being thirteen at the time. He was a devil with the girls even then. Do you know Maria still asks about him? And her with two bambini of her own now? It's disgusting, the effect baby brother has on unsuspecting girls. And he never confesses all of his sins, that one, never!' Bella sounded indignant but was grinning all the same.

Luigi had that effect on most people, women especially, even his sisters who should have known better. Paulette said it was because he was the baby, that and he was just plain lovable, despite everything. He was also gorgeous, everyone agreed on that. All the Campanini children had turned out good-looking and as Auntie Maggie said, 'After all those practice runs, it stands to reason that Mamma and Papa had perfected the art by the time they got to Luigi.' Although she never said it if there was a Campanini about; feelings might have got hurt.

I was tired after my hard afternoon's play and big nosh-up. That didn't stop me from trying to carry on well into the evening on the grounds that I might miss something, and that would never do. In the end, though, I just had to go to bed and leave them all to it, and I hardly argued at all, which shows just how knackered I was. However, I did manage to stay awake long enough to hear that Betty Potts had finally got a job, at one of Maltese Joe's clubs, and that he had changed her name for professional reasons.

'Betty Potts' didn't conjure up the right image for a glamour-puss hostess, according to Uncle Bert, who broke the news to Luigi and the assembled company, so Maltese Joe had come up with a name that was far more exotic and expensive sounding. 'Chinchilla O'Reardon he calls her. Chinchilla on account a coat of the same costs an arm and a leg and that's what she's cost him since he clapped eyes on her and it's got him nowhere fast. The O'Reardon's on account she looks Irish to our Joe, even though she ain't, and anyway he says she's got a great arse. I didn't get it till he wrote it down for me. Silly sod spells it R-e-a-r, as in back end. He's got her billed as "the Emerald Isle's brightest jewel", would you believe? No one's had the heart to tell him that a chinchilla's some kind of rat and that arse or no arse that's not the way to spell O'Riordan. Still, nobody's ever been able to tell Joe anything, except his mum of course, and maybe Bandy now and then, if he gets her mad enough.'

'Well, he can call her what he likes, the old pervert, but she'll always be Betty to me,' declared Auntie Maggie firmly to a chorus of agreement.

I yawned at that point, which told Auntie Maggie that it was way past my bedtime, so I missed the rest of the evening's fun.

9

Smiley Riley had been a bit slack in passing on my message and T.C. didn't show up at the cafe until Monday. By the time he and Sharky had had a bit of a chat about the Mangy Cow and Mr Robbins it was dinner time, and he offered to pick me up from school and escort me home for my nosh. Auntie Maggie didn't like to tell him that I was big enough to make my own way home. She said it hadn't seemed kind, as he was obviously dying to see me.

I must admit I felt a bit of a fool when he took my hand and I had to hiss at him that hand holding was for babies. He understood right away, and dropped my mitt toot sweet. We agreed that putting my arm through his was just about OK, but simply walking side by side was better. He looked a bit disappointed and said it was a long time since he'd had a pretty girl on his arm. So I took pity on him, and got a grip once we were well away from sneaks like Smelly Smales. I told him everything I could think of that had happened since I'd last seen him. He listened carefully to all my news and even asked the odd question about Sugar's latest sequined creation and Betty Potts to show that he really had taken it all in. T.C. was good at that, just listening as if you were the only person in the world.

By the time we'd got back to the cafe and he'd been talked into stopping for his dinner with me, we'd got on to Jenny. He was particularly interested in hearing how I felt about my friend being ill. It was a tricky one to answer, that, because I hadn't really *thought* about how I felt about it, I just felt it. I was tucking into lemon syrup pud, my favourite, when the tears welled up and started to drip into my plate. Until that moment, I hadn't realized how frightened, sad and lonely I felt about it. Next thing I knew, I was on his lap, thumb in mouth and sobbing my heart out. He was very kind, didn't point out that blubbing was for babies, just handed me his hanky and cuddled me tight, muttering 'There, there' from time to time until I hiccuped to a stop. It was only after he had escorted me back to the playground that I realized he hadn't once told me that everything was going to be all right, the way grown-ups are supposed to do when you're blubbing. Of course I wasn't to know where telling T.C. was to lead and the trouble it would cause him in the end. By the time I did know, it was far too late to keep my mouth shut anyhow.

Now, a sighting of Maltese Joe during daylight hours was as rare a thing as seeing Bandy before sunset. Sometimes he could be spotted driving his old ma to Mass in the Roller on a Sunday morning. Occasionally, sunlight caught him on the hop before he managed to get home from one of his clubs and now and then he went to the races, but that was about it. So you can imagine what a surprise it was to see him sitting at the corner table with my uncle Bert when I got home from school. Judging by the virtually empty ashtray in front of him, he'd only been there for a short while.

According to Uncle Bert, he'd just missed bumping into T.C., which was a jolly good thing as there was no love lost between the pair of them. Each knew the other was a family friend, but was too well-mannered to mention it, or so Uncle Bert said anyway. Very occasionally, they both turned up at one of our parties, but they managed not to notice each other and one would always leave quickly. It was fascinating to watch, because there would be no discussion: one of them would simply start saying goodbye to people and then go. The first to arrive was the first to leave. Uncle Bert said it was bad for Maltese Joe's reputation to be seen hobnobbing with a copper, and Auntie Maggie said that socializing with criminals didn't do a lot for T.C.'s either. Still, everyone seemed to cope somehow, and we managed to keep friends with both of them.

I loved T.C. and quite liked Maltese Joe. I'm not sure why, although it didn't do not to like him. T.C. always treated me as if I was a grown-up when we talked, and as a child if I needed comfort in the form of a cuddle. He took what I said seriously and never, ever fobbed me off with remarks like 'You'll understand when you're older', or 'You're too young'. I always hated that. It seemed to me that grown-ups were just too lazy to come up with a better excuse to leave me out of things.

Maltese Joe also treated me like a grown-up female, but that wasn't saying much, because he treated nearly all females as if they were children, or at least mentally retarded. He was always patting women on the bum and telling them to 'run along and powder your nose or something while the men get down to business', in exactly the voice grownups use when they're telling kids to 'run along and play'.

Uncle Bert always said that the only exceptions to Maltese Joe's 'women are idiots' rule were his old mum, Auntie Maggie and Bandy Bunyan. Auntie Maggie said the only reason she'd been included in the list was that Uncle Bert made Joe put her there by beating him up soon after Uncle Bert and Auntie Maggie had started 'walking out'. It almost ended their friendship, apparently, but Joe's mum had joined in the argument on Uncle Bert's side by saying that showing respect for Auntie Maggie was a way of showing respect to her man and anyway Joe didn't have so many good friends that he could afford to lose one. So it was settled: Auntie Maggie was officially tolerated by Maltese Joe. Over the years they had grown used to each other, and had finally grown to like each other, after a fashion. But Auntie Maggie never did approve of Maltese Joe's general attitude to the fairer sex.

Naturally, being nosy, I wanted to know why Bandy was OK with Joe, but whenever I asked Uncle Bert he only laughed and said, 'Would you try telling Bandy to go and powder her nose? I know I wouldn't. She'd have me minced and diced before the words left me mouth. Anyway, with a hooter the size of hers, she could be gone for a week.' Which was unkind, but true; Bandy did have a big nose. She looked like an eagle, and about as friendly.

Still, I didn't mind being told to take a hike by Maltese Joe, because he always slipped me a half-crown as 'a little sweetner'. Betty Potts said he was the same with the women, except that they got a nice, big, crisp white fiver or two for their obedience.

Of course, he needn't have troubled,

because even big strong men ran away to play when told to by Maltese Joe. It didn't do to argue with him on account of his temper. He could turn very nasty indeed if crossed by a man, a woman or even a child. I once saw him clip one of Luigi's young nephews around the ear'ole so hard, he sent him clear across the room, so that he bounced off the wall. Said he'd caught the boy beating up his little sister, and when he'd told him to stop the boy had got lippy and sworn at him. Not a wise move, that, and one Giovanni would not make again in a hurry.

There were lots of stories about Maltese Joe losing his rag and people winding up so badly hurt that they never came back to bother him again. It was true that Dave Potter was still in a wheelchair years after an altercation with Joe over the rightful ownership of a large suitcase full of forged tenners. Joe won the argument after what Uncle Bert described as a frank exchange of blows, kicks and finally army-issue bullets between Dave and Joe and his 'boys'. And Lenny-the-Gimp did owe his nickname to the time he was caught with his hand in one of Joe's tills. In fact, as far as I know, my uncle Bert was the only person ever to biff Maltese Joe and get away with it and he had old Ma Joe to thank for that.

Anyway, Maltese Joe was at the cafe when

I got home from school and I couldn't help wondering why. Auntie Maggie was out and the place was empty apart from Joe and Uncle Bert, which was probably just as well. They took no notice of me as I scuttled behind the counter for my glass of milk and a couple of digestives.

Maltese Joe was well dressed as usual. He wore a smart Savile Row three-piece suit in a dark blue wool with the tiniest fleck of maroon, a sparkling white shirt and a blue and maroon striped silk tie with a fat Windsor knot. A white linen hanky peeped out of his breast pocket. He wore a heavy gold wedding ring on his left hand, the way the Italian blokes did. Auntie Maggie said that she thought it was terrible that Joe's old mum still bought all his clothes, despite his being married and everything. She said it showed he was a bit of a mummy's boy, but she said it quietly, in case she got her head bashed in. But everyone agreed that it was unusual for a married bloke to have quite so much to do with his mum. Everyone put it down to him being Maltese, but nobody said why. I knew other Maltese blokes who didn't even seem to have mums at all.

Instead of keeping up the regulation short back and sides most blokes had, Maltese Joe wore his hair slightly long, so he kept his barber in Dean Street busy doing his nails once a week and shaving him twice every day instead, once at noon and again at six in the evening, ready for the working night. Maltese Joe always seemed to have a seven o'clock shadow, no matter what time it was.

I didn't have to wait long to find out why Joe was visiting us. He wasn't used to kids, so he forgot they have ears, and was soon carrying on his conversation as if I wasn't there. I could tell by the way his eyes were bulging, and how red the veins were, that he was angry.

'So, where is he now, does anyone know?' Maltese Joe glared across the table at Uncle Bert as he took a hefty drag on his fag and flicked the ash in the general direction of the ashtray.

'We're not sure, Joe, but last seen he was in a coma at Ruby's. We reckoned she'd keep him out of our way while we had a think. We was hoping to come up with some sort of plan that didn't involve too much in the way of mess and bother, while he was occupied, like.'

'You're wrong there, Bert. He's been occupied in poking about the manor, and only a day or two ago. And when *were* you planning to give me the news, huh? I had to hear it from Hissing Sid's bint when I was giving her one in the office last night. Woman goes like a rabbit. It's an eye-opener, I can tell you. She talks while she's at it and she was talking about this funny Yank. Talking a blue bloody streak, in fact. The more she said the more I was reminded of the Widow. So, I'm asking you again, Bert, when were you planning to tell me that Stanley was back and looking to shove a shiv in me back right up to the sodding hilt, eh? Or have you come to some arrangement with the man himself, is that it?'

'Now, you've no call to make insinuations like that, Joe, no call at all. I've never come in on the wrong side in all the bloody years I've known you and I resent you even thinking it.' Uncle Bert was getting angry too. He jumped to his feet, knocking his chair over with a clatter, and glared down at Joe, his fists clenched by his side. Joe stood up slowly and took a long, hard look at Uncle Bert. Their noses were almost touching. Then he shrugged, walked to the door and stopped with his hand on the doorknob.

'And this plan, it's sorted is it?' Maltese Joe's eyes were glittering dangerously, just like the time when he clouted Giovanni. I hoped like mad that he wasn't going to clout my uncle Bert because I didn't know what I would do if he did.

Uncle Bert took a deep, calming breath before answering. I could tell he was working really hard not to lose his rag. 'Not exactly, Joe, no. I haven't had much of a chance, to be fair. I s'pose I was hoping that

that would be the end of it, and was waiting and seeing. But of course it won't be the end of it, not really. He's like a bleeding terrier, that one. Never lets go of anything.'

'So, no plan, eh? Time to get one going then. Stanley'll be back, no question of that, and – thanks to you – I might not be ready when he gets here. I still say I should've killed the sod while I had the chance, but you soft buggers wouldn't let me. It would've been a bloody sight easier to tart it up as an accident in the blackout than it will be now.'

'Hold your water, Joe. Now do you see why I kept my gob shut? I knew you'd go overboard. Me and Bandy have discussed that much and we say no killing, even if it is so richly deserved. If anyone is going to top Stanley, let's make sure it's the government that does the deed and not us, any of us. But I agree, I have been putting things off, and I'm sorry. I just thought it was for the best, that's all.' Which wasn't quite true. It was Auntie Maggie who had thought it best, and had made Uncle Bert keep quiet. He really hadn't wanted to. I wondered why Uncle Bert wouldn't just say that Auntie Maggie had put her foot down and be done with it. Except that you never grassed up your own, and Auntie Maggie was more to Bert than his lifelong mate. It must have been hard to fall out with his friend, but he kept his gob shut just the same.

Maltese Joe's eyes bulged a bit more and the little vein in his forehead throbbed. 'Let's hope your thinking hasn't done any permanent damage, shall we? But I wouldn't put your pension on it, Bert, or on your chances if he fucks me over.'

'Are you threatening me, Joe?' my uncle demanded, his voice dangerously quiet.

'I suppose you could say that, Bert,' Maltese Joe replied. 'You could say that. You'd better start praying it turns out right, hadn't you?'

Uncle Bert had his mouth open to reply and had taken a step towards Joe when he spotted Auntie Maggie coming towards the cafe door with Madame Zelda and Betty Potts in tow. Maltese Joe smiled a tight smile, shrugged and pulled the door open, stepping to one side to let in the chattering women, and walked out into the street. He didn't turn back for one last joke with Uncle Bert, like he usually did. In fact, there had been no jokes at all, and Uncle Bert watched him go with a sad look on his face. Then he, too, shrugged and walked slowly back to his kitchen with his head bowed low.

10

The atmosphere around our place was just so awful it was a real pleasure to go to school. I missed meeting Jenny in the churchyard, but took to waving to her instead while I waited for Kathy Moon to turn up. Jenny also liked feeding the pigeons only now she was so poorly she fed hers on her kitchen window sill. Her mum let her, even though she said they were filthy things. Jenny's favourite was called Peter the Pigeon and was brown and white instead of grey. He had a dodgy beak which grew over just like an ingrowing toenail, and Jenny and her mum had had to grab poor old Peter and file his beak down with a socking great nail file so that it didn't grow so far over it was stuck closed. Still, he seemed to appreciate it, because he kept coming back for his grub.

Every morning, I'd look up and wait for Jenny's head to poke out of the top window and I'd wave like mad and she'd wave back. It wasn't the same as walking to school with her and sitting next to her in class, but it was better than nothing. Since I'd last seen her I'd been thinking about a simple code language, with coloured hankies or hand signing or something and planned to talk it over with her next time I saw her. I had a really good book about codes and semaphore and stuff. I loved all that. I could pass on all sorts of bits of good gossip if we could find a system of secret signals. I could keep her up to date with poor Luigi's unrequited passion for a start. Jenny had a bit of a crush on Luigi, but then most females did, it seemed to me. Except Betty Potts, that is. As it happens, there was about to be a bit of action on that front at last.

After a week of gloomy silences at home, it was Saturday again, and as it happened I was the only one there, apart from Mrs Wong that is, and she showed no interest at all. Auntie Maggie, Madame Zelda, Paulette and Sugar were well cheesed off, but I was next to myself with the deepest of joy. It wasn't often that I got to come up with a bit of red hot gossip, so you can imagine my unholy glee.

Madame Zelda and Paulette had just left to go in search of some incense to pong up Madame Zelda's consulting room. It added atmosphere, or so she said. Personally, I thought she used it to smother the whiff of wintergreen in the horse liniment she used on her poor feet. As I've said, Madame Zelda was a martyr to her feet, especially in winter when they were smothered in chilblains as well as the rheumatics that made her hobble so. Anyway, there was a shop in Bloomsbury that supplied churches with candles, chalices and stuff, but it closed at dinner time on Saturdays, so they were in a rush.

Auntie Maggie had nipped out to get some cucumber for Mrs Williams's Sunday tea. We always had cucumber sandwiches with the crusts cut off when Mrs W. had tea with us, even in the winter when it was almost impossible to get. As luck would have it, our mate Ronnie knew a bloke who knew a bloke who supplied the Ritz, so that was all right, as long as he got plenty of warning. As Uncle Bert said, they had to have time to tell the bloke who knew a bloke to get his bloke to start growing the damned thing, but Auntie Maggie said he was laying it on a bit thick. Still, it was a right old performance, getting cucumber in winter. Cucumber sandwiches were something to do with Mrs W. being in service before the First World War, and before she married Mr Williams and took over the grocery next door to the paper shop. Mr Williams had been killed by flying shrapnel while visiting his mum in Bow in 1942.

I wasn't that keen on cucumber sandwiches. They were titchy for one thing, apart from being disgustingly boring. Still, it made the local pigeons very happy, because they got the crusts. Personally, I liked a nice bit of Spam, fish paste or a fried egg in my sandwiches, but I didn't count when we were entertaining.

Down the alley round the corner, Sugar was asleep in his bed above the club, Friday nights being long and busy. Uncle Bert was in his kitchen, getting ready for the dinner-time rush, so there was only me and Luigi at our table, Mrs Wong behind the counter and a few of the Saturday morning punters. They were usually a fairly quiet lot, being busy trying to focus their poor eyes and get their brains to work through the fog. It's not easy thinking up new and original excuses for being out all night splurging the pay packet on booze, women and gambling when you have a hangover. Or so Luigi was explaining to me as I sipped my milk and swung my feet.

I was bored, jittery and thoroughly fed up with all the trouble about. Uncle Bert and Auntie Maggie were barely speaking. Maltese Joe was avoiding Uncle Bert, Jenny was poorly and there was nothing I could do to change any of it. There was no one to play with. Kathy was being made to stay in and scrub the kitchen floor on account of being caught playing knock-down-ginger the day before on the way home from school. I told her it was stupid to ring her own bell, her mum being no fool, but she wouldn't listen. I wasn't caught as I'd had the brains not to poke my head round the corner, but Kathy just had to see her mum's face when she stuck her head out of the window to an empty doorstep. Kathy was never over-burdened with the grey stuff when it came to playing tricks; she just couldn't resist a gloat. So no Kathy that Saturday, and I was bored rigid and in a deep funk. At least I was until the door opened and Betty Potts strode in.

It was always interesting watching Luigi when Betty hove into view. His face lit up like a petrol dump hit by a doodlebug, or so Auntie Maggie used to say; personally, I'd never seen that, but I took her word for it. He certainly glowed a lot. He also leaped to his feet and shuffled chairs about to make sure that she parked herself as close to him as was decent in broad daylight.

Luigi was not usually given to glowing and leaping; that's what girls did when *he* arrived, so it made a nice change to see him at it. Then he'd either get stuck for words or gabble on and on about nothing at all for ages before winding down like a clockwork top. Somewhere in the gabble there was usually an offer of a trip to the flicks or a dance or a night at his favourite jazz spot. Poor Luigi was always turned down, in the nicest possible way of course. It had become a sort of ritual in the short time that Betty had been around. This Saturday was no different.

'So, Betty, how's it going? New flat all right, is it?'

'Yes thanks, Luigi, it's fine. Apart from that trumpet player above me, that is. He can make a row sometimes but, thank God, he spends most of his time around at his girlfriend's. She's a singer, I forget her name.'

'You mean Johnnie's girl? She's called Annie. She sings with the band he plays with.'

'That's her. Nice girl. Good singer. You'd think they'd see enough of each other, working together six nights a week and twice on Saturdays. It's gotta be love. Still, it keeps the racket down. But they must have had a row because he's in this morning, blasting away like a good 'un. I couldn't stand it a second longer, so I came here for a bit of peace and quiet. Last night was busy, and Mr Joe was like a ruddy octopus. Kept me dodging and weaving until I thought my legs'd drop off.'

'You'd think he'd get the message, but then Joe's never one to get messages he ain't interested in,' said Luigi with a laugh. 'He thrives on a challenge, and let's face it, gel, you're one hell of a challenge. You should try going out with me, that might cool him off. How about the pictures tomorrow?'

Luigi and me, we almost missed it, we were so used to her coming up with some variation on thanks but no thanks.

'That'd be nice, Luigi. What time will you pick me up?'

'OK, Betty, another ti–What? Did you just say yes?'

'Well, if you'd rather not...'

'No, no. I mean yes! I'm buggered if I know what I mean. 'Scuse the French. I'll pick you up at six. P'raps we can grab a bite and a whistle-wetter after the flick.'

'Lovely. I'll look forward to it. Now, Rosie, what do you recommend for my dinner, you being the resident expert and all?'

And that was it. I could hardly wait to tell Auntie Maggie, Madame Zelda and Paulette that Luigi had finally cracked it. As it was, I had to make do with Uncle Bert until my beloved aunt got back. He tried to look suitably impressed with my news, but I could tell his heart wasn't in it. He was still too busy worrying about the Widow Ginger, Maltese Joe and everything. Still, Auntie Maggie and the others more than made up for it.

Auntie Maggie got back first, Berwick Street market being a lot closer than Coptic Street. Even so, she'd taken her time, but then it was impossible for her to get two yards down the road without finding someone to chat to, as I knew to my cost. I hate to think of how many years I've wasted hanging about beside her as I listened to views on the weather and bits and bobs of gossip I already knew.

Even when she was back, I couldn't pass on my news until Luigi and Betty had left, and I was hopping from foot to foot in my impatience. Poor Betty's knife and fork had barely hit the plate before I was whipping away her empties and getting Mrs Wong to force her tea on her. She'd decided against the apple pie and custard on account of her figure. Not that there was anything wrong with it, as Luigi gallantly pointed out. Betty supposed there wasn't, yet, but there would be if she kept guzzling Auntie Maggie's wonderful puds. Auntie Maggie blushed with pleasure at the compliment and insisted Betty have a second cuppa to make up for it. Meanwhile, I wished like mad that she'd minded her own business so that I could blurt out Betty and Luigi's. It was so frustrating. I was in like a ferret up a trouser leg as soon as the door closed behind them.

'Guess what?'

'What?'

'Go on, guess,' I insisted.

Auntie Maggie sighed and rolled her eyes to heaven. 'The Queen's coming to tea.'

'Don't be daft. It's not that.' Everyone knew the Queen was far too posh for the likes of us.

'The donkey broke his leg.'

'Now you're being really stupid. What donkey?'

'And who are you calling stupid, young lady? Watch your manners with your elders and betters or I'll make your little bum glow. So what is it, this bit of news of yours?'

I wasn't ready to give it up yet. 'Promise you'll let me tell the others and you won't just blab it out.'

'Tell what others? And would I blab?'

'Madame Zelda, Paulette and Sugar. And yes, you'll blab. You won't be able to help it, unless you promise.'

'Well, if that's your attitude, young lady, I'm sure I don't want to know.'

And she had me there, she knew she did, because I was fit to burst and I simply could not have borne to keep my gob shut. 'Luigi's taking Betty to the pictures tomorrow and for a bite and a whistle-wetter after. Now promise you won't tell the others.'

'Well, I'll be blowed. Yes, yes, I promise. When did this happen? Who said what? Tell me everything from the very beginning.'

I'll say this for my aunt, she really knew how to enjoy a bit of news. I told her everything and she kept her promise to let me tell the others. They were also suitably astonished, except Sugar who'd already heard it by the time he dropped in a few days later. But by then Betty had given us all the interesting details about what she wore, where they went and what the film was like. She wore her navy two-piece with the pencil skirt, with a white blouse and flat emerald green shoes so's not to be too tall. She carried a matching clutch bag and she had her hair up in a French pleat. Luigi wore his best blue worsted suit with a two-tone blue striped tie.

There was a choice between several war pictures, cartoons or *Roman Holiday* with Gregory Peck and Audrey Hepburn. Naturally Betty chose *Roman Holiday* and who wouldn't? As she said, she was sick of war and had seen enough cartoons to last her a while. Personally, I don't think you can get enough of Mickey Mouse and his pals, but then nobody consulted me. They went to Luigi's cousin Giuseppe's place in Brewer Street for their meal afterward. Being a greedy little sod, I insisted on a rundown of the menu. They both had the same thing, which was minestrone soup, ravioli and green salad, with a bottle of Chianti between them, fresh fruit, on account of Betty's diet and strong black coffee. They followed it up with a couple of drinks at the Red Lion in Fitzrovia, then they went for a stroll around the manor and, finally, he saw her home.

To everyone's amazement and disappointment, Luigi was a perfect gentleman all evening, according to Betty. Madame Zelda said that she hadn't realized Luigi had an ounce of gent in him, since he had never shown it before with any of his other conquests. Sugar said that that proved he was serious about her and everyone except me agreed. It seemed to me that Luigi had been serious about everything ever since he'd met Betty. Up until then he'd been a jolly soul, full of laughter and a wonderful sense of fun, but the second he fell in love with Betty all laughs were off. I couldn't help wondering why he bothered if it was so hard to squeeze any joy out of it. I remember asking Paulette to explain it to me but all she would say was that Luigi was having a different sort of good time, one that didn't involve playing the fool. As an explanation of the workings of grown-up romance, I have to say it was as clear as lumpy porridge and about as interesting.

11

On the Sunday morning of Mrs Williams's tea I was suddenly excused the dreaded cucumber sandwiches. Jenny's mum had asked me to visit again. I wasn't to go for the whole afternoon, just for a little while before another picnic tea. Jenny was too knackered for a long haul.

I was thrilled; not that Jenny was knackered, of course, but because I was spared those ruddy awful sarnies. I liked Mrs Williams well enough. When I went in the shop she always gave me some broken biscuits from one of the big square tins with the glass tops that she kept on a long, narrow trestle table in front of her counter. She'd give me a brown paper bag and let me choose from the custard creams, rich teas, digestives and my favourites, the ones with the pale brown, coffee-flavoured icing sugar on the top. The trick was to get the icing sugar off in one lump and suck it until it dissolved. Heaven!

Although Mrs W. was kind, I did find her visits a bit boring. I had to be on my best behaviour and sit up straight, hands folded in my lap. I was to be seen, in my best frock, but definitely not heard. Well, not a lot, anyway. So to escape to Jenny's was a treat.

Once again, we provided the picnic on the insistence of my aunt. I helped get it ready and spent a happy morning in the kitchen beating up fairy cake mixture with a fork and licking the bowl afterwards. Bowl licking was one of my specialities. Auntie Maggie cut the bread for the sandwiches and I was allowed to slather meat paste over the slices. Then we finished making a trifle that Auntie Maggie had started the night before. We split the sponges – soaked in orange juice instead of sherry – between two bowls, one for Mrs William's tea and one for the picnic. My tongue was busy again, finishing up the last tiny scraps of custard and cream from the blue and white striped bowls. I loved those bowls, because they meant baking and puddings. Auntie Maggie said there was no need to wash them, or the spoons, forks and saucepan, because me and my tongue were champion washer-uppers. I think she was joking, though, because they all wound up in the sink anyway. The trifles were covered with clean tea towels and put in the cold larder to set. Later, when it was ready, Auntie Maggie said I could sprinkle pastel-coloured hundreds and thousands on the one for Jenny and me. I could hardly wait, because it was hard to do without scattering them all over the place and I got to crunch up all the tiny sugar bombs I collected from the table-top – although not those that skittered across the floor.

At last it was time to go, and Uncle Bert was volunteered to do the lugging of the picnic basket. He popped in to see how Jenny was doing and found some gob-stoppers in her ears. She'd lost some weight and her normally quite squinty eyes looked enormous, with dark circles underneath. Still, the thrilled look on her little pale pointy face when Uncle Bert made a deep bow and presented her with the bright, sugary balls made her look quite shiny and well for a moment. I felt a bit of a fool when my minces filled up with tears that threatened to spill over on to my cheeks and I didn't know why. I was forced to rummage in Uncle Bert's pocket for a hanky to blow my hooter good and hard and wipe up the salty stuff while I was at it. Uncle Bert and Mrs Robbins didn't notice, I'm thrilled to say, and Jenny was too busy oohing and aahing over her gobstoppers to take it in.

I couldn't wait for Mrs Robbins to show Uncle Bert out, so that I could tell Jenny all about Luigi and Betty. We had a lovely time wondering what they'd do and whether they'd get as far as a snog on the doorstep.

'Everyone says Luigi can get a girl flat on her back without even offering her dinner, so I should think snogging would be dead easy.'

'Yes, but Betty's been playing hard to get, and it's taken him this long to get her to go out with him. I reckon she'll stay upright all right, but she might let him have a little kiss. I bet he doesn't make it in to her place, not right off. Not on their first date. What do you reckon, Jen?'

'What does "getting 'em flat on their backs" mean, anyway?'

I tried to look as if I knew what I was talking about. 'I reckon they mean ... er ...

sex and that.'

'Yes, but what do they actually do?'

She had me there. I had never got past wondering why girls would want to be flat on their backs waving their legs in the air. This was something girls of any age were discouraged from doing, on account of showing their knickers. Knicker flashing was a very big no-no. We were trained long and hard in the art of keeping our knees clamped together and our skirts pulled down from the moment we could stand or sit unaided. Nice girls kept their knickers to themselves until they were married, and that was a fact that everybody knew.

Reality was often very different, especially in our neck of the woods. Brasses were often nice girls, but the women's magazines suggested otherwise. Nice girls didn't 'go' with men until they had the gold band. Round our way they did. Paulette was always a smashing person, tart or not. We'd always loved Paulette, whether she was on the streets or being a Nippy at her Corner House. My very own mother was not known for keeping her drawers on either. She'd gone with more than her fair share of blokes. Madame Zelda said she'd go with 'anyone with a wallet and a heartbeat' when the bevvy was upon her. Yet she was a really nice person when she laid off the booze.

It was tricky, dealing with my mum. She

could be awful one minute and wonderful and exciting the next. There was no telling with her, so sometimes I found her frightening. I never knew if she was going to grab me and slobber all over me, or blub the place down because I wasn't pleased enough to see her. Luckily, I didn't have to do it all that often. Perhaps that's why I never got it just right. Still, that's another story – but it did get us on to something else that had been troubling me.

'You know my mum wasn't married when she had me, so that makes me a bastard, right?'

Jenny nodded gravely. This was serious business.

'Then how come people call Maltese Joe a bastard and Luigi's cast-offs are always calling him one too? How come they're bastards when their mums and dads were definitely married? I don't get it, do you?'

Jenny couldn't explain that one, either, so after a bit we gave up on it. Then we got on to Romance, capital R and all. We found the topic thrilling, but a bit puzzling too. If, as the song said, love and marriage went together like a horse and carriage, how come that round our way, in our experience, they didn't necessarily go together at all?

'I mean, look at Sugar and Bandy. My auntie Maggie says they love each other dearly, but they ain't married nor showing any signs of it.'

Jenny nodded, 'Yeah, I know what you mean. Look at my lot.'

It was my turn to nod. Her lot didn't bear thinking about, what with the Mangy Cow in the picture. We needed something more cheerful to concentrate on. 'Who do you reckon would wear the frock, anyway? You know, out of Sugar and Bandy? Can you imagine Bandy in a frock?'

We gave it a go, but we couldn't see it. We howled with laughter as we tried to picture the event. In the end, we decided that Sugar should wear the dress as usual, and that Bandy could have the top hat and penguin suit if and when they ever tottered down the aisle. We kicked up such a din with our shrieks of merriment that Mrs Robbins came in to find out what all the fuss was about. We couldn't tell her, of course, but every time we caught each other's eye we howled some more, until she gave up on us with a resigned shrug.

Before I left we managed to work out a very simple signalling system involving Jenny's waving tea towels in a variety of sequences depending on whether she wanted chocolate, comics or a visit after school. I, in turn, would wave my arms about: two arms up meant a visit after school, one meant 'Message understood', and dancing around like an Apache on the warpath meant 'Hot news, see you later'. Gossip, we decided, was too complicated for signals, and anyway poor old Jenny was so tired by then, she wasn't able to raise the enthusiasm to work it out.

I was just leaving when it occurred to me that we ought to have a sign for 'Help' because all the best secret agents had one. In the end we decided she'd dangle the red scarf she'd knitted for her mum's Christmas present out of the window and I'd wear my red gloves, should help be needed by either side. Red, we decided, was just the thing: red for danger. Simple and to the point.

12

I knew the Widow Ginger, or Stanley Janulewicz as his parents probably preferred to call him (that's if he ever had any; Auntie Maggie always said he was Satan's spawn), the minute he walked into the cafe. The hair stood up all along my arms and my knees turned to jelly as soon as I spotted him. It was late one Wednesday afternoon. There was no big kerfuffle; he just slid in and he was there. Auntie Maggie gave a start when he spoke to her. 'Hi, Margaret. Albert out back, is he?'

'Oh! Hello, Stanley. No, don't come round.' Auntie Maggie placed her mighty bulk across the end of the counter, the route through to the kitchen, happy in the knowledge that the neat, slight man wasn't going to be able to shift her without a bulldozer. 'I'll give him a shout. Take a seat, I'll bring you some tea. Bert. BERT! It's Stanley to see you.'

Auntie Maggie watched him all the way to his seat, the way a mongoose watches a snake. I'd seen it at the pictures; they watch the snake's every move. Well, Auntie Maggie was watching the Widow just like that and all the colour had drained from her usually rosy face. I realized that the cafe had gone absolutely silent, apart from the faint hiss and bubble from the tea urn. Everyone in the place had sensed the tension and was waiting. I found I was cringing slightly, the way you do in a Western or war film when something's about to explode and you know but the blokes on screen don't. The Widow sat down and carefully removed his black hat and laid it on the table. He smoothed his hair with a delicate, almost girlie, hand. It was the palest hair I had ever seen, except on Jean Harlow maybe. Only the Widow's was cut short and was very neat.

Uncle Bert finally came out from his kitchen and joined Auntie Maggie behind her counter for a moment; a second mongoose, same snake. Then, wiping his hands slowly on his apron, he walked over to the table and sat down opposite the Widow, who was busy arranging his trouser creases. He didn't trouble to look up or speak until he was absolutely satisfied that there'd be no baggy knees to ruin the line. Uncle Bert waited patiently and didn't say a word. He wore a faint smile, but his stare was hard. Auntie Maggie delivered two teas to the table and Uncle Bert's pipe and tobacco.

My uncle Bert could make a real production out of lighting his pipe. Sometimes, when I was in trouble and Auntie Maggie thought his two penn'orth would help to make me see things her way, she made him give me a good talking to. Other times, when the situation was really bad, he thought of it himself. Either way, he pulled the pipe stunt. He'd concentrate hard on each stage, looking up at me every now and then, but saying nothing. The more stages, the deeper the trouble. If he took his pipe tools out, it was the full monty, which meant very big, very deep trouble. The pipe tools were out now as he and the Widow sat there, saying nothing.

It got so that the silence got on my already jangled nerves and I wanted desperately to whoop and yell, or drop a load of plates or something, anything to break the tension. But I didn't dare. I was too afraid.

At last the American spoke. 'Nice little operation you got here, Albert. Must bring in a few bucks – knicker, I should say.' The familiar voice sent a trickle of ice right down my spine. I felt sick as a flash of that menacing moment outside the church came back to me. He was a Yank all right; he sounded just like some of them on the films or the Pathe News. Except the Widow's voice was very, very quiet.

'It's a living,' Uncle Bert replied.

'I should hope so, Albert. I should hope so.'

'What's that supposed to mean?' Uncle Bert sounded tired.

The Widow's smile was tight and for his mouth only. His eyes were looking round the room as if he was pricing the place up to see what it'd fetch. They stopped at the corner table where Luigi, Madame Zelda and I were sitting. That's when I realized just what was so frightening about him. It was the expression in his eyes. There wasn't one. They glittered so coldly, there was no reading them. They acted almost like mirrors so that when they lingered on you, you saw yourself like a bug under a microscope. As if you were a specimen and not a person at all.

'I mean that I should hope so. You're a family man now, Albert. You have responsibilities. Insured, is it, all this?' The Widow waved a hand, taking in everything like a bailiff on the make.

'I don't think my arrangements are any of your business.' Another hard stare, then Uncle Bert stood up. 'What can I get you, Stanley? I think there's some shepherd's pie left, if you fancy that. There's nothing else on offer.'

Absolutely everyone in the place was riveted. We were watching every move. Listening to every word.

'I was only thinking, Albert. Grease fires, nasty things in a catering establishment such as this. Live above, do you? Just you, Margaret and the kid is it?' There was a long, long silence as Uncle Bert stared hard at the Widow and the Widow stared just as hard back at him. Uncle Bert had the advantage of being the one standing. It was just like a Western. I expected someone to start blasting away with their Colt 45 at any minute. Only this time, it wasn't John Wayne or Hopalong Cassidy squaring up to the black-hearted villain, it was my uncle Bert. Suddenly, I couldn't bear it a second longer. I hurled myself at Uncle Bert, clamped firmly on to his legs and glared around his long, white apron at the Widow. I hadn't forgotten being grabbed by the scruff of the neck and my knees were wobbling badly, but Uncle Bert was mine and I wanted to be on his side. Luigi,

116

Madame Zelda, Auntie Maggie and several punters also stood up and walked over to Uncle Bert and ranged themselves in a semicircle behind him. Nobody spoke. Nobody needed to. The message was loud and clear.

The Widow stood up, shook out his beloved creases and with another long, slow look round the place smiled that icy smile, picked up his hat, settled it comfortably on that pale hair and started to walk towards the door. Then he stopped, deep in thought, and turned to look at Uncle Bert again.

Concern was etched deep on his face, but missing those cold eyes completely. 'I mean it, Albert. Watch out for grease fires. I would take out insurance if I were you. Yes sir, I surely would.' And with that, he was gone. His untouched tea steamed gently, the only sign that he had ever been there. Well, perhaps not the only sign; there was also the deathly silence from everyone that seemed to go on and on.

Luigi was the first to react. 'Christ! I see what everyone means about that geezer now. A chilly bastard, ain't he?'

It showed how seriously everyone took the Widow's visit that Auntie Maggie didn't notice Luigi's 'bastard' and failed to shoot him the usual 'watch that gob of yours' look she had when people swore in front of me. She was especially touchy about the word 'bastard'; I suppose because I was one and she didn't want my nose rubbed in it.

'He is that, Luigi. He is that.' Madame Zelda's voice was thoughtful. 'Was it just me grabbing the wrong end of the stick or was that bugger threatening you, Bert?'

'He was threatening all right, Zeld, and he's not one to be idle about it neither, but I reckon we're safe enough until he states his terms. He wants something from me, that's as certain as I'm standing here. The only question is what?'

'Use your loaf, Bert. What do people usually want? Dosh, gelt, filthy lucre, the folding, whatever you want to call it, that's what he's after,' Madame Zelda said firmly. 'Bound to be.'

'No, it's not money, Zelda. Well, not just money, anyway. Did you see the whistle he was wearing and them shoes? He ain't short of a bob or two. No, it ain't just the readies he's after; he wants more than that.' Luigi looked worried as he turned to my uncle Bert. 'What are you going to do, Bert?'

Uncle Bert stared long and hard at his cold pipe before he finally answered, and when he did he sounded bone weary. 'I'm blowed if I know, Luigi. Wait and see, I suppose. It's all I can do for the minute until he gets to the point and tells me what he wants. I reckon Maggie's right: he's after Joe's businesses and he thinks he can force me to help him get them.' He sighed, and my heart ached for my beloved uncle. Despite Auntie Maggie's attempt to keep Uncle Bert away from the Widow Ginger, it seemed that the Widow was determined to come to him. I wondered if it was all my fault, that by stamping on his foot I had tipped the Widow over the edge. He had been very angry at the time and everyone said he was a nutter, so it might not take much to set him off.

Uncle Bert seemed to shake himself slightly, then he smiled a rather tight smile. 'What he thinks I can do is another question. But that's why he's threatening me. He wants me to co-operate and he knows I'm not willing; that, and the fact that he enjoys turning the screws just to watch you squirm. He told me once that as a nipper he used to torture cats and things, to see what would happen and how much they could stand before they pegged out. Fair made me sick to hear it, I can tell you. He called it his "spirit of inquiry". Personally, I call it sadism. He's a twenty-four-carat gold nutcase, that much is certain.' Uncle Bert stared at the floor as if he could see the mangled remains of some poor pussy cat. My eyes filled with tears as, just for a second, I saw it too. It was our lace-eared old Tom and I wanted to rush out to make sure he was all right, but I knew he was curled up in his box next to the warm oven, so I didn't. Maybe my accident with the Widow's toecap really had shoved him right out of his trolley. If he was already three-quarters there, it wouldn't take much. Dimly, through the miserable guilt of wondering why I could never watch where I was going, I heard Uncle Bert's voice continue.

'The only thing I ever saw that worried that one was currants, of all things.' When everyone looked blank he went on to explain. 'Not the currants you get in spotted dick, but currant buns as in nuns. Turned white he did when he bumped into a pair of 'em begging for the poor outside the Ritz. Couldn't empty his pockets into their little mitts fast enough. Cleaned him out they did. I had to lend him the price of a drink to calm him down and even then he shook so bad he slopped it. Said he was brought up by the Sisters back in New York, at some orphanage or something. Said that was after his folks died in a fire that burned down their ... what did he call it now?' Uncle Bert's brow creased in concentration as he looked back across the years to that conversation. 'Their "apartment block". That's a block of flats to you and me. I remember thinking at the time that it wouldn't surprise me if he turned out to be the bug who set the fire in the first place. I dunno why I thought that, but I did.'

It was then that Auntie Maggie noticed my teeth chattering and me shivering all over with fright and called a halt to the conversation. But it was too late. I was back on that pavement, head being forced down and down. I was really and truly frightened, and what made it worse was that I knew I wasn't alone. Everyone at that table was frightened, even my uncle Bert.

13

Daylight wasn't Bandy Bunyan's natural element, so you can imagine how surprised I was to see her, large as life and twice as ugly, sitting in the cafe when I got back from playing with Kathy Moon. Actually, it wasn't quite daylight – more twilight – and Bandy wasn't ugly at all; what she was was deeply unfashionable. Women were supposed to be made up of soft curves, fluffy hair-dos and pretty, doll-like faces. Bandy was all hard angles, with wild, wiry hair like a wayward Brillo pad and a handsome, imposing face.

According to the women's magazines at the time, a real woman devoted her life to providing a comfortable home for her man. Her job was to greet the master of the house at the door, bathed, fragrant and attractively dressed, with her hair neatly brushed and her slap freshly applied, his slippers warming by the fire and his tea ready and waiting for the warrior's return. Any children should be safely tucked up in bed out of the way in case they disturbed their old man's well-earned peace and comfort. In other words, she was to give the impression that her day had been a doddle and that her well-kept little mitts had been nowhere near mop, broom, duster or smelly nappy.

Try as I might, I could not imagine Bandy ever doing any of those things. If there was a lord and master in her house, it certainly wasn't Sugar. It was her. If any slaving over a hot stove, sink or duster was to be done, it was done by Sugar. If any hair was coiffed, or slap applied, it was Sugar's bonce that got it, and all the curves were his. And they seemed to love it that way.

Everyone knew that Bandy was as tough as old boot leather, but few realized that she had a soft, soggy side that she kept for Sugar, kids in general and me in particular. Every year she threw a Christmas party for the local 'tackers' as she called us. Sometimes she'd lob in an Easter one as well. We'd had a really good one the year before, to celebrate the end of the official sweet rationing. Not that Bandy had ever let a little thing like rationing stunt her style in the past, certainly not. Uncle Bert had been roped in to do his magic tricks, Sugar and Auntie Maggie did the catering, Madame Zelda and Paulette were the waitresses (despite Madame Z.'s poor plates and their glowing chilblains) and Bandy was the entertainment. She was a gifted clown and seemed to be made of India rubber as she threw herself around her club doing pratfalls and tripping over her huge clown shoes into giant custard pies. She didn't seem to mind being smothered in goo or landing on her bum. Looking back it's a miracle that she could hurl herself about like that, given the gallons of gin and the number of pink packets of Passing Clouds she got through in an average week. Still, her guests loved it, and more than one of us left with damp gussets after all that hysterical laughter.

We also left the club clutching a neatly wrapped parcel, with a carefully selected gift inside. That Easter, she gave us each a selection of sweets, each wrapped separately in bright tissue paper, all fancy like the stuff the French use on their bonbons. At Christmas she was at Hamley's riffling through tin whistles, yo-yos, spinning tops, jacks, clockwork trains, cars and aeroplanes looking for just the right thing for each child. Nobody ever got a doll or a stuffed bunny, but the very young might get a teddy or possibly a dog. Bandy wasn't keen on dolls or any other girlie-type toys but teddies and dogs were all right as they were loved by all. She spent hours wrapping parcels with hands that looked as if they should be wielding a sledgehammer rather than dainty little bits of ribbon. Sugar said that she had a wonderful time and loved every minute of it. It showed, too. The parcels she gave us were really beautiful, flashes of sparkle and colour in a generally very dreary grey world.

It was very cold as I came home from Kathy's, and to my surprise the cafe door was locked, although light poured through the windows streaming with condensation. Bandy was there, sitting at our corner table with Sugar by her side and Madame Zelda, Paulette, Luigi, Auntie Maggie and Uncle Bert in close attendance. Everybody looked serious as they listened to something Uncle Bert was saying. Then Bandy spotted me at the door and her face lit up like the sun bursting through black clouds.

'Rosie!' she roared, and Sugar leaped to his feet to unlock the door for me. Bandy flung her arms out in welcome and before I knew it I was gathered into an enormous hug. Suddenly, my worries about the Widow and Jenny's illness didn't seem quite so bad. If Auntie Maggie's hugs pillowed you against life's knocks, then Bandy's stood in trouble's way, threatening to smack it in the teeth. Either way, it was a comfort in hard times.

'And how is my favourite girl, apart from being frozen? How's school? My spies tell me that you are a jolly fine student just bulging with brains. Is that true? Of course it is, of course it is. Any fool could see that you were brainy even when you were still dribbling round your dummy. Now let me see, where is it? I know I had it somewhere. Sugar, where did I put the first clue, can you remember?'

I forgot to mention two other things about Bandy. One is that she rarely bothered to wait for an answer to any of her barrage of questions – unless it was important, of course – and the other is that she loved setting up treasure hunts and used any old excuse to get one going. I am thrilled to say that I was often just the old excuse she needed.

'Left hand pocket,' Sugar replied promptly.

'Ah yes. Have a rootle, Rosie, there's a good girl. There should be a scrap of paper in there. Found it? Excellent. Now, what does it say? Read it out, you clever little tyke you.'

I did as I was told toot sweet. 'The frogs call them "apples of the earth" and you'll find them in the kitchen.' Which meant that clue number two would be in the spud barrel. Off I galloped to have a delve and came back waving a rather muddy bit of paper. 'Where you lay your weary head to dream.' I shot off to my bedroom and looked under the pillow and found clue number three, 'Where Uncle Bert parks his skinny derriere.' Number four was under the cushion on Uncle Bert's armchair. I knew from previous experience that there would be ten clues in all and that the clues would get harder as I went along. I realize now that clever old Bandy was giving me French lessons while I was at it. Proper ones, not the ones advertised by 'Yvette, Strict Discipline' on a grubby card in Moor Street. Thanks to Bandy, I was already quite proficient in French by the time I went there with my school.

While I was dashing about hunting down clues I was too busy to wonder why Bandy and Sugar were round at our place and why the cafe had closed early. Had I given it any thought at all, I would have realized that the meeting was about the Widow Ginger's veiled threats. However, nobody was talking about anything important while I was within earshot. They confined themselves to idle gossip – which turned out to be pretty fascinating as it happens.

I heard Bandy's plummy tones telling everyone about Sharky's solution to Mrs Robbins's money troubles as I puzzled over clue number four, 'Under the joanna in le petit salon'. It was tricky working out what the French meant while trying to eavesdrop at the same time and it took a while before I realized the next clue was hidden under the toy piano in the living room of my doll's house. I paused before I hared off to my bedroom to listen to Sharky and T.C.'s brilliant scheme.

'We had Hissing Sid and that skinny creature that I believe the lovely Rosie refers to as the Mangy Cow in the night before last. Personally, I like my women with a bit of meat on them. And my men, come to that.' There was a hefty thwack as she slapped Sugar's bum playfully as he passed with a tray of drinks.

Sugar was indignant. 'Watch it, Band. I'll have scorching tea all down me good bits if you're not careful. Still, skinny or not, it didn't stop you giving her one now and then, did it? You really are a sex-crazed old bag. We should change your moniker to Randy Bunyan and have done with it. Half a bottle of Gordon's and a toast rack starts to look good to you, doesn't it, sweetie? Do you reckon Hissing Sid realizes what a shagnasty that Mary is?'

'I shouldn't think so. But hold hard there, Sugarpie. I do have some standards, as you well know. Anyone I bed must have a heartbeat, be human in origin and over the age of consent. Apart from that, given the right circumstances, I'll try virtually anyone. Where was I? Oh yes, they were whining about being raided by the vice boys. Seems that they were cleared out of their entire stock only to discover that the self-same books had turned up round at Cliff's place. Seems the chaps in blue simply sauntered round the corner and flogged the lot to the grateful Cliff at a very healthy discount. When I asked Cliff about it later, turns out the whole scheme was dreamed up by Sharky and T.C.'

Madame Zelda's voice asked what the scheme was, exactly.

'Apparently, the arrangement was that apart from the usual chunk going to the boys in blue, and Cliff's bit of profit, the rest had to go to Hissing Sid's cast-off and that poor little mite of a daughter of his. Said they'd make it a fairly regular arrangement until Jenny was out of the woods. Quite right too. That Mary's a voracious little twat, and I should know. She's always on the make, that one.'

Which left me wondering what Jenny was doing in the woods when she wasn't well. Then I wondered what woods they could possibly mean, Soho not being known for its trees. Still, I didn't like to ask and draw attention to myself, because the conversation was so fascinating that I just knew it'd stop if they realized I was listening.

Finally, the subject turned to the trouble that Paulette was having with the new manager at the Lyon's Corner House at Marble Arch where she worked as a Nippy. He had a bad case of the desert disease, or wandering palms, if you prefer. A lively discussion followed as to ways and means of getting him to keep his hands to himself. After listening for a bit I got bored and carried on with my treasure hunt while filled with wonder about what clever blokes T.C. and Sharky were. I was glad that Mrs Robbins and Jenny would finally have some money and I was even gladder that they were getting it from Hissing Sid and the Mangy Cow.

In case you were wondering, I did solve all ten clues, and my prize was tiny models of Toady, Ratty, Mole and Badger from *The Wind in the Willows*, my favourite book. I loved them to bits and still have them, which is a miracle because that night, and for many nights after that, they slept under my pillow and it's a wonder they weren't broken. Then it was time for bed. Everyone kissed me goodnight. I was in the middle of *The Railway Children* at the time and fell asleep to the sound of Bandy's deep, plummy voice reading it to me. It was remarkably soothing for a woman whose personality certainly wasn't.

14

Now, when God created the world in general and schools in particular, He laid down, in tablets of stone, that school heating should be switched on on the first of October and off again on the first of May. Blizzards in September, an Indian Summer in November and snow in April changed nothing; the heating went on and off at the official times and nothing and nobody could alter it.

So when, a few days before the official Easter holiday, the ancient boiler at my school finally blew, there was much joy and jubilation. After half an hour spent paddling and freezing, it was decided to close the school. Those who were sure to find a parent at home could leave at once and the rest would have to huddle in the upstairs classrooms with as many electric fires as could be found. Even old Welbeloved could tell that we couldn't write or even think when our fingers were blue and we were ankle deep in water. I was one of the lucky ones who went home. I fair bounded down the road, brimful of glee. An unexpected day off school was always a treat. The fact that it would run into a fortnight's holiday made it even better.

T.C. was sitting at the corner table with Uncle Bert and Auntie Maggie as I rushed through the door into the steamy warmth of the cafe. I was mightily surprised when nobody looked delighted to see me, which they usually did. T.C.'s crinkly blue eyes failed to sparkle and Uncle Bert and Auntie Maggie simply looked startled. I'd obviously strayed into a serious and very private conversation and it took them all a moment to take in the fact that I was there.

Auntie Maggie was the first to pull herself together. 'Rosie, love, what are you doing here? Why aren't you at school?' Without waiting, for an answer, she whisked me upstairs so I could hang my coat up and change into my slippers and my civvies. School clothes were precious and kept only for school.

Once we were safely out of earshot of Uncle Bert and T.C., I heard the deep rumble of their voices begin again, but not what they said until T.C. roared, 'He said what?' He sounded furious, which was really unusual for T.C. who was normally quiet and calm. Earwigging was out of the question on account of Auntie Maggie's sticking to me like a poultice to a carbuncle. It was a bit annoying because it was clear that something important was going on. My

131

mind shot back to the Widow Ginger and his threats and I was sure that they were talking about him. Half of me felt a stab of fright and the other half felt relieved that T.C. was going to be in the know. There were times when knowing a copper – and possibly being related to one – was a jolly good thing, even round our way, where such a connection would normally be seen as worse than a dose of pox, chicken or otherwise. This was obviously one of those times.

Auntie Maggie looked distracted as she tried to find things for me to do to take my mind off what was going on downstairs. Trouble was, she couldn't get her own mind off it either, so mine naturally followed. In the end, we gave up trying to play snap and made do with knocking up some early elevenses instead. There's nothing quite like a biscuit at difficult moments, except perhaps another biscuit. I was beginning to wish I was back at school, baking my front by an electric fire and freezing my bum off at the same time, when I heard footsteps on the stairs. T.C. came into the room and at last I got the twinkly, crinkly smile that I was used to.

Looking hard at him, it wasn't difficult to see why everyone thought he was my dad. We had the same blond curls, only his were shorter, and our eyes were the exact same shade of blue. Although he wasn't fat or anything, there was a sturdiness in his build that was mirrored in mine, which was a pity really, because I longed to be tall and willowy and what I was was short and, if not stocky, at least well made. My legs weren't about to snap in a high wind, let's put it that way.

'So, young Rosie, bunking off are you?' T.C. asked in a voice that was just a shade too hearty. I knew my grown-ups. False heartiness always meant something was up and, whatever it was, it wasn't good. 'Have you got plans for her, Maggie, or can you spare her to keep me company? Pat's at her brother's for a week and today's a rest day, so I have it all to myself. How about a trip out to the funfair at Battersea? It's been a long time since I threw up my dinner on a big dipper. Can you spare her?'

When Auntie Maggie nodded, smiling a funny sort of sad smile that I didn't understand, T.G. turned back to me. 'Fancy it, do you?' What a stupid question. Of course I fancied it. Who in their right mind wouldn't?

It was the first day we had ever spent together, just T.C. and me, and we had a truly wonderful time. Before we made our way to Battersea we trawled around Hamleys, my favourite shop in all the world.

133

Trouble was, T.C. had been given strict instructions by Auntie Maggie not to spoil me rotten, so I didn't manage to wheedle any new toys out of him. Still I left him in no doubt about what he could get me for the next three million birthdays and Christmases and he solemnly took notes in his copper's notebook so that he wouldn't forget. We had a really good time poking about, though, and trying out the clockwork cars and train sets. But we got thrown out when we tried to race two of the cars and they crashed into the floor manager's highly polished brogues. Luckily, we didn't scratch either the cars or the brogues, or we'd have been in even more trouble. I tried to explain that it was all right, T.C. being a copper and all, but the manager showed no interest and anyway T.C. grabbed my hand and yanked me towards the way out before I could mention the word 'policeman'.

'I can't let the villains know I play with toy cars and get thrown out of toy shops, now can I, Rosie? They'd laugh me off the streets and out of the spielers. I'd never get any work done. No, sweetheart, I reckon this one's our little secret. What do you say?' So we shook hands on it, and I was struck by how large, firm and comforting his mitt was, and how sparkling with fun his blue eyes were.

Next we had our dinner at Paulette's

Corner House, and when I told T.C. about the manager's attack of wandering palmitis he took the opportunity to have a little chat. Paulette said afterwards that she didn't know what T.C. had said but that whatever it was it put the fear of God into Sluggy Weatherall because after that he'd barely even look in her direction, let alone touch her. We called him Sluggy because he had fat pale fingers, like peeled slugs. Yuk! No wonder she didn't want them anywhere near her.

We took the bus to Battersea, and sat on the top deck right at the front so that we could see everything. I loved looking in the windows of the flats above the shops to see what people were up to or at least what sort of wallpaper and curtains they had. We made a game out of counting how many plaster Alsatians we could spot on people's window sills. I was bouncing up and down and crowing because I'd counted ten and T.C. had only got nine but he was firm. 'That last one was a Scottie; you can't have that. It's nine all.' And he wouldn't budge, although I explained that some Alsatians *look* like Scotties on account of being Alsatians from Scotland. T.C. gave me full marks for inventiveness, but the score stayed at nine all and that was that. The squabble kept us busy all the way to our bus stop.

At last we arrived at the funfair and we enjoyed every second of our time there, despite the air being so cold that our breath was all huffy. We rolled round and round in the looper, a funny caged wheel thing, then we whizzed about on the waltzer and the dodgems until we felt sick. Once we'd settled our tums with an ice cream cone, we screamed up and down on the big dipper and swung so violently backwards and forwards on the gondolas that I felt sure we had to swing right over the bar and drop out on to our heads. Only we didn't. But we almost did.

I had a go on the rifle range and didn't hit anything, but T.C. managed to win me an enormous doll with hair and everything. I called her Lita after Lita Roza, the singer, and she was almost as tall as me. I spent many happy hours messing about with her hair over the years. I loved it, because she had long, straight hair that I could plait, bunch or put up in a bun.

My curls would never do anything like that, because even the tiniest hint of damp in the air would make them spring out of any clips, bows and slides and back into bubbles. It was really annoying, although nobody could quite understand that. They just kept telling me I'd be glad to have my beautiful barnet when I grew up because it would save me a fortune on perms. Huh!

Auntie Maggie was always promising that if I ate my crusts like a good girl, or sometimes it was my greens, then my hair would magically straighten. It never did, despite the tons of crusts and acres of greens she conned me into choking down my reluctant gullet. She could be devious could my auntie Maggie, even though she was the most wonderful woman in the world.

Finally, after scoffing the biggest and pinkest candyflosses you ever saw in your life, we made our weary way back to the bus stop. Once again, we managed to nab one of the top front seats, but this time I leaned against T.C. with my thumb in my mouth and just watched the streets go by.

Battersea was foreign territory to me. All I knew about it was the funfair, the dogs' home and of course the gigantic power station. London's always been like that, cut in two by the Thames, despite all those bridges that are supposed to make a whole of the two halves. South of the river was almost as alien to me as the moon. There were no familiar landmarks to ease the feeling of strangeness. Streatham, Tooting and Balham might as well be the South Pole to someone from the West End, while a person from Penge would feel at a loss in Soho, Mayfair or Fitzrovia. The language might be the same, but the houses, food and people were different.

Where they had loads of little roads stuffed with terraces of tiny houses and shops built – according to T.C. – around the turn of the century, we had tall, narrow houses that were now mostly flats, built more than a hundred years before that and, in my opinion, much better looking. Ours had interesting details like fancy plaster-work or Dutch gables, whereas theirs were more squat and solid looking. They had little gardens, front and back, and we had window boxes if we were lucky. They had greengrocers' shops, we had Berwick Street market. They had grocers' shops with tasteful displays of things like bottles of Camp Coffee, packets of Bird's Custard Powder and Atora shredded suet. Although we had one of those, too, run by Mrs Williams, mostly we had delicatessens run by the Campaninis and their rivals. The delis filled their windows with mounds of ravioli and spaghetti piled high in bowls and had salamis, hams and strings of garlic hanging from hooks, like weird Christmas decorations. Lumpy packets of coffee beans and bottles of olive oil were dotted about, to complete the picture.

I didn't see even one Turkish coffee shop, French pâtisserie or newsagent selling *Paris Match*, *The New York Times* or anything at all in Chinese, Russian or Arabic on the south side of the river, whereas we had all of those, and more, in the Street where I lived. To be fair, round our way only the parks had bright yellow daffodils waving about and purple and yellow crocuses studding the grass, while lots of people in Battersea had their own in their very own little patches. I liked that a lot.

There were still loads of ragged holes in the rows of houses, where Hitler's bombs had struck. They looked like shattered teeth, spoiling the set, only much worse. Sometimes wallpaper still fluttered like faded flags and stairs ran up walls to nowhere. It was ever so sad. I hated bombsites and so did my auntie Maggie on account of her mum and dad copping a direct hit in the war. She said she knew how many broken hearts went along with those broken houses, and then she'd blub a bit.

T.C. and I talked very little during the journey home. We were happy just to take it all in.

15

Now, if T.C. hadn't insisted on stopping to talk to Brian the butcher in Poland Street, we would probably have been home long before the fire started.

I was sitting on T.C.'s shoulders and hanging on to his lugs and wondering if T.C. and Brian would ever shut up as I was nearly falling off my perch with exhaustion. I was also heartily sick of staring at the gutted rabbits dangling at my eye level from the striped awning outside Brian's shop. Their poor dead eyes, drooping whiskers and ears and dull, bloody fur weren't making me fancy rabbit stew for my tea at all, as Brian probably intended. They were making me fancy cod and chips in a big way. It's hard to feel snuggly towards a cod, whereas bunnies are an entirely different matter. I blame books for that. Nobody ever wrote a book about a cuddly cod, whereas bunnies in bonnets get everywhere. On and on the men droned as I struggled to keep my eyes turned away from those pathetic little corpses and longed for them to belt up and let me get home.

Unfortunately, I was brought up never to

interrupt grown-up talk for anything less important than sudden death, the need to spend a penny or, worse, tuppence, or mortal danger from runaway trains, horses, cars or any kind of armed nutter, but I was getting desperate. So I gave it some thought and discarded death and mortal danger on the grounds that T.C., being a copper, would know I was fibbing, and chose the middle way, the khazi option, happy in the knowledge that T.C. couldn't prove that I wasn't about to pee down his neck. I tugged on his lug and whispered discreetly into it. It worked better than I could have dreamed and we were off in seconds, yelling our goodbyes to a surprised Brian as we fair galloped along Poland Street towards Broadwick Street.

Although the stalls were empty in Berwick Street, the gutters were choked with bits of old cabbage, tired carrots and onion skins, waiting to be collected and carted away. One or two tramps rummaged about, looking for the choicer bits before some other bugger got them. The covered stalls looked lonely without the stallholders and the seething mass of customers that usually milled around them, getting in each other's way and yelling cheerful insults at one another.

We'd got to the tag end of Berwick Street before we smelt smoke. As soon as we turned the corner into Peter Street we saw Maltese Joe standing in the middle of the dark, narrow road, with Betty Potts towering over him in her black evening frock and silver high heels and Mick the Tic, one of his 'boys' twitching quietly beside him. All were watching gusts of black smoke belching out of the doorway of one of Maltese Joe's clubs.

Nobody spoke as we stopped beside the little group. T.C. took in the situation immediately. He lowered me to the ground and gently placed my hand in Betty's.

'Look after Rosie, will you, Betty, and stand well back? Has anyone called the fire brigade?' Betty nodded, eyes still wide with shock, but she did as she was told, and with a firm grip on my mitt moved back to the opposite pavement. I clutched my precious doll. Smoke was rapidly filling the street. My eyes began to stream and I started to cough. Betty moved us upwind of the billowing doorway as T.C. galvanized Mick and Maltese Joe into action by asking if the upstairs rooms had been cleared.

'No? We'll start by leaning on the bells then. Has anyone got a key to that door?' T.C. waved at the brown door that stood next to the club entrance. A row of bells and name-plates were crammed down one side of the frame. According to the name-plates, nearly all the rooms were let to French teachers or Swedish models, but that was a fib. They were what Auntie Maggie called 'working girls' from Rotherham, Slough and Birmingham and had been no nearer to either France or Sweden than Piccadilly Circus. You could tell that when they opened their gobs to order tea and a fry-up at the cafe; they were as English as their fried bread. The only man with rooms there was old Mr Rabinowitz, who was a bow restorer from Russia and hardly spoke at all except when the subjects of bows, violins, cellos, violas and double basses came up, which wasn't all that often.

Maltese Joe, who still hadn't said a single word, nodded and started fumbling with an enormous bunch of keys. He looked like a warder from the Scrubs, only shorter and better dressed. He finally found the one he wanted and stuck it in the lock, and before T.C. could stop him he was gone. He'd shot into the doorway yelling that they were 'his girls' and that he'd better get them out. We could hear him roaring at the top of his lungs as he thundered up the stairs banging on the doors each side of the tiny landings as he went. 'Get the hell out of here *now!* The club's on fire.' He yelled it over and over again until he got to the top landing, then he started down again, banging as before.

When Joe reappeared through the smoke,

he was shoving half a dozen underdressed women and two semi-naked men in front of him.

By now the little street was choked with people and Joe had a quick look round, counting heads. 'That's the lot, all present and, if not correct, at least accounted for – except for old Rabinowitz.' And he disappeared once again into the dense smoke. Nobody said a word as we waited for him to come out again, our eyes straining and streaming as we stared at the door. It seemed longer than a school assembly before we heard stumbling and choking and at last Maltese Joe tottered out into the air carrying what looked like a large bundle of black rags.

He staggered over to our little group and placed his bundle gently down on the pavement. He could hardly speak; his chest heaved with the effort of getting some air in. He just waved a hand at the heap at his feet and croaked, 'Do something, can ya?' Just then, something deep below us exploded and flames and smoke billowed from the club's doorway like dragon's breath. 'We'd better get out of here before something else blows. Give us a hand with Rabinowitz, can you?'

Betty let go of my hand and bent down to examine the bundle and found old Mr Rabinowitz somewhere inside it. He was still breathing, but his eyes stared blindly ahead and he seemed unaware that he was surrounded by people, some of them semi-naked and smothered in embarrassment. Very gently, she and T.C. helped the old gentleman to his feet and hung on to him so that he stayed upright.

Maltese Joe found a bit more voice. 'Just as well it's early. No punters in the club yet and the girls hadn't really got going either,' he remarked to no one in particular. Then he jerked as if someone had stuck his finger in a socket and turned the juice on and barked, 'Has anyone banged up the lot in the building on the other side?'

T.C. assured him that he and Mick the Tic had, and sure enough a small frightened group huddled at the end of the street, blocking the entrance so that the fire engine that was clanging along Wardour Street didn't stand a snowflake's chance in hell of getting through. T.C. was masterful. He urged us all along the road, clearing the blockage as we went.

We regrouped in Wardour Street a few minutes later, and stared at the dark, empty space we'd just left. Great clouds of choking black and grey smoke swirled about, trying to find an escape from the narrow tunnel of tall buildings. The last stragglers reached our pavement just in time to let the engine squeeze into the narrow street and hook up to a hydrant. I know this because a nice fireman, who was keeping people away from the entrance to Peter Street, told me, Betty and my doll Lita what they were doing as they did it.

It took mere minutes to put the fire out, but much, much longer to clear up the mess afterwards. In fact, it was weeks before the club opened its doors again, it having copped most of the damage. Everyone said later that it was a miracle that nobody died or was even seriously hurt.

Once T.C. was sure everything was under control, he claimed me back from Betty and we all trooped down Old Compton Street to the cafe, even Maltese Joe and Mick the Tic, who seemed to have forgotten for the moment that T.C. was a copper. We made a strange group as we trudged down the road. Maltese Joe was in front, his dapper suit smothered in soot and ash. He had angry red eyes, like the Devil, and was followed by Betty in evening dress, me, T.C. and half a dozen scantily dressed women who supported old Mr Rabinowitz and several tons of goosepimples between them. Behind them came the tenants of the building next door and a whole load of idle nosy parkers. Gigi's and Ingrid's punters had melted away, despite wearing little besides their underwear. How they explained themselves away on the tube or to their wives was a matter for intense speculation at the cafe for some days after.

Nearly all of us made for the cafe but I noticed that Maltese Joe and Mick the Tic didn't join us. Maltese Joe and my uncle Bert still weren't speaking, even in an emergency.

Pretty soon, the girls were wearing various garments rounded up from Auntie Maggie, Madame Zelda and Paulette and we were all wrapped around bacon and egg butties and steaming cups of tea rustled up by Uncle Bert. All except Mr Rabinowitz, who had black tea and salt beef sandwiches from Nosher's Salt Beef Bar, supplied on Maltese Joe's instructions via Mic the Tic as he hurried past to round up 'the boys'. Mick asked Nosher to make them specially, it being well after closing time, or so Nosher explained as he bustled in with his steaming parcel. It seemed that old Mr Rabinowitz was a valued customer and fellow member of Nosher's synagogue, so he was happy to oblige and to offer the old man a bed and a bath into the bargain. I discovered that I was very partial to salt beef sandwiches that night; I liked a smear of strong mustard on mine. 'A very sophisticated taste for such a young lady,' according to Nosher.

We talked about the drama in Peter Street until it was late and I was positively dropping with tiredness. It had been an amazing day, one way and another. I lay half asleep in T.C.'s lap, thumb comfortingly in my mouth, and listened to the voices recounting every second of their escape. It was Rita from the building opposite who cleared up the mystery of how the fire started. She just happened to look out of her kitchen window when she was washing up after her tea and saw a bloke dart into the club doorway, strike a match and set light to something with it, then stand back and sling it through the door, followed by some rags he pulled from a bag. Then he scarpered.

'It was all over in a flash, if you'll pardon the pun. Took no more than four or five seconds from start to finish. It was me what yelled down from the door for you three to get out quick. Just as well there was that back way out. You weren't going to get up them stairs in no hurry. They was ablaze in the time it took me to get down into the street.'

'There's no doubt your prompt action saved everyone from serious injury or even death.' T.C.'s voice rumbled above my head. 'Any bright ideas who the arsonist might be, anyone?' He waited a moment then continued into the crushing silence that had stolen over the place. 'I asked Joe the same question, and, amazing though it may seem, he couldn't come up with a single soul who bore him any ill will. Extraordinary thing, because I for one could name a whole load of people queuing to do him down.'

Which made me wonder why he was being so dim, if he knew so much. Even I knew just who was at the head of that queue. Amazed at his stupidity, I squirmed upright and said, in loud, ringing tones, 'What about the Widow Ginger, then? Everyone knows he can't stand Maltese Joe at any price.' My voice echoed around the quiet cafe and I suddenly wished I could disappear.

Uncle Bert obliged by lifting me off T.C.'s warm lap, plonking me down in front of my auntie Maggie and muttering, 'Bedtime for this one, I think.'

At this I was whisked away, undressed, washed, tucked up and kissed goodnight in double-quick time, so I missed the rest of the evening.

16

It took me ages to get to sleep that night, even though I was so tired I was almost propping my eyelids open with matchsticks. There were so many different things going on in my bonce. I'd had a wonderful day with T.C., so a whole chunk of me wanted to think about him and whether he was my dad or not and how I felt about it if he was. But the rest of me was too worried about the Widow Ginger to do anything but shiver and shake every time he popped into my head. I knew a nutter when I saw one, and there was no doubt in my mind that the Widow was so far round the bend he was in danger of meeting himself on the way back. There are nutcases who are mostly harmless and then there are NUTCASES, who aren't. They're the sort you never turn your back on, even when they're smiling, laughing and having a joke. The Widow was one of them.

I must have dropped off eventually because the next thing I knew, I was woken up with a start. For the second time in a few weeks, Uncle Bert and Auntie Maggie were yelling at each other downstairs. That in itself was enough to set the gnashers rattling, I can tell you. My aunt and uncle were not in the habit of screaming at each other, and even if they were they'd make sure I didn't hear them. It showed how upset they were that they had forgotten to leave me out of it. I tiptoed to the stairs and listened. My thumb crept into my mouth and I sucked and sucked as if my life depended on it.

'I'm telling you, you stupid bloody woman, that the fire would never have happened if I'd warned Joe in time. He would have been better prepared. But no, you had to nag me into keeping my trap shut. Now I'm on the outs with me mate and that bleeding firebug is playing fast and loose with sodding matches.' Uncle Bert spluttered to a stop to get his breath back, and Auntie Maggie was in like a rat up a drainpipe.

'Don't you call me stupid, Bert Featherby. If you didn't have such dodgy mates in the first place we'd never even be involved in all this. It's hanging about with the likes of Joe that has brought this trouble on our heads, and you know it!' Misery and fury were fighting for control of her voice, and it trembled badly, but in the end fury won.

'I wondered how long it would take you to slag off my mate. You've never liked Joe, but I didn't see you complaining when his good offices brought all that gear to our door in the war. How do you think we'd have kept this place going without Joe? You just tell me that.' Uncle Bert's voice was shaking with rage and he crashed his fist down on the counter with such force that the teacups tinkled and at least one crashed to the floor.

That was my cue. I couldn't stand hearing my beloved aunt and uncle fighting for one second longer. It was bad enough that we were all scared to death, but the Widow had got everyone at each other's throats with no trouble at all. I'd seen enough Westerns and war films to know that, in times of real trouble, sticking together is better than not. Look at the wagon trains in the Wild West. The minute the Indians turned up, the wagons formed a circle and the men, women and children defended that circle and each other to the last gasp. It seemed to me that we ought to be doing the same, so I stepped out of my hiding place and waited for them to notice me and belt up.

'I want you to stop fighting now,' I said firmly. I was good and cross, as well as scared half to death. 'You've always told me that families stick together when there's trouble,' I went on, while they stood there with their gobs open. 'You told me that families are made up of people we love, whether we actually always like them or not, and you told me that you can't always choose your family.' I was hitting my stride now. What I was saying made sense to me, and as it was made up of all the stuff they had taught me they couldn't even argue with it.

'It seems to me that Maltese Joe is family, whether you like it or not, Auntie Maggie. He came with Uncle Bert when you married him.' Then I wobbled a bit, because I knew I was on very dodgy ground. I was about to defy my auntie Maggie, something

I hadn't really done before, not seriously, and anyway she'd always won any battle of wills. But this time I knew I was going to dig my heels in, and I was afraid. I'm not sure what of; perhaps that she wouldn't love me any more. 'I think we should form a circle, like the covered wagons do when the Indians come. If you go to see Auntie Flo and leave Uncle Bert behind, then I'm not coming with you,' I shouted. Then I burst into tears, and they almost knocked each other over in their rush to get at me.

There was a long silence after that, broken only by the occasional hiccup from me. Uncle Bert and Auntie Maggie stared at each other, then at me, and then at each other again and at last Uncle Bert spoke. 'Out of the mouth of babes, eh?' he said, whatever that was supposed to mean.

Auntie Maggie seemed to understand because she nodded, dabbed her eyes with her pinny and said, 'She's right, of course, Bert. And I'm sorry about Joe. I thought it was for the best, but...' And she left it at that.

I was reassured that nobody was going anywhere without the others; that I wasn't in trouble for shouting at my auntie Maggie and that I did indeed have a point about sticking together. To top things off, I got to sleep with them in the big bed, a rare treat saved for times of special need. We all agreed, this was definitely one of those.

Everyone was tense over the next few days as we waited to see what was going to happen next. There was little or no doubt about who set the fire at the club. What nobody knew for sure was what to do about it. Nobody knew where the Widow Ginger was or exactly why he set the fire in the first place. Some people thought it was a simple case of a nutter being a nutter and enjoying setting fires, especially if it involved an old enemy and a spot of vengeance. Uncle Bert said that although he had long suspected that the Widow had enjoyed playing with matches since childhood – look what had happened to his parents – and wasn't against arson for fun in principle, there was more to it than that. He thought it was part of a carefully thought out plan to get Maltese Joe rattled and force him into a position of either doing something stupid or negotiating some sort of settlement. He also thought it would be a good idea if Bandy, Sugar, Maltese Joe and our little household kept our eyes and ears wide open, because he was convinced that the fire at the club was far from being the end of it. 'Mark my words, it's just an opening shot. There's more to come. That bleeder can hold a grudge like you wouldn't believe. He's had all that time in his cell to plot and scheme

154

and he's a meticulous bastard, that one. He'll have polished that plan until it's a blinder. He'll definitely want us to suffer before we hand over our assets, so he'll do his best to build up a nice head of terror.'

'Well, Bert,' said Bandy, 'that's a point of view that's sure to get all our gussets in a right old tangle. But I think you're right; the shit does want us gibbering with fear and ready to give him anything. The man may be a psychopath, but he's no fool. Vigilance is the order of the day. Meanwhile, let's put the word about, quietly, that we want to know where the sewer is hiding himself. And when we find him, in no circumstances must he discover that we know where he is. It might be handy to know his movements and his cronies – if he has any, that is.'

And so it was agreed. The word trickled out until everyone we knew in Soho was on the lookout for sight or sound of the Widow. Meanwhile, life went on, even if it did twitch a bit and keep looking over its shoulder.

With school officially over for Easter, Luigi's nieces and nephews were at a loose end, too, so I was invited to the flat above the delicatessen to play. This was a few days after the fire and what I always think of as T.C. day, because it was the day I knew for sure that he was my very own dad. Not that he said so, but I felt it, and have never stopped feeling it. I don't think the penny had quite dropped before.

So, despite being afraid of the Widow, worried about Jenny and still nervy about the rows at home, I was about three-quarters full of the joys of spring when I went to play at the Campaninis'. It was always great fun there, because Mamma never bothered her head about little things like noise or mess. Auntie Maggie said that with her tribe she'd have driven herself completely loopy if she had. I think that Mamma just adored kids, and her grand-children in particular, and loved to see us having a good time, and that not driving herself round the twist was simply a bonus.

We were soon playing hard, screaming up and down the stairs in a game of 'he'. This involved choosing someone to be 'he' and leaving them to count to a hundred while the rest got away; then 'he' had to track us down and chase us until we'd either been caught or made it safely 'home'. The first one to be caught took over the job of being 'he'. Sometimes we played a more vicious variation where the caught ones joined 'he' until we were all caught or 'home'. However, 'home' was only safe for the count of a hundred; then you had to make a break for it and attempt to reach another safe haven and so on until everyone was caught.

The last person standing then became 'he'. The vicious variation was more fun by far, although having a howling mob baying at their heels did tend to frighten the tinies. I'm ashamed to say that just added to the fun for us bigger ones, who enjoyed scaring them witless. Still, they got comfort and lap time with Mamma and the odd sugared almond or lump of chocolate, so it wasn't all bad.

We'd played this at top volume for at least an hour when, to my surprise, Luigi appeared from the bathroom wearing only a towel round his waist and a black eye. Now, a Luigi who slept in his own bed was a rare and wondrous thing, so it took me a moment to recover from the shock of seeing him at home and half naked to boot. He yawned blearily and greeted me with a 'Wotcha, Shorty' before disappearing into his bedroom. I noticed that even a black eye couldn't make Luigi less gorgeous. His olive skin glowed with health and his glossy dark hair was wet and all spiky. I'd never seen that before. When Auntie Maggie washed my hair it still curled into corkscrews. Hers was so fine that it just hung there like limp lettuce, while Uncle Bert's bonce had very little hair at all, as he kept it very short and it was a bit thin in places, so spikes were out of the question. I must admit, it struck me as very odd the first time I saw it and it almost took my mind off the eye. The one good one was brown and soft like a cow's, and fringed with a thick set of black lashes about a yard long that were the envy of every female within a ten-mile radius. The other was dimmed slightly by its red, yellow and purple bruise and the swollen and puffy eyelid. But its lashes were intact, thank goodness.

'Who clobbered your Luigi?' I demanded, good manners hurled to the wind. Here was hot gossip and I was blowed if I was going to miss out.

It was Serafina who answered. 'Maltese Joe hit him when he saw him leaving the club with Betty.'

'Why?' I was mystified. Why shouldn't Luigi walk Betty home after work?

What felt like twenty pairs of soft brown eyes looked at me with pity, the silent message being that I didn't know anything. They were right, I didn't. But I made up my mind that that was about to change. 'So tell me, why did Maltese Joe clout your Luigi? They're friends.'

Giovanni, who was all of twelve and therefore a man of the world, answered this time. 'Where women are concerned, Rosie, men are never friends. Maltese Joe wants her but Uncle Luigi has her, so naturally they fight. Except that Uncle Luigi didn't fight, he just stood there like a girl.' His tone showed his disgust, and for some reason I felt the need to defend his uncle.

'Perhaps Maltese Joe got away before Luigi could do anything,' I offered.

Scorn soaked Giovanni's reply. 'No, Maltese Joe didn't run. Betty told Uncle Luigi that if he made a fight of it she'd see herself home, so he just stood there and didn't even try to defend his honour.'

My sense of fair play overcame what passes for my common sense at that moment and I remembered that Giovanni had also been on the wrong end of Maltese Joe's fist and why. 'I didn't notice you defending your honour when Maltese Joe clobbered you. At least Luigi doesn't beat up girls.'

This was a big mistake because, of course, Giovanni had no such qualms. Next thing I knew I was flattened by an enraged boy and we were surrounded by a host of yelling Campaninis. The girls were chanting 'Rosie, Rosie' as I scratched, kicked, tugged hair out by its roots and bit anything that came anywhere near my gnashers. Queensberry rules, what Queensberry rules? Who the hell was Queensberry anyway? I didn't know and I didn't care. All that mattered was winning, and getting that great lump off of me.

The boys were on Giovanni's side and were also shouting encouragement – 'Go on, bash her, Vanni. Hold her arms down, you twerp,' and other handy hints – but I was beside myself with fury and he couldn't get a grip. At last, after what felt like a week, the weight was lifted from me and I opened my eyes to see Giovanni hanging from Luigi's fully dressed arm and Mamma standing behind him, arms crossed over her enormous bosom. Nobody was smiling, although I swear that Luigi's one good eye gave me the tiniest of winks.

Mamma was furious with Giovanni, being of the opinion that no amount of provocation justified beating up little girls. Giovanni was sent to Luigi's room on account of his own being several streets away and I was sent home in disgrace. Which wasn't fair, in my opinion. Auntie Maggie was all for making me apologize to Giovanni and Mamma but I was rebellious. I would apologize to Mamma gladly, I told her, but nothing on God's earth would make me apologize to that oaf Giovanni. I really was pushing my luck. Two acts of defiance in swift succession. Luigi saved me from further punishment.

'It wasn't Shorty's fault, Maggie, honest. Even if I say so myself, that Giovanni is a nasty piece of work. Gets it from his dad.' (Who was not a Campanini, naturally, but a Rossi.) 'Giovanni was calling me a sissy for not beating the hell out of Maltese Joe in return for the shiner and Shorty here reminded him of his own ... er ... short-comings in that area. He took exception to a blast of the truth and decided to prove his manhood by slapping her about a bit. You'd have been proud, Maggie. Shorty here was definitely winning when I hauled the bugger off.'

Auntie Maggie thought for a bit then reluctantly decided that Luigi had a point; nice girls should stand up for their friends and Luigi was my friend. 'All right, young lady, although by the sound of it I can hardly call you a lady. You can write a note to Mamma apologizing for turning her living room into a bear pit and we'll leave it at that. But Gawd help you if I catch you fighting again.' She always said that, but nothing ever came of it, because whenever she caught me fighting I always seemed to have a good reason. Gawd never needed to help me, thank goodness; a really angry Auntie Maggie was a terrifying thing.

Still, I didn't get away with it scot free; I was made to tidy my bedroom from the floorboards up. Instinct told me that shoving it all under the bed wouldn't do this time, and I resigned myself to sorting everything neatly into cupboards and drawers. It took all of the rest of the day. It was punishment enough. I hated clearing up and, anyway, what a terrible waste of a day's holiday!

17

The Easter holidays seemed to fly by, as my grown-ups took it in turns to amuse me. I spent a couple of days at Southend, visiting one of Madame Zelda's friends, who told fortunes at the end of the Longest Pier in the World. There was a little train that would take you almost to the door of her snug little booth, in case you couldn't face the walk. We took the train for fun and then walked back. It was funny looking through the gaps in the planks and seeing the grey sea curling and frothing beneath our feet. Funny, and a bit scary too. I decided it might be a good idea to learn to swim before I stepped on to another pier.

We decided not to bother with the Kursaal on the grounds that I had recently been to Battersea funfair. At least, when I say 'we' I mean Madame Zelda and Paulette decided. Me, I'd've made the sacrifice, but Madame Zelda said there was no need, because she had every intention of hanging on to her fish and chips, thank you very much. So we had a great time freezing our toes off having a paddle, making sandcastles with moats and turrets and everything, and eating winkles with a bent pin and plenty of vinegar instead.

Then I spent a whole week with my great-aunt Dodie and Mr and Mrs Filkins, the butler and housekeeper who ran her house for her and looked after it when she was away – which was a lot. Great-aunt Dodie had very itchy feet sometimes, especially in the winter. She hated our weather. She said she didn't mind being up to her neck in the burning sands of some desert or ditto in snow in the Himalayas; what she couldn't stand was the 'half-arsed winters that old Blighty knocks out, all monochrome days and bloody endless rain, mud and fogs'.

In London, we had smogs, when the fog mixed with the coal smoke from millions of fires. The pea-soupers in London were awful. The smog would get so thick that you literally couldn't see a foot in front of your nose, and it was absolutely filthy. It could be so dirty that if you put a clean white hankie over your nose and mouth and walked down the road, it would be grey and black with smuts by the end. It stank of sulphur, too, like the pits of hell.

The name 'pea-souper' might suggest a green tinge, but the split peas used for soup were yellow, and so was the smog. Like soup, it was tricky to breathe in, and lots of people got bronchitis or even died. Sometimes it was so bad that the school would be closed because the teachers couldn't get there, with buses and trains being cancelled and Shanks's pony being out of the question. Those pea-soupers could hang about, too. Sometimes you didn't see the sky for a week or so. So I could see Great-aunt Dodie's point: English winters did leave quite a lot to be desired.

Still, she was back by Easter, which was lucky for me because, to be frank, I was a bit fed up with home. What with the frights, the fights, the fire and my best pal being too ill to play out, it was good to get away. When I was out and about in Soho I couldn't help looking over my shoulder all the time, on the watch for a slight figure with pale hair. I noticed all the grown-ups were the same. It was unsettling, and I didn't like it. I knew that the Widow would not be in Bath, though. What's more, Great-aunt Dodie and Mr and Mrs Filkins liked a good time and knew how to play exciting games.

I had my own, big room at my great-aunt's house. It had been my mum's when she was little, but we'd changed it so that it became mine. It had high ceilings with fancy plasterwork around the light fitting. I loved picking out the birds that hid among the leaves and flowers that twined round and round. The windows were enormous, and light flooded into the room at all times of the day.

Best of all, my bed had a roof and its very own curtains, so that I could pull them closed to make a cosy cave for a bear and her cubs, or a cavewoman and her children. Or, better, it became a secret camp where I was a member of the French Resistance trying to send coded messages back to Blighty. Great-aunt Dodie and Filkins were awfully good at being the Gestapo, crashing in on me and scaring me half to death, but I always managed to fool them and escape their hideous clutches. Other times, the bed was a pirate ship afloat on the endless sea, and I tried to spy land before the rum and ship's biscuits ran out. I spent many happy hours on wet, miserable days, simply playing in that bed.

Great-aunt Dodie took me to Bristol in her lovely, low silver Lagonda. We swept over Clifton Suspension Bridge and back again with the roof down and the wind blowing in our hair. I loved everything about that car. I loved its throaty throb as it belted along, and its dull silver paintwork, gleaming chrome fittings, and the AA badge clamped to the front bumper. Even the headlamps were handsome at the end of the long, low bonnet. I loved its little windscreen with the funny little wipers that clicked as they wiped, and the walnut dashboard with its swirls and whorls. There was a gleaming knob that

Great-aunt Dodie said was the choke, which I wasn't to touch, and lots of businesslike but good-looking dials. Great-aunt Dodie did try to explain what they all were, but it was lost on me. Best of all, I liked the smell of the dark red leather seats and the canvas roof that would be folded down like a pram hood on dry days.

We had our tea in Clifton Village at a posh tea shop with ladies in black dresses and little white pinnies to serve us. The cakes were scrumptious and I had three. I had a vanilla slice, a custard tart and another vanilla slice, then I felt sick and we had to go home. I never did get a proper look at the Gorge, but Great-aunt Dodie said that it wasn't going anywhere and we would see it another time.

Another day we went to Bradford-on-Avon, a tiny place in a deep hole. It had a very old bridge and loads of ancient houses and shops. It looked like a toy village to me. We went into this funny little toyshop there. It was minute but crammed to the ceiling with good things.

Finally, after a great deal of thought and rummaging about in my purse to check on funds, I bought Jenny a book made up of a cardboard cut-out theatre, with actors and actresses complete with cut-out costumes and what's called 'props' and everything. It had the costumes and props for three whole stories, Cinderella, Jack and the Beanstalk and The Sleeping Beauty. I thought that Jenny might be bored, stuck at home all day with no one to play with, and that the theatre was something she could do by herself or with someone else. I was right, too; she got a lot of mileage out of that theatre.

For Kathy Moon I bought a thinner cut-out book with just a couple of dolls, a girl and a boy and their weird clothes. For some reason, cut-out books nearly always had Edwardian or Victorian people and their clothes in them. Still, it didn't seem to spoil the fun any. In fact it made it better. The hours spent cutting out and being very careful not to cut off the tabs that you folded over to attach the clothes to the doll were almost half of the attraction. Many's the time my tabs got lumpy with Sellotape or glue because my scissors had slipped. They never worked as well once they'd been mended, either.

In all the time I stayed with Great-aunt Dodie I didn't once think of the Widow Ginger for more than a minute or two on waking up or dropping off to sleep. I was simply too busy the rest of the time; Great-aunt Dodie saw to that. Every day we did something different. We'd slide into the Lagonda, picnic hamper in the back, and we'd be off. When we weren't sightseeing,

167

my great-aunt just loved a good garden and she taught me a good deal about what she called the 'noble art' as I trailed around behind her. I can hear her now, her voice passionate as she told me her views on the subject.

'Rosa dear, gardening is such a *generous* pastime as well as being good for one's spirit. Generous because most people and most creatures enjoy a welcoming spot to throw off the hurly-burly of the modern world...' there'd be a pause while she launched a slug into orbit over the garden wall, and then she'd carry on, 'and it's good for the spirit, because growing things is so hopeful. It's an investment in the future, don't you know.' And then she'd grab a dandelion by the scruff of the neck and yank it out from between some paving stones. It seemed to me that there was an awful lot of killing things involved in this generous and spiritual hobby. Still, her small garden was gorgeous, full of scented honeysuckle climbing the walls along with vanilla-smelling clematis. The borders were planted with blowzy pink peonies, bit fat oriental poppies and stately delphiniums. Pink phlox filled in some gaps and pinks hugged the edges. It was a riot of colour in the summer, but just then, at Easter, the buds were just beginning to swell and only the hellebores and the bulbs were flowering their heads off.

I knew it was time to go home when I found Filkins solemnly packing my bag after I'd had my breakfast one morning. Straight away I had a blinding vision of a pale head, immaculate trouser creases, shiny shoes and cold, hard eyes. Suddenly, I was dreading being home again and that had never happened to me before.

I told Great-aunt Dodie all about the Widow Ginger on the drive up to London. Every now and then her face would harden as I spoke and she'd remind me even more than usual of Bandy Bunyan, right down to the big nose and Brillo pad hair. Funny thing was, they weren't even related, but they might have been. Bandy looked a lot more like Great-aunt Dodie than my mum did, even though she really was her niece. I got to the bit about the Widow's shoe and she roared, 'The filthy sewer!' with such ferocity that I jumped out of my seat.

Great-aunt Dodie was very angry by the time we got to the fire. 'Oh I say, that's hardly cricket. Fire's a coward's weapon, like poison. They do it secretly, like the slinking creatures that they are. And bullying an innocent child! The swine should hang. May a thousand dogs defile his ancestors' graves! Mark my words, young Rosa, you mark my words, behind every bully there's a coward skulking just below

169

the surface. The trick is to winkle the bastard out and then face the blighter down.' She paused, then gasped. 'Oh, I do beg your pardon, Rosa. I know that your good aunt wouldn't like me bandying foul language about while you're aboard. Let's keep cave about that little error, shall we?'

And we changed the subject. But I don't think she ever forgot it, because it wasn't long after that that she started talking about my education and perhaps looking into decent schools. She was subtle about it, she didn't press, but every now and then, after that, she'd deliver a report on a school she'd 'just happened' to hear about. She was ever so well informed for a woman with no kids of her own. If I'd kept my mouth shut, I'm pretty sure the subject of my going away from home to live in a school would never have come up.

Back home, Sugar took me to the cartoons and we decided that Bugs Bunny was our very favourite rabbit in all the world. Bandy threw a slightly late Easter party and we ate chocolate and played silly games until we were practically sick with excitement and then she sent us home for our families to deal with. I remember Auntie Maggie saying, 'Thank you very much, Bandy Bunyan,' as she tried to scrape me off the ceiling and calm me down enough to get me to bed.

I went to play with Jenny several times during that fortnight and each time she seemed a little smaller and a little paler. She loved her theatre, though, and we had one wonderful afternoon when she had enough energy for us to have a good long play with it. We ignored the given stories and set about making up one of our own.

Needless to say, it got very complicated. One doll, dubbed the Mangy Cow, turned out to be the wicked stepmother. Maltese Joe was another character, who became Grand Vizier of Soho. Luigi was Prince Very Charming Indeed. We squabbled a bit over who should be his princess, but in the end I let Jenny take the part on account of her being ill. Uncle Bert and Auntie Maggie were Soho's king and queen, naturally; it was a concession that Jenny readily agreed to once she'd nabbed being the princess. I wound up as a sort of naughty younger prince who was called, you've guessed it, Prince Not Very Charming At All, who was always on hand to get in the way whenever it looked as if Prince Very Charming Indeed and Princess Jenny were likely to wind up in a clinch. I wasn't at all keen on the notion of Princess Jenny getting into too many clinches, even though she was ill; I wasn't sure why.

Before we knew it, it was time for me to

get off home. According to Mrs Robbins, Jenny was so worn out that she fell asleep as soon as I'd gone, and spent most of the next day too knackered to bother with anything much. So I didn't get to play with her for several days after that. I spent some of the time writing out the story we'd made up as I remembered it and drawing pictures to go with it. Then I made a cover for it out of cardboard and I called it *Princess Jenny and the Handsome Prince* in my very best handwriting.

18

The cafe was humming with the news when I came downstairs for my breakfast on the first day of the new term; another of Maltese Joe's clubs had been set alight in the night. Luckily, a punter had noticed a small fire on the stairs and had stamped it out as he was on the way in. No one was hurt and the club hadn't even had to close. Madame Zelda said it was something in the stars, all this trouble with fire or, in the case of the school boiler, the lack of it.

'Stars be damned,' said Uncle Bert. 'It's more likely the Widow Ginger with an oily rag and a match.'

Auntie Maggie spotted me and clucked at him to shut up, but the damage was done. I'd been reminded that there was a firebug on the loose, and, worse, one with glacial eyes who didn't like us. It was scary and my breakfast wouldn't get past the mysterious lump that had suddenly appeared in my throat.

Now, I loved my grub and had to be really poorly before I went off it, so the congealing bacon and egg on my plate was another cause for concern for Auntie Maggie. She looked at it, then she looked at me, then she cupped my chin in her hand and turned my head this way and that to get a closer look and to check what colour I was. Her cool hand felt my brow. Finally, she decided that I was a bit pale round the gills and, despite the new term and the mended boiler, I'd better stay home from school that day. I almost leaped with joy until I realized that any leaping had better wait until school was well and truly under way, otherwise I'd find my bum at my desk toot sweet. Madame Zelda, Paulette and Uncle Bert began muttering among themselves the minute Auntie Maggie led me back up the stairs to the comfort of my still warm bed.

Auntie Maggie and I had a lovely comforting routine for the times when I was a bit under the weather. She started by putting a match to the fire in my bedroom. The fire was always laid for action but only lit when I had to stay in my room for some reason, usually illness. I normally loved that fire but this time I really didn't think I fancied it. I'd had enough of fires for the time being, even a friendly one. Auntie Maggie tutted a bit, because there was always a fire in a sick-room, sometimes even in August. She understood, though, when I explained that I was a off fires for a bit. We agreed that the weather was warm enough as long as I wore my winter nightie and Auntie Flo's most recent bedjacket when I sat up to read or eat. The plump eiderdown was to remain on the bed at all times. Once terms were agreed, we were free to get on with the next bit of our ritual.

I had three winter flannelette nighties with little rosebuds, one pink, one blue and my least favourite, the yukky-coloured yellow one. That day it was the pink. The blue was in the wash, and the yellow was neatly folded in the airing cupboard waiting for emergencies. Once on, the nightie reached to my ankles, and the long sleeves and high neck were buttoned up until the only flesh showing was my mush and my hands and feet. Next came the pink knitted bedjacket, a rather boring part of my Christmas present from Auntie Flo and Uncle Sid, who lived in a boarding house by the sea. At least it was boring until I was stuck in bed;

174

then it was snuggly, warm and wonderful. Auntie Flo knitted all my bedjackets over the years and she made a point of using the softest, cosiest wool and pretty ribbons to tie them at the throat. She was all right, was my auntie Flo.

Once Auntie Maggie had me tucked up in bed, she made sure I had plenty of reading matter, paper, pencils and crayons on the bedside table, ready to ward off the dreaded boredom. It helped Auntie Maggie if I was busy and content because she could carry on downstairs in the cafe without worrying too much about me.

When I was settled with my heap of books, comics, notebook and drawing book, the radio was ceremoniously brought in from the living room and plugged in. Then I could keep abreast of Mrs Dale and her Jim. *Music While You Work* was all right as background noise and, if I was desperate, *Listen With Mother*, which was actually meant for the little kids but was followed by *Woman's Hour* which I just loved. It was full of inspiring stories of women doing amazing things like knocking up a three piece suite from pipecleaners or walking across the Himalayas with a yak.

The schools programmes could be fun. I liked to work up a good gloat that I wasn't prancing around being a tree or a fairy with my skirt tucked into my knickers. At such moments, I really pitied my school chums in a self-satisfied sort of way. If the programmes were about history or nature, they could be very interesting. I liked to hear about Florence Nightingale, Good Queen Bess, the Romans or the life of the common newt. I would wait with varying degrees of patience for my favourite programme, which came on at five in the afternoon: *Children's Hour* with David Davis reading the stories and serials. I just loved his voice. Then on Saturday mornings there was good old Uncle Mac who was an absolute must. Of course, to really appreciate this feast of radio fun, I had to be feeling relatively well. Yaks, newts and pipecleaners were no good at all if I had a raging fever, because they all sort of melted in together and got confusing. In fact, to enjoy being off sick from school I had to be in pretty good nick, because there was so much to do.

Then there was the grub. My personal favourite invalid foods were soft boiled eggs and Marmite soldiers, Mrs Wong's home-made chicken noodle soup and Mamma Campanini's special ravioli. Swollen tonsils responded well to Italian chocolate ice cream, I always found, and lemon and honey was bliss for a cold. Homemade egg custard was also a favourite, especially if it had a sprinkle of nutmeg on the top and a vanilla pod added to the boiled milk and fished out before it went into the oven. Auntie Maggie was a dab hand at egg custard. But then, my beloved auntie Maggie was a dab hand at most things.

At last I was settled, with the radio burbling hymns quietly in the background as I waited for something good to come on and Tom, our lace-eared old cat, snoring and purring gently at the end of the bed. I'd eaten every scrap of my boiled egg and soldiers, and at last Auntie Maggie was satisfied that I'd be all right for an hour or so on my own. With a last feel of my brow and a kiss on the top of my curls, she was gone. I was utterly content all morning and after dinner – ravioli from Campanini's – all through *Woman's Hour*. But then, once that was over and there was only boring music to listen to until Mrs Dale came on, I remembered Uncle Bert saying that it was the Widow Ginger with his oily rag and matches who had set fire to Maltese Joe's clubs, and all peace and contentment drained away, leaving a feeling of dread I could neither shift nor put a name to. Just as I was feeling as if a rat was gnawing at my belly, Paulette came into the room and I hurled myself at her, sobbing and hiccuping with relief.

The good thing about Paulette was that she never told me I was daft to worry. She just listened seriously to my garbled terror and agreed that the Widow Ginger was a frightening man, but she also pointed out that he was not stupid enough to try anything in broad daylight, and that anyway it was Maltese Joe he was really after. She also thought that he wouldn't do anything else until he had seen how well his first efforts had paid off.

This reasoning made sense to me and I calmed down quite a bit. Then I threw up my dinner, and realized I probably really was ill.

The last thing I remember was Paulette wiping my forehead with a cool wet flannel and changing my nightie for the yukky yellow one, still warm from the airing cupboard. Then it was night time and Auntie Maggie was sitting by my bed with her knitting and the radio tuned quietly to *Book at Bedtime*. I don't know why Auntie Maggie was knitting, because she wasn't very good at it and only made what she called 'toe covers'. These were scrappy little bits that served only to keep her hands busy in times of crisis. When the crisis was over, the scraps were carefully unravelled and the wool saved for the next time. That poor ball of grey wool must have been knitted up a thousand times before it finally got too thin to use.

I was boiling hot and the glands in my throat were huge and bulged like an overfed hamster. It turned out that, like half of my school, I had mumps.

I had a lot of nightmares during that illness. I'd wake up red hot and sweaty, convinced that the cafe was on fire and that any minute now the flames would creep up the stairs and burst though my bedroom door and eat me alive. That's when I didn't think the Widow Ginger was lurking in my wardrobe just waiting for a quiet moment to jump out with a huge pair of tweezers ready to fix me on a slide under a giant microscope. I could see a puzzled cold fish eye gazing down at me though the eyepiece, wondering what manner of bug I was and whether I should be swatted or dropped into the fire so that I fizzled and hissed and burned until I popped. It was awful.

The daylight hours were nowhere as bad because the bogeymen tend to hate the full glare of the sun, and anyway, I had lots of visitors. Luigi often came and read to me. He was good at reading aloud and did all the actions and voices. Madame Zelda said that he should have been an actor, what with his looks and everything. Gina Lollobrigida was a very famous Italian actress at the time and Madame Zelda reckoned that Luigi was a sort of blokey equivalent. I suppose she was right, although Luigi didn't have the same sort of chest as 'La Lollo' –

which Paulette said was just as well.

Madame Zelda and Paulette took it in turns to look after me when Auntie Maggie was busy in the cafe. Sometimes, when I was feeling particularly poorly, they looked after the cafe while Auntie Maggie soothed me. Uncle Bert made regular trips up the stairs when he could get away from his kitchen for long enough. He always managed to magic something interesting from my nose or lug'oles. When I was still feeling sick he found cigarette cards for my albums, always just the one I wanted to finish off a set or to start another one. When the queasiness left me, gobstoppers and sherbet dabs mysteriously appeared from here, there and everywhere. Sometimes he would just sit in front of the cold fireplace, with me wrapped in a blanket on his lap, and tell me stories about when he was a little boy and the scrapes he got into. I loved those times the best. Even better than sherbet dabs, and I was devoted to them. I can still feel my cheek resting cosily against the rough cloth of his waistcoat and smell the combination of Lifebuoy soap, pipe tobacco and fry-up that clung to him almost as closely as I did.

19

Just because I was poorly, it didn't mean that I missed out on what was going on in my world. Well, I didn't once the worst of the fever was over; my constant stream of visitors and my terrible nosiness saw to that. If information wasn't volunteered, then I asked endless and very pointed questions. Auntie Maggie always said that asking questions was rude, but I took no notice and asked away without a trace of shame. I think that secretly she was glad, because she got to find out quite a bit as well.

Take the romance between Betty and Luigi. Being laid up in bed, I hadn't had the chance to watch what was going on and draw my own conclusions, so I was forced to use more direct means. I grilled everyone who came through that bedroom door. I learned from Paulette that there had been two more dates. Once they'd gone to Luigi's favourite jazz club and the other time they'd spent a Sunday at Richmond Park. I learned from Madame Zelda that, despite the legendary Campanini powers of persuasion, Betty had stayed upright on her own two feet at all times, except when she was sitting down. At no point had she been flat on her back, with or without her legs in the air. What's more, Luigi still hadn't even managed to get into her flat, let alone her knickers. Unfortunately, Auntie Maggie came in and tutted at her pal at that point, so I got no more juicy speculation on that visit. However, I wasn't above giving Betty and Luigi the third degree either.

I started with the black eye. Knowing how touchy men can be about such things, I decided Betty was the best one to pump for more information on that score. I lulled her into a false sense of security first, asking politely about her health and so on, then I pounced. 'Why did Maltese Joe black Luigi's eye, Betty?' There's nothing like suddenly going for the direct approach. It catches people unawares.

'Because he was jealous, love. He'd heard that Luigi and me had been stepping out a bit and he didn't like it. Still doesn't. Poor Luigi has to wait outside the club to take me home now. Joe won't let him in, the silly man.' You'd expect Betty to look pleased with herself, with two men after her but she didn't. She just looked a bit worried.

'Which one do you like the most?' I thought it was best to clear this matter up from the start.

'Well, they're both nice in their way, Rosie, but Joe's married, so as far as I'm concerned, that's that. Take my advice, Rosie dear. When you're a big girl, never trouble with a married man. A man who betrays his wife is a man who will betray anybody. That's what I've come to think, anyway. Course, not everyone would agree with me, especially married blokes with roving eyes, but it's always served me all right as a general rule of thumb.'

I couldn't work out what thumbs had to do with it, but I didn't want to spoil the flow by asking, so I didn't. For all her many faults, my mum didn't breed any dumbos, so I knew when I was being sidetracked. Betty hadn't answered my question, but as Uncle Bert always said, I'm like a 'bleeding terrier' when I get my teeth into something and I wasn't about to let go. 'Yes, but which one do you like best?'

Betty looked at me for a long time with those bird's egg eyes of hers, a tiny worried frown creasing her perfect brow. I gazed back, stunned by just how beautiful she was. Even I could see why men would be fighting over her, and for the first time I found myself worrying about poor Luigi's safety. Everyone knew that Maltese Joe was several scruples short of a conscience and wouldn't think more than twice about maiming Luigi if he got in his way.

When at last Betty answered, she chose her words carefully. 'Rosie, I like them both. But I don't love either one and that's the honest truth.' It seemed a relief for her to blurt it out. 'I know Luigi's really smitten, and if I could, I'd be smitten back. He's a really nice boy, kind, gentle, sweet, but...'

I kept my gob shut and we just carried on staring at each other in a sad kind of way. I don't know what she was thinking, exactly, but I know that I stopped worrying about Luigi getting his bones broken and started worrying about his poor heart being shattered instead. Somehow I just knew that would be a far more serious injury for him to bear. All the cafe women and Sugar Plum were agreed, we had never seen Luigi in such a state about a woman before, it was as if he was mesmerized. I knew that when it dawned on him that he was getting nowhere he would take it hard, very hard indeed.

Betty shuddered and beamed me a gorgeous smile, full of perfect teeth and warmth. 'I'm working on it, though, Rosie. He's a good man, one of the very best, and I know he would make a terrific husband and a lovely father, so I'm working on it. I'm not that much of an idiot that I don't know when I've got hold of a good one. Decent blokes are about as common as hen's teeth, I know that...' Betty's voice trailed away to nothing again, and instead of staring at each other, we both got lost in the dancing flames of the fire for a bit.

I decided that she had answered my question. She preferred Luigi, but that wasn't saying much, judging by how sad it seemed to make us both feel. Then she said, 'How about a game of beat your neighbour out of doors?' And the mood was broken.

I told my beloved auntie Maggie all about that conversation later on, when she came to tuck me in and kiss me goodnight. She also looked sad for a moment, but then got all hearty. 'Well, I keep telling you not to ask people personal questions. It's like listening at keyholes. You don't always like what you get to hear. Now, snuggle down like a good girl and, if you play your cards right, I'll let you listen to *Take It From Here*.'

I played my cards right. It was only when the programme was over and I was well and truly kissed goodnight, that I realized that Auntie Maggie had failed to assure me that everything was sure to turn out for the best. I fell asleep determined to find out from Luigi how he felt about Betty. I was still plotting how best to approach the subject when I must have fallen asleep.

The next thing I knew was Auntie Maggie was rattling the poker, trying to coax some life back into the fire, opening curtains and singing out, 'Morning love. Uncle Bert'll have your breakfast up in a jiffy. P'raps you can get up later if you feel like it. The water's hot. You can have a nice bath and a hairwash.'

I could never understand how Auntie Maggie could get the words, 'nice', 'bath' and 'hairwash' into the same sentence. Hairwashing always meant stinging eyes, a cold, wet neck and much tugging and yanking on my curls. I hated it, especially in cold weather. But the thought of wet curls reminded me of Luigi with his surprising spikes when his hair was wet, and my plan to ply him with cunning questions about Betty.

I knew the direct approach was less likely to work with him, on account of him being a bloke and therefore incapable of talking about his finer feelings. It would take what Uncle Bert called guile, and as I gronfed my scrambled eggs on toast, I laid my plans. Complicated they were, and as it happened, totally unnecessary, because life was about to overtake me in all sorts of ways. When I thought of it again, it was perfectly obvious how Luigi felt, so there was no need to ask.

20

It was my first trip downstairs in what felt like months, but was not much more than a week. I was sitting at the corner table with Madame Zelda and Luigi and munching my breakfast, when one of Luigi's brothers-in-law walked in.

He saw Luigi immediately and hurried over to our table. 'Luigi, we've clocked him. Last night, coming out of Ruby's place.' The urgency in his voice made everyone pay attention, even though only Luigi seemed to know what he was talking about.

Madame Zelda soon put that right. 'You two may know who you're muttering about, but the rest of us are looking for enlightenment, so cough it up, Luigi.'

Before opening his mouth, Luigi took a careful look around the cafe, to see who was earwigging, then he leaned forward and hissed just two words: 'The Widow.' Immediately, an army of penguins with frozen feet seemed to be marching down my back. I shivered and I swear my teeth began to rattle.

'Did you follow him? Did you find his gaff?' Now Luigi's voice was sharp.

'Yes, we followed him, but no, we didn't find his place. He lost us when he grabbed the only cab in bleeding Streatham. We didn't even hear where he told it to go. Sod gave us a little wave as he drove past. We did find out one thing, though. We went back to Ruby's and one of the lads there said he was a regular. In at least once a week. A fiver bought us the whole story. They're scared shitless of him but he pays well for what they call "special services", which seem to be more than a little light bum-slapping. I'll leave it for you to work out. Makes me feel uncle just thinking about all that sort of stuff. I mean, I don't mind giving a geezer a bit of a slap if he's earned it, like, but to do it for the jollies, well, as I said, makes me wanna heave. If you ask me, there's not much wrong with your old woman, your basic missionary and a nice Woodbine after. Still, it does mean that he'll have to go back there or somewhere similar, and, let's face it, there ain't too many houses that cater for the pervs. And being foreign, he most likely doesn't know about the others, so Ruby's it'll be, I reckon.'

I could not for the life of me work out what they were talking about, except that the Widow had been spotted. Neither Madame Zelda nor Luigi would explain, either, and then Auntie Maggie came over to the table and decided I was getting over-excited, and maybe a little lie down was in order. In desperation I asked her what 'special services' meant, but when she heard why I wanted to know she went all vague on me.

'It could mean anything, lovey. They say special services in church for people who are very poorly or something. In a caff, special services would mean something like silver service, I expect, like what Paulette does at the Corner House: a little black dress, a white pinny and a cap and messing about with all that silverware. You know, serving a cake with a pair of silver tongs or two silver forks. It's having all the right knives and forks and spoons for everything and serving the soup from a tureen and having proper soup spoons and fish knives.'

I always knew when my auntie Maggie began to babble that she was avoiding answering one of my questions. I sighed. I was never going to find out what Ruby's special services were, and I resigned myself to the fact. By the time I was settled comfortably on the bed, Auntie Maggie was on to silver sugar tongs and I fell asleep. There's only so much babble a person can take.

When I woke up again it was dinner time and I was starving. Downstairs the cafe was full of punters, talk, laughter, fag smoke and steam. Mrs Wong's little figure was darting about in the fug with plates of food balanced all the way up her arms and I had to dodge smartish so as not to get under her feet. According to my auntie Maggie, one of the secrets of being a good waitress is being nimble and able to dodge and weave because it's a law of nature that there is always some so and so ready, willing and able to trip you up and send good food and crockery crashing to the lino. And there's no profit in that, so I learned from nappyhood how to get out from under flying feet fast. Uncle Bert always said that as a baby I was the fastest bum-slider in the west. I expect all cafe kids are the same, otherwise we'd spend our lives covered in gravy, custard and bits of cabbage.

I was so busy trying to get to the corner table without getting in the way that I didn't see the Widow Ginger come in. I felt the draught from the open door and when I looked round he was standing there in the doorway, smoke and steam billowing around him as it made a rush to escape the crowded room. I felt like joining it, because, just for a moment, the Widow looked like the Devil at the gates of hell. It was his stillness in the doorway that was so frightening. Only his eyes moved; he appeared to be looking for somebody. Then they stopped at me, with a brief, blank stare followed by the coldest smile I had ever seen. I was rooted to the spot as he stared at me and I stared back at him.

It seemed like a hundred years of quaking in my slippers before, thank God, I heard Madame Zelda's voice cut through the distant sound of the hissing tea urn and the chatting punters. 'Oi, you, move your arse. We've got a starving mob backed up behind your carcass.' And the Widow Ginger was shot sharply forward into the room by a dig in the back from Madame Zelda's handbag. Nothing and nobody was allowed to get in the way of a hungry soothsayer with a whiff of the trough in her nostrils – or so Sugar said later, when relaying the story back to Bandy. I scuttled for the safety of the corner table and the reassuring company of Luigi, Sugar and, once she'd muscled past the Widow, Madame Zelda.

When I looked again, the milling about around the doorway had stopped and the Widow Ginger had gone. I almost thought I'd imagined the whole thing, until Luigi muttered to no one in particular, 'I wonder what that bastard wanted. I think I'd better get hold of Joe.' He stood up and headed towards the door, then turned and added an afterthought. 'Sugar, warn Bert and Bandy that he's about, will you?' And he too was gone.

It wasn't often that I was struck dumb, but I was left feeling really shaken and frightened, and with no way to explain it to anyone. Nothing had actually happened, but I still felt as if he gave me his special attention. On the few occasions I'd seen him he'd always given me strange looks. That was it; nothing more than funny looks. I'd seem a right wally if I told my nearest and dearest that I was all rattled because he'd looked at me. But I was. It seemed to me that the Widow hated just about everything and everyone round our way, and that for some reason I couldn't understand he seemed to hate me too, which wasn't fair; stepping on someone's shoe isn't *that* bad, after all. And I wasn't even born until the war was over, and whatever it was that had got so far up his nose that it had twisted his brains was nothing to do with me.

I was convinced that those glittering eyes sought me out for special attention and it made me deeply afraid. I hoped and prayed that I wasn't going to be on the receiving end of any of those 'special services' nobody would talk about.

Luigi wasn't able to find Maltese Joe at any of his usual haunts, but then it was a bit early in the day for that, so he had to content himself with leaving urgent messages for him with various henchmen. It was Betty Potts who suggested that Luigi try at Maltese Joe's flat. Now, nobody visited Maltese Joe at home unless they were a priest or a nun or were invited to do so by the man himself. It just wasn't done, because he was funny like that. Most people weren't even sure where he lived most of the time, because he moved around a lot just so he could confuse business rivals and the police. Still, there was the flat that his mum lived in. He was often there, but even Uncle Bert had always waited for an invitation before visiting it.

So Luigi was reluctant to go ringing on the doorbell, what with that and the fact that there had been no love lost between the two men since Betty had appeared on the scene. That made visiting Maltese Joe an even dodgier manoeuvre. Everyone at the corner table agreed on that. It was Uncle Bert who suggested telephoning first. Owning a telephone was still a relatively rare thing – we didn't have one at the time – but Maltese Joe did, and so did Sharky Finn, so Luigi nipped next door clutching a piece of paper with the number on it.

He was back quickly. 'No answer,' he explained.

Uncle Bert was puzzled. 'What do you mean? It ain't Sunday, is it? So Joe's mum should be there at least. She never goes out if she can help it, except to Mass, of course. There's always someone there. Joe makes sure of it. You're certain there's no answer? Did you let it ring? The old girl's a bit slow on her scotches nowadays. Maybe she didn't make it.'

So back Luigi went. He was away considerably longer this time, but the news was the same. 'No answer.'

Uncle Bert was worried, and the deep frown showed he was thinking hard. At last he came to a decision. 'Look, Luigi, I don't want to leave the girls or this place, not with that nutter roaming about. He's already scared our Rosie by just walking in here.' (Now how did he know that? I hadn't said a word. Later, Madame Zelda said I did look a bit white around the gills, but Auntie Maggie said that he just knew his little girl like the back of his hand.) 'Can you stay on here while I nip round to Joe's flat and make sure everything's all right? I've got a bad feeling about this.' Luigi simply nodded once and Uncle Bert whipped his apron off and slipped out. I noticed that Auntie Maggie pressed her lips tightly together, so as not to say a word.

She was all business once he'd gone. 'Betty, would you mind sitting with our Rosie for an hour or so? Looks to me as if she could do with a rest and I know she'll be messing about up there if she's all on her tod. We've got the dinner-time rush to clear up after and it won't clear itself.'

I was still a bit jittery at first. The Widow had unsettled me that much. But Betty

194

cosied up beside me and began telling me stories about her childhood on the chicken farm deep in the Sussex countryside, somewhere near a place called Bolney. She told me how, even when she was tiny, she'd dreamed of getting away from chicken poo and becoming a dancer or a film star. She didn't mind which. After a while, the soft drone of her voice soothed my jangled nerves, and I was almost able to forget about the Widow and the nameless dread he made me feel.

I especially liked the story of her dog, Jack, and how he saved her from getting squashed flat by the tractor at the farm at the top of her lane. It seems that she had just learned to walk and was busy putting her new-found talent to good use. She got everywhere: in the barn, in the chicken coops, in the dung heap and, finally, out of the farmyard and into the lane. 'What you don't realize, Rosie, being brought up in the Smoke, is just how many dangerous places there are on a farm. There's the hayloft, for a start. Get up *there* and fall, and it's a broken leg at least; land on something, and you could be run through into the bargain.' Betty knew I was keen on gore in theory, if not in practice, and usually managed to include some in her stories.

'Then there's the duck pond; easy to drown there. God, there's a hundred and one places for a toddler to get hurt or even killed stone dead on a farm, and according to my mum I found all of them. Luckily, though, I had my faithful old Jack, who stuck to me like glue and managed to get me out of most dangerous situations. He'd just grab me by the nappy, or my cardigan, and drag me away. But this particular day he couldn't get a grip on anything because there was nothing to sink his teeth into. I was stark naked; not a stitch on, no nappy, no cardie, no nothing, and I was headed straight under the wheels of next door's tractor. Farmer Cattermole saw the whole thing from his cow byre. He yelled to try to warn the tractor driver that I was in the way, but the engine drowned him out, and just as he'd started to run across his yard he saw Jack round me up like a naughty sheep and then drive me back all the way down the lane to home by nipping just a fraction behind my bare bottom. His teeth didn't make contact once. He was that clever.'

We played a few games of snakes and ladders and then it was time for tea. Now that I was getting better and there wasn't a mump to be seen, I was expected to eat my meals in the cafe to save Aunt Maggie the trips up and down with loaded trays. I was keen to oblige, because it was more interesting downstairs once I was in a fit state to sit up and take notice.

Betty and I entered the cafe at exactly the same moment as Uncle Bert. He had been round at Maltese Joe's for an amazingly long time for somebody who was uninvited and not on speaking terms with his host. He should have got what the American soldiers called the 'bum's rush' in very swift order. Paulette explained to me that a bum had nothing to do with backsides in America; a bum was a tramp or something like it. I wasn't at all sure that she'd got that right; after all, getting 'the bum's rush' and getting 'your arse out of here' sounded pretty similar to me. Still, the point is, Uncle Bert had been gone for ages and we soon found out why.

Uncle Bert didn't trouble to stop at the corner table, and I knew things were serious when he began encouraging the last few punters to leave. Even Betty said she had some shopping to do. Soon the place was empty except for Luigi, Uncle Bert, Auntie Maggie and me.

'Go and pull the door blind down, Rosie, and turn the sign to Closed, there's a love. I'll get your tea. Boiled egg and soldiers do you?' And he disappeared back into his kitchen.

For some reason, none of us spoke, even though he was being infuriating not telling us what had happened round at Maltese Joe's place. We simply waited in silence until

Uncle Bert came back carrying a tray with my tea, several glasses and a bottle of whisky on it. He began handing out food and drinks and I remember being struck by the wonderful colour of whisky as it sloshed into the glasses. Needless to say, I got milk, which is nowhere near as good-looking. Once everyone was served, Uncle Bert sat down heavily with a deep sigh and took a large swig of his drink. 'OK, I'll tell you what happened.' Which is what we were all longing to know.

Uncle Bert thought for a long time before he spoke. Truth to tell, I was getting bored with waiting and almost blurted out 'Get on with it!' But I didn't, because they would almost certainly have sent me upstairs to get me out of the way.

'I knew I was right and that something was up as soon as I got up the stairs to Joe's door,' Uncle Bert began at last. 'It was ajar. Now Joe's never that sloppy, so I called out and got no answer. Gave me the creeps, I can tell you. Anyway, I pushed the door right back, in case there was someone behind it, but there wasn't. What I thought I was going to do about it if there was, I'm blowed if I know; but there wasn't any problem, so that was all right. I waited a bit, to see if I could hear anything, but there was nothing but this funny little tapping noise. Once I was sure I was on me tod, at least in the hallway, I stepped in.

'I saw the pile straight away. It was a great heap of what looked like Joe's clobber. Suits, shoes, shirts, the lot, and they reeked of petrol. Sure enough, somebody had left the empty jerrycan right next to the pile. That and a box of matches. On the wall behind it, written in what looked like blood, but might well've been ketchup, seeing there was a bottle of it on the hallstand, was a message. "Joe, I'll be seeing you ... but will you see me?" The bloody Widow knows how to make you sweat, I'll give him that. The bastard's been planning this for a long time.

'Meanwhile, that tapping noise was getting on me nerves, so I thought I'd better look into it. In the end, I tracked the noise down to the broom cupboard in the kitchen. It was old Ma Joe. Trussed up like a Christmas goose, she was, just had the strength to tap the chair leg against the floor. If the place hadn't been so quiet, I never would've heard her. Poor old duck had a gag and everything. It's a wonder she didn't suffocate.

'Anyway, I figured I couldn't just leave her there so I calmed her down a bit and took her to your mum, Luigi. I didn't think the poor old darling would like to be faced with a cafe full of punters so soon after what had happened to her. I thought she'd feel safer away from the flat, you see. She was able to tell Mamma what happened while I went to find Joe. You'll never guess where he was? Not in a million years. Go on, have a guess.'

Auntie Maggie gave Uncle Bert her old-fashioned look. 'Don't be a prat, Bert. If you're going to tell us where Joe was, just bloody well tell us and get it over with, there's a dear.'

Uncle Bert whipped out his pipe, stared at it for a minute, then smiled. 'Suit yourself. Where was I? It turned out that old Ma Joe answered the door to what she thought was the postman first thing. But it wasn't; it was the Widow. He pushed his way in, tied the old girl up, arranged his bonfire in the hall, wrote his message and then told her to tell her son that he should keep his boys away from him and that he would be back to light the matches. Then he buggered off. Poor old dear had been there all day, practically. She couldn't walk. I had to carry her to Mamma's.'

Auntie Maggie was anxious. 'Is she all right now? Should I go round there?'

'No, no. Mamma's got everything sorted. Ma Joe's staying the night with her. She was tucking into a plate of spags when I left. She'll be all right. She's too sparky to let something like that get her down for long. Right now, she's telling her Joe just what he's got to do to the bugger when he catches up with him, and believe me, it ain't pretty. Last I heard, she had the Widow's orchestras flying through the top of his head, and that was just for starters. Joe says that he'll be along for a word in a bit, when he's got his mum settled.'

Auntie Maggie looked uncomfortable, but held her peace. Uncle Bert and Maltese Joe had some ground to make up, and she knew it. She also knew that in no circumstances was she to interfere. It was between the two men.

Nobody seemed inclined to ask the question that was bothering me. There was a long, long silence while everyone thought about what they'd heard. Except me, that is. I was busy thinking about what I hadn't heard. In the end, I could bear it no longer. 'Uncle Bert, I give up. Where was Maltese Joe?'

He laughed, eyes sparkling in merriment. 'He was having a violin lesson, Rosie, with old Rabinowitz. Seems he's been at it for years, but he keeps it very, very quiet. I mean, who ever heard of an arch spiv playing the bleeding fiddle? Classical at that, according to his mum.'

At that moment Maltese Joe walked in the door, closed it behind him and shot the bolts top and bottom. If he noticed me at all, he gave no sign. I tried to make myself as small and still as possible. I stuck my thumb in my mouth and, like the others at our corner table, I waited.

At last Maltese Joe spoke. I had expected plenty of ranting and raving, because that was his style, but in fact he was very quiet and serious. 'Thank you, Bert, for sorting my mum. She could've died in that cupboard.' He took a few deep breaths and continued. 'Like she said, if you hadn't dropped by, sure as hell nobody else would've had the front to come to my private place. So, I owe you one, Bert, a big 'un.' He walked over to our table then, and stuck out his hand.

Uncle Bert stood up, wiped his hand on his trouser leg, and shook briefly with Maltese Joe, looking solemn. They looked into each other's eyes for a long moment, and nodded slightly at each other. Then Uncle Bert said, 'Take a load off, Joe. I reckon we've got a lot to talk about. Maggie, how about a cuppa? And Rosie, you've been up long enough. Time for you to have a nap, if you ask me.'

Which I hadn't, and neither had anybody else, but I was hustled up the stairs by Auntie Maggie anyway. The last thing I saw was Maltese Joe hooking a chair over to the table with his foot and sitting astride it, resting his arms on the back. 'Right, now that's out of the way for the time being, we'd better talk about what we're going to do about that mad fucker Stanley. Luigi, nip round and get Bandy, will you? She'd better be in on this.'

I missed the next bit, because Auntie Maggie was busy settling me under my eiderdown for a kip. However, I could tell that her mind was downstairs with Uncle Bert and Maltese Joe and it wasn't long before I got a swift kiss on the curls and she was gone. Of course, I was out of that bed almost before the door closed and her heavy step sounded on the stairs, and it was only moments before I heard Maltese Joe telling Uncle Bert and Auntie Maggie what was going on.

'I've got my boys out now, combing every inch of the manor. There ain't a club, knocking shop, boozer, dive or doss house within a five-mile radius that they ain't turning over as we speak. The bastard's in and out so quick, he's got to have his base nearby. I've told the lads not to hesitate to break arms, legs or even backbones, if required, to loosen any tongues. Some bugger knows where he is, or is hiding him; if creating a few cripples helps us find out who and where, I say the effort's worth it. Now's the time to bung your loose change into a wooden leg factory, Bert, because demand's about to fucking well go up.'

'Now, hold your water there, Joe. I've told you before, I won't be a party to any maiming or killing.' Uncle Bert paused for a moment. 'Well, p'raps a little maiming, seeing what he did to your poor old mum. But restrict it to him, eh? He's the sod that did it all, so he's the one that should suffer. Any others he might have aboard, well, they're probably scared shitless and will do anything he wants. You know what he's like; he frightens people into things. And anyway, the lads might maim a total innocent and that ain't never right. You'd be no better than him and that ain't right neither, Joe, and you know it.'

There was total silence for what felt like a week, while we all wondered whether Uncle Bert was likely to leave the table with his bonce on. And then, out of the blue, there was a brief burst of applause and Bandy's plummy tones saying, 'Hear, hear, Albert. Well said. I agree with you. Something must be done about Stan, and I agree with Joe as well, a permanent solution is probably best. But as the man says, Joe, we needn't start a run on wheelchairs.

'Maggie dear, any chance of a slug of the hard stuff to get my gears shifting? Young Luigi here dragged Sugar and me from the land of nod and I'm not all present and correct yet.'

I heard Auntie Maggie's chuckle and the rattle of glasses. 'Looks as if Sharky's bottle has gone the way of all Sharky's bottles, into the bin. I'll just nip upstairs to get another.

Hang on a tick.'

It's just as well Auntie Maggie wasn't built for nipping, because I was safely tucked up under my plump eiderdown reading Swallows and Amazons when her head popped round my bedroom door.

21

Poor Jenny had the mumps and had been laid even lower. I felt awful, even though Auntie Maggie kept telling me it wasn't my fault. I was after all the only mump-stricken person to visit her, so it stood to reason that I took them there. Mrs Robbins said it was pitiful to see her. All I could do was send in comics and little notes in the hope of cheering her up a bit.

Betty got a bit odd after the day old Ma Joe was found in the broom cupboard. Luigi didn't understand it because she'd gone very quiet and started turning down his dates again, with lame excuses about hair washing and cleaning her flat. He was upset because he couldn't work out why she'd cooled down so suddenly. He confided in my auntie Maggie, as everybody did. 'We seemed to be doing all right. You know, low-key but all right. Then out of the clear blue, she doesn't want to know. What's all that about?'

'I really couldn't say, Luigi. Maybe you should ask her.' My auntie Maggie was a great believer in 'talking things through'. It sometimes got up my uncle Bert's nose, but she did it anyway.

'I have, but all she keeps on about is Maltese Joe and the Widow Ginger and how she can't be doing with all the violence and mayhem. Now what's that got to do with me, I ask you? I can't make sense of it at all. Still, no Campanini's ever been known to beg, so I reckon I'll stop asking soon. What do you think?'

Auntie Maggie was cautious. 'That depends, Luigi, on just how keen you are. If you stop asking, she may think you've lost interest, and I hate to say it, but there's plenty to step in. There's been a queue forming ever since she got here. On the other hand, pestering her will do no good at all. Why don't you compromise and ask her out along with other people? Maybe she just needs a bit of time. Perhaps she feels things have been going a bit fast. You've behaved yourself, I hope. Been a gentleman and all that, have you?'

Luigi managed to look hurt and innocent at the same time. 'Of course I've behaved meself. I can if I put me mind to it, you know. I like this girl, Maggie. Why would I ruin it by jumping on her? I'm not a total prat.'

Auntie Maggie was soothing, 'Of course you're not, Luigi. I never said you was. My advice is take things slow. Take a good old-fashioned chaperone with you. You can borrow Rosie here if you like. She'd be a good chaperone, and it might put Betty more at her ease if she feels you're both taking Rosie out instead of you taking just her. You can always ease Rosie out as things develop.'

Thank you very much, Auntie Maggie! All this talk of easing made me sound like an old wellie. Still, it did mean I was likely to get more first hand gossip on the Luigi and Betty front, to pass on to Jenny when she felt better. And, of course, to Auntie Maggie, Madame Zelda, Paulette and all the other devoted Luigi and Betty watchers, although I expect that consideration was a million miles from the Auntie Maggie mind when she made her generous offer. I don't think! She knew she could rely on me to take careful note of all romantic developments on account of me being the nosiest kid in London, England, Europe and possibly the world.

Less thrilling was the fact that I was finally pronounced fit to go back to school. Which I suppose was OK really, because it gave me less time to brood on what the Widow

Ginger was going to do next.

Now the weather was warming up a bit, we began to limber up for Sports Day. We always had Sports Day at the end of the summer term, and practice started early. Suddenly, PE lessons leaned heavily towards sack racing, running, jumping and swimming at the Marshall Street baths. It was all go. Everyone in the school had been put into a house when they started, a fact that we forgot about a lot of the time, until Sports Day, or the swimming gala, or the netball, football, rounders or cricket matches came round. Then house loyalty became fierce and everyone – well, almost everyone – strove to make their house victorious in the various competitions. So out came the gym knickers and plimsolls ready for action. I quite liked running and jumping and had made up my mind that I would learn to swim as well, which came in handy, because it gave Luigi and Betty somewhere to take me when I was on chaperone duty.

But the Widow Ginger still lurked at the back of my mind, icicle eyes fixed on me and a box of matches in his hand. He was a regular feature of my dreams, and once or twice I was so frightened I snuggled up in bed between Uncle Bert and Auntie Maggie. Uncle Bert swore that fairies came in the dead of night and sharpened every one of my ninety-four elbows and two hundred and fourteen knees to vicious points, so that I could dig them all into him. Auntie Maggie was less critical. She just said I was a wriggle-monster, and left it at that.

But the anxiety still gnawed away at me the minute I wasn't busy enough to keep it away. The Widow Ginger had done nothing but cause trouble and fear since his shiny shoes had hit our Soho streets once again. He'd even managed to get Auntie Maggie and Uncle Bert at each other's throats, and that wasn't easy. He'd been behind the trouble between Uncle Bert and Maltese Joe, too, when you got down to it. It might have been Auntie Maggie who pulled the trigger but the Widow definitely loaded the gun. I kept seeing him standing in the cafe doorway, pale hair glinting to match his eyes. Or he'd have me by the scruff of the neck again and I'd feel such terror, I'd almost wet myself. He was, without doubt, the most frightening person I had ever met, and, let's face it, Soho wasn't short of frightening men; the war and circumstances had seen to that. But I wasn't afraid of them the way I was afraid of the Widow. He was one on his own, thank you God. The world couldn't stand too many people like the Widow, in my opinion.

I knew that every single one of Maltese Joe's boys was looking for him, but the trouble was, nobody would venture a guess as to what would happen when he was found. Uncle Bert's face just got hard and closed off when I asked him, and Auntie Maggie looked anxious and scrunched up her pinny in worried hands. So going back to school came as something of a relief. Even old Welbeloved's kisser was a reassuring sight, so you can imagine just how bad I felt, underneath it all.

22

The Widow Ginger must have been clever, because none of the landladies, landlords, hotel managers, maids or madams would own up to having seen him. Which, according to Bandy Bunyan, meant one of two things: either he wasn't staying locally, or the person or people housing him were too afraid of the consequences to grass him up. Either was possible.

'Let's face facts,' said Bandy, settling her bony frame more comfortably in her chair. Her giant hooter and Brillo pad hair made her look more like my Great-aunt Dodie than anyone who wasn't related should do. She even sounded like her; it was amazing. 'Everyone knows the sewer is a firebug, and nobody wants to lose either barnet or business in a conflagration, now do they?'

'That seems a reasonable deduction, my dear Bunyan,' agreed Uncle Bert, pretending to be Sherlock Holmes and waving his pipe around. I *told* Madame Zelda that I should have bought him a Sherlock Holmes special when I was in Southend; it would have suited him down to the ground, especially when he was showing off. However, he managed to be just as pompous with his bog-standard briar.

Maltese Joe was less patient. He was in the cafe daily to check progress and was given to ranting at no one in particular and everyone in general when told that there was no progress. In the end, Auntie Maggie got shirty with him. 'Will you stop barging in here and shooting your mouth off, Joseph? There's our customers to think of, not to mention poor Rosie's nerves, so just calm down, will you?'

Her tone made it quite clear that it was an instruction and not a suggestion. I almost felt sorry for the man, having been on the receiving end of a similar tone in my time, but I was also very worried that Maltese Joe would take exception to being told what to do, especially by a woman.

Sugar soothed my fears. 'It'd take more than an irate Maltese midget to put the wind up your auntie Maggie, sweetie, don't you worry your little curly top about that. Your auntie Maggie is a force of nature when she gets her dander up, and it's well up now. Old Ma Joe did not foist a fool on the world when she dropped her boy and he does know when to push it and when not to. Mark my words, little 'un, he'll let it pass.' And let it pass he did.

Auntie Maggie's scheme to lend me out to Luigi as a chaperone turned out quite well for Betty and me, but less well for poor Luigi, because although Betty wasn't at all reluctant to go out with him as long as I was there she wouldn't go out with him alone. This pleased Betty and certainly pleased me, because I got to go to all sorts of interesting places and, more to the point, I became the source of all gossip concerning the couple. This swelled my sense of importance, and my chest was puffed up like a pigeon's when I was being grilled by Sugar, Madame Zelda, Paulette and Auntie Maggie.

'So, where did they take you?' Madame Zelda asked after our first outing.

'The cartoons. We were supposed to go to the park, but it was raining, so we went to Leicester Square instead. Then we went to the deli for a cassata and then we came home.'

'Any hanky-panky worth a mention, was

there?' Paulette wanted to know.

'Nope.' I liked to make 'em work for their info.

'What, even in the pictures?' Paulette's voice rose in disbelief. 'Luigi's definitely slipping.' And everyone agreed that he was, except my auntie Maggie that is, who thought he was behaving very well indeed.

'What do you mean, slipping? He's hardly likely to get an attack of the wandering mitts when our Rosie's there, now is he? That would be on the verge of corrupting a minor, that would, and he'd never do that. He does know how to behave, you know, when he has to. His mother saw to that when he was a growing lad. Very moral people, the Campaninis.'

She ignored the frantic eye rolling that passed between Madame Zelda and Paulette. They knew when Auntie Maggie was looking for a high horse to get on to and decided not to help her. Anxiety always inclined Auntie Maggie to shirtiness and high horse clambering. Uncle Bert said it made her feel more secure when she was bossing people about. She liked to think that everything was under control, especially when it wasn't.

And it definitely wasn't. Maltese Joe's daily visits proved that. It wasn't just the Widow Ginger business, either. Things were obviously much less smooth with Betty and

Luigi, and nobody was quite sure why. I hadn't had the chance to get her alone to ask her, or Luigi either, for that matter.

Just to add to the feeling of doom and gloom, Jenny wasn't getting any better. In fact, what with the mumps and everything, she was getting more poorly and weaker by the day, or so Mrs Robbins said when asked.

'Do you think a visit from our Rosie'd help perk her up a bit?' Auntie Maggie asked in a sad, tired voice. The strain was beginning to tell on my aunt, and my almost nightly visits to her bed, with all my elbows sharpened and kneecaps in place, weren't helping a lot, either. Sleeping with a wriggle-monster cannot have been easy.

'Could she catch the mumps back again, do you reckon?' Mrs Robbins asked, reminding me that it was me that gave them to poor Jenny in the first place.

'No. You can only catch 'em once, I checked. So it'd be all right from that point of view, but it's your Jenny we've got to think of. Will it do more harm than good, or more good than harm? That's the question.'

Auntie Maggie and I waited quietly while Mrs Robbins gave it some thought. 'I reckon it'd be all right, as long as Rosie leaves the minute Jenny looks like she's getting too tired.'

Which was how it was decided that I would pop in to see my pal the following Saturday morning. I was armed to the teeth with comics, sweets and my second favourite teddy, working on the theory that any girl confined to bed would want a good read, something sweet to suck and something soft to cuddle when the need arose for a bit of comfort. I know I should have given her my first favourite teddy, on account it was my fault she was mumpy in the first place. And I did get him out of my bed, honest. I even gave his hair a good brush, and then I gave him a long goodbye cuddle, but when it came to getting him out of the door I simply couldn't do it. My eyes filled with tears and my nose began to drip the minute I was on the landing and I had to take him back to the safety of my pink eiderdown. I struggled with myself for what felt like hours but in the end I realized I really loved my teddy. We'd been friends all my life and no amount of guilt was going to get me to part with him. Even parting with number two bear was a wrench. However, I was so ashamed of being too mean to part with Eddie Bear, and of seriously considering giving Jenny my least favourite soft toy, Ugly Blue Monkey, or Uggers for short, that I forced myself to make the sacrifice. So Dingle it was, so called because he had a rather fetching blue ribbon collar with a bell attached. He was almost as well loved as Eddie, and rubbed almost as bald with all the strokes and cuddles he'd had over the years.

Once the decision was finally made, I was ready to go. I was almost out of the door when Auntie Maggie spotted Dingle dangling dangerously by one arm from the pile of goodies. She was curious. 'Why're you taking Dingle with you? I think you'd better leave him here, dear, in case you lose him. He doesn't look very safe hanging off that lot. Anyway, I don't think Jenny's feeling much like playing actual games at the moment, pet. P'raps you can save that for next time.' With that, she plucked Dingle from the pile and settled him comfortably on top of the till.

'I thought Jenny might need something to cuddle, you know, when she's feeling lonely or poorly,' I mumbled, grabbing him back. I didn't want to enter into a discussion about why she was only getting my second-best teddy, because I really, really didn't want to be persuaded to do the decent thing and cough up my beloved Eddie Bear.

'So you're planning to give him to her, are you? Or is it just a loan?' Now, a loan had not occurred to me. My heart leaped. Here was a way out. If I lent her Dingle, I wouldn't have to part with him either. But then I remembered Eddie Bear and Uggers and felt ashamed all over again. No, Dingle had to be a gift. I told Auntie Maggie that Dingle was, in fact, moving out.

'It's very kind of you, Rosie, to want to give Jenny your bear, but why don't you give her that blue monkey? You never play with him, and he's very soft and cuddly and has plenty of hair left. I'm sure she'd like him, and he looks newer than Dingle.'

My heart leaped again. If Auntie Maggie thought it was OK to fob my pal off with an unwanted and truly hideous toy, then maybe it was. Just as quickly my heart sank again because it knew that it wasn't all right. Auntie Maggie didn't understand that I had to give Jenny something precious to me because it was all my fault that she'd been laid so low.

A reject wouldn't do at all. I knew what was right; it was bad enough that she was being given second best. Bottom of the heap Uggers wouldn't do at all.

I couldn't explain because I had no words to describe the great lump that caught in my throat whenever I thought hard about how ill my friend was and how I made things worse. In a peculiar sort of way, I felt that if I made a sacrifice, gave up something I loved, somehow Jenny would get better. And I did love Dingle; his bald spots were testimony to that. I was trying to buy a miracle, only I didn't know enough to understand it, let alone explain it. I realize now that I was bargaining with God. But as it turned out, He didn't think much of the deal, and in my heart of hearts I knew He wouldn't. Like my beloved aunt, He knew second best when He saw it.

A quarter of an hour later I was at Jenny's, sitting beside her narrow bed, while she lay still under her brown blankets. She would keep dropping off. It was odd because she'd suddenly snap out of it, open her eyes and see me sitting there, and her pale little face would be lit by an enormous smile. She was so pleased to have a visitor who wasn't her dad, the Mangy Cow, the doctor or, believe it or not, old Welbeloved that it would have been wicked to tiptoe out of there while she was snoring. Me and Mrs Robbins agreed on that. So I stayed.

Jenny said you could have knocked her over with a feather when old Welbeloved walked in. She said that she thought for one terrible minute that the old trout had brought her school work to do at home, but she hadn't. It was just a visit. Mind you, if you ask me, you wouldn't have needed a whole feather, or old Welbeloved either, to knock Jenny over. She was so thin and pale she looked like a wisp of smoke with big panda eyes, and simply breathing heavily probably would have done it. The moment I clapped eyes on her I knew it would take more than a second-best bear to make her better.

Each time Jenny nodded off, I got bored, and looked around the dreary little room for something to do while I waited. Trouble was, I'd read all the comics I'd brought and I hadn't thought to bring a book. I played noughts and crosses with myself for a bit, but I kept winning, so that got boring, too. Finally, I noticed a pair of binoculars beside Jenny's bed. They were army issue, and I figured that they'd stuck to Hissing Sid's fingers when he was demobbed. A lot of soldiers had sticky fingers after the war. That's why there were so many guns and stuff around Soho at that time. I spent an interesting hour or so spying on the people in the street and the flats opposite, which I suppose was what Jenny had been up to. It was good fun. It's amazing how many people pick their noses and scratch their bums when they think they're not being watched. Jenny and I had a good old giggle about that when she woke up briefly. She also tipped me the wink about watching the very top flat almost opposite. It had big windows and no curtains, so it was easy to see almost everything.

'There's a couple of blokes there. I know one of them because he works for my dad sometimes, and anyway he's lived there for months now. Dad calls him Kid, but I don't know why because he's ever so old, thirty at least my mum says.' I nodded. Everyone knew Kid.

'But the second bloke's new,' Jenny went on. 'Kid's a right old scruff-bag normally, and he stinks to high heaven.' I nodded again. The smell was one of the reasons everyone knew Kid. You often got a whiff of him long before he actually arrived anywhere, and you definitely knew where he'd been.

Although she was obviously tiring again, Jenny was keen on finishing her story. After all, her chances for a good gossip had been pretty thin since she'd been poorly. 'Anyway, my mum says she hates to think what his place must be like. She reckons it must be stiff with creepy crawlies – yuk! Well, all that changed when the second bloke turned up. Kid's place was a pigsty; you could tell by all the dirty crocks in his sink. Piled higher than Big Ben they were; you could see the heap as clear as anything from here. Then the second bloke moved in and now everything's different. All the crocks have gone and Kid's slaving away day and night, washing, scrubbing and polishing while the other bloke just sits there bossing him about. But the really good bit is that the new bloke makes Kid dress up like a...' And then, would you believe it, she fell asleep, and me with my tongue hanging out wondering just what it was that Kid had to wear.

I settled down to some serious watching. For ages, nothing happened, and eventually I let the binoculars wander away from the top flat down to the street – just in time to see a squeaky clean Kid, laden with bags of fruit and veg from the market, letting himself in on the ground floor. Jenny was right; gone was the claggy hair, the scuffed old shoes and the grubby, baggy khaki trousers, and in their place was a scrubbed and stylish Kid in a smart new whistle, barnet cut and tidily combed. Through the binoculars I could see that even his finger-nails were clean, and that was unheard of in Kid world. Jenny was right; something was definitely up.

I had to wait a bit while Kid climbed the stairs. I saw his flat door open, and there he was. His gob was moving as if he was saying something to someone I couldn't see. Then a second bloke appeared with his back to the window, and I felt a jolt run through me. I knew that pale hair and those narrow shoulders. I knew the cut of that whistle as if it was Uncle Bert's Sunday best. For one thing, Americans' trousers never seemed to be on speaking terms with their shoes, because they rarely met. Their turn-ups were always just shy of their laces, leaving a bit of sock on show. No Englishman wore his trousers like that, not on purpose. If they were hand-me-downs from a runt, that was different; but their own trousers, never! It simply wasn't British to show socks on purpose, unless you were a girl in a skirt or a bloke wearing sandals. I'd noticed the trouser business in American films. Even Gene Kelly's socks were on show to the world, and I bet *he* wasn't wearing hand-me-downs. So I reckoned they must like their trousers short, and it wasn't a mistake at all.

My mind flashed back to the night outside the Catholic church, when I was forced to stare at the Widow's shiny shoes, and sure enough, there were his black socks, just peeping out from beneath his turn-ups. Kid's new friend was the Widow, there was no doubt about it.

Suddenly, the Widow exploded into movement. He shot across the room and fetched Kid such a clout around the bonce that I screamed out, 'Bloody Hell,' as if he'd attacked me. He was waving his arms about and shouting and then his right hand flew out, index finger rigid and pointing at the floor. To my absolute amazement, Kid dropped to the deck on all fours. The Widow turned to get something hanging from a hook on the door and I looked him straight in the face.

I stepped back as an alarmed Mrs Robbins came in from the kitchen. 'For goodness sake, Rosie, what is it?' Her eyes flew to the bed. She was reassured to see Jenny sitting up, wild-eyed – my yell had woken her with a start – and turned back to me. 'Will you watch your language. Nice little girls don't blaspheme or swear like that.' Now, I wasn't at all sure that saying 'hell' was actual blasphemy. I thought you had to take the Lord's name in vain, but I didn't like to argue because Mrs Robbins had got religion since Jenny'd been ill and I thought she might know better than me. Jenny said she spent a lot of time on her knees, and when she got a chance she went to church as well.

I must have looked stricken because she immediately apologized. 'I'm sorry, Rosie, I didn't mean that. You're a good girl, and a good friend to my Jenny, but really, dear, you must try not to swear.'

'I'm sorry, Mrs Robbins, really I am, for swearing. I didn't mean to. But I've gotta go. Sorry, Jen. P'raps I can come tomorrow and explain it all then, but right this minute I've really got to go.' I was still jabbering at them as I made for the door, but then Auntie Maggie's training came back, and I stopped long enough to say, 'Thank you for having me, Mrs Robbins. I'll see you tomorrow, Jen, if that's all right, Mrs Robbins?'

Jenny's mum nodded just once and I was gone, running down the stairs and then the road as if all the devils from hell were snapping at my bum like Betty Potts's dog Jack – which they were, in a way. I certainly had no trouble seeing the Widow, with red glowing eyes and a tail, rising from the flames of hell.

I panted into the cafe almost too breathless to speak, but managed to keep enough of my wits about me not to blurt out the news to the room full of punters. I looked around and saw to my great relief that Maltese Joe and Mick the Tic were both sitting at the corner table with Uncle Bert.

I rushed over to them. 'It's the Widow Ginger. He's at Kid's place,' I managed to gasp.

It was as if I'd shoved five million volts through the three men. As one, they leaped to their feet and almost trampled me into the lino in their rush to get to the door.

Auntie Maggie managed a 'Bert Featherby! You stop right where you are! Let Joe and his boys handle it,' but she needn't have troubled, because Uncle Bert ignored her. He charged out of the cafe, then sprinted back in, vaulted the counter like a cowboy in a Western, grabbed his sharpest kitchen knife and was gone again before she could say anything else. I never knew my uncle Bert had such a turn of speed in him, let alone the leaping abilities of a young gazelle.

Auntie Maggie and I spent an anxious half hour worrying about what was going on at Kid's place. All Auntie Maggie could do was wring her pinny and keep muttering, 'Please God, don't let my Bert use that knife,' over and over again until I was thoroughly rattled. Thank goodness, Madame Zelda came in after about the ninety-fifth mutter and took charge of the situation.

'Pull yourself together, Maggie, you're scaring the little 'un. Now you just sit there and give the girl a cuddle while I get rid of the punters, just in case we don't need any witnesses when the lads get back.'

I wasn't used to Auntie Maggie losing her grip like that and I wished and wished that I hadn't seen the Widow Ginger – or that, having seen him, I'd kept the news to myself. But it was too late. I found myself taking up Auntie Maggie's prayer with an added bit. 'Please God, don't let Uncle Bert use that knife and let him come back safe.'

When I wasn't imagining what was going on in Kid's flat, I kept seeing Jenny's pale, pointy face and enormous panda eyes. It scared me, the way she kept falling asleep as we talked. I wanted Auntie Maggie's reassurance desperately, but I knew that, with Uncle Bert out struggling with that nutter the Widow Ginger, reassurance was out of the question.

Our cafe began to feel like a flimsy little rowing boat, adrift on the ocean with no hand on the tiller, while sharks circled lazily around, just waiting for it to ship water and tip us into their gaping, razor-toothed jaws. I shuddered, and tried praying for us all instead of letting my imagination drive me mad.

23

Uncle Bert and Maltese Joe came back to the cafe in a temper. Maltese Joe was ranting while Uncle Bert was tight-lipped and silently seething, I could tell. The new, improved Kid was wedged between them, looking white and scared.

Auntie Maggie forgot she had me on her lap and jumped to her feet as soon as they came in the door. I hit the deck with a thump as she rushed forward. 'You didn't do anything with that knife, did you, Bert?' I think she was afraid that they might have left the Widow Ginger dead or bleeding on Kid's squeaky clean kitchen floor.

Uncle Bert sounded strained. 'No, love, I didn't do anything. Seems that Stanley

226

caught a glimpse of our Rosie the same time she saw him, and put two and two together when he saw her racing down the road. He legged it quick. It's just a matter of persuading Kid here that it's in his interests to tell us where the man went. Trouble is, at the minute, he still finds Stanley more terrifying than us.'

Maltese Joe grinned with his teeth, but not with his eyes. 'But that's just about to change,' he said, giving Kid a hefty shove towards the door again. 'When Mick gets back with the boys, tell him that we've decided to take Kid to Bandy's place instead for our little chat. No bloody great windows there, see. More privacy. He's to follow us round there. C'mon, Bert. It's time to tango with this toe-rag.'

Auntie Maggie put her hand on Uncle Bert's arm, trying to stop him from leaving, but he wasn't having it. Gently, he took her hand away and said quietly, 'I've got to do this, Maggie. It involves us all. If we let Stanley wander about, then he's free to use his matches and oily rags again, and next time someone might be killed. And Maggie, love, that someone could be us, or Joe here, or Bandy or Sugar. Let's face it, he could incinerate a whole club full of innocent people. We can't let him carry on, now can we? Use your loaf, gel. The man's a bleeding nutter and that makes him unpredictable

227

and dangerous. I don't need to tell you that, now do I?'

'Can't you let the coppers deal with it? It is their job, after all.' Auntie Maggie's face was all white and pinched. The fact that she was suggesting calling the police told me all I needed to know about how serious the whole thing was.

'Don't be daft, girl. What are we going to tell 'em? All about our war work? And what about the bloke in the blackout and all that? They'll want to know why it wasn't reported years ago, and that makes me an accessory to the blackout thing. On top of that, how can we prove the swine's responsible for the fires? We might know it's him, but where's our proof? No, love, we've got to have a little natter with Kid here. Lives depend on it, especially ours.'

'Come on, Bert. The sooner we've broken a few bones, the sooner we'll know where that slimy git Stanley's hanging out.' There was a glint in Maltese Joe's bulging eyes. The veins showed bright red in the whites, like the arterial roads on a map.

'Just a tick, Joe. Zelda, look after my girls for me, will you?' Uncle Bert turned to Auntie Maggie. 'Try not to worry, love. I'll be back as soon as I can. Look after your auntie, Rosie, there's a good girl.' And with a swift peck on Auntie Maggie's cheek and a pat on my curls he was gone, along with

Maltese Joe and Kid.

Auntie Maggie started pacing as soon as they left, her pinny wrung almost to rags. Madame Zelda tried to calm her down. 'It'll be all right, Maggie, you'll see. Your Bert's not given to being too hasty and he'll be able to keep Joe in some kind of order. You'll see, it's going to be OK. Now get a grip, there's a good girl. Poor little Rosie here's in a right old two and eight and you ain't helping.' That got Auntie Maggie to stop pacing for minute and have a good look at me. Large tears were streaming down my mush. I could tell by the steady drip, drip, drip from my chin on to my blouse.

'I didn't mean to let him see me, Auntie Maggie, honest I didn't.' And then I began to blub in earnest. Everything was my fault: Jenny being so poorly and Uncle Bert being mixed up in nasty business with Maltese Joe and the Widow. I wished and wished I'd been more careful, that I hadn't hared back from Jenny's flat, gob flapping the minute I got in the door, telling them I knew where the Widow was hiding. I was so pleased with my discovery, I just didn't stop to think as usual. I didn't think that I might be seen, or what might happen when Maltese Joe got his hands on anybody connected with the Widow. But it was much too late to be sorry.

Then I began to wonder and worry about

what my uncle Bert had meant when he talked of the bloke in the blackout, and him being 'an accessory'. But Auntie Maggie's kisser closed up tighter than a miser's wallet when I asked her, and I knew it was no use to nag. She wasn't going to tell me and that was that.

The men still hadn't got back to the cafe by the time I had to go to bed. We'd sent Mick the Tic and the rest of Maltese Joe's boys round to Bandy's place ages before. By the time I was tucked up, Paulette had come to join Madame Zelda and Auntie Maggie in the long wait. Bless her heart, she realized I wouldn't be able to sleep and felt sorry for me all alone upstairs, so she joined me for a chat and a cuddle.

'So, Rosie, what's going on with Luigi and Betty?' And so I told her all about our most recent trip to the swimming baths in Marshall Street and how Betty in a bathing costume caused even more of a stir than Betty in proper clothes. I told her that Johnnie the Horn, so called because he played the trumpet in a jazz band, had been there with his girlfriend Annie, the band's singer. We'd had a great time playing with a huge beach ball until we were so tired we had to nip into Campanini's for coffee for the grown-ups and ice cream for me.

'So, no hanky-panky yet again. Do you

230

reckon the fire's going out with those two? That's if it was ever lit in the first place. Of course, we all know that Luigi's burning hot still, but Betty never really managed much more than a bit of a smoulder, did she?'

Sadly, I had to admit that I thought she hadn't. It worried me, because I knew that if Betty dumped poor Luigi he would be very upset. Still, it gave Paulette and me something to talk about while we waited for Uncle Bert to come home. It was a long, long wait, and by the time he finally did turn up, I was sparko.

Nobody was saying much the next morning. Auntie Maggie and Uncle Bert were obviously worn out from lack of sleep and plenty of worry. I tried to keep the chatter going, but it was such hard work that even I shut my trap in the end.

I had just raised the last mouthful of scrambled eggs to my mouth when Maltese Joe hammered on the door. Uncle Bert let him in and Auntie Maggie's lips thinned. She chomped down on her bit of toast with a snap like a trap closing on a rat. She was definitely not happy to see him.

Maltese Joe ignored her and spoke only to Uncle Bert. 'The bugger's not saying much. I don't know what Stanley threatened him with, but whatever it was it was worse than even I can manage. Nothing'll shift him. I left Mick working on him all night and Mick's a man who enjoys his work. Trouble is, Kid likes it more, so upping the persuasion ain't going to do it. He looks as if he's been hit by the bleedin' Flying Scotsman at full tilt. He won't be using that arm again in a hurry, neither, but still he's keeping schtum as to Stanley's probable whereabouts. Best we could manage was to get him to swear to drop the word in me shell-like the minute he hears from Stanley. But we can't trust him. By then he'd have said anything to get out alive.

'We dumped him on the steps of the hospital come the end. You can't do anything with a fucker like that. Bleedin' pervert *enjoys* a good slap. I've got the boys taking it in turns to watch him and his gaff. I reckon if we can lull him into a false sense of security, he'll try and get in touch with Stanley, or Stanley'll get in touch with him, one of the two. What d'you think?'

'I think it's worth a try, Joe. It's definitely worth a try. You had breakfast?'

Uncle Bert and Maltese Joe went upstairs after that and Auntie Maggie and I were left alone. We sat in silence for a long, long time and then Auntie Maggie heaved a huge sigh and said, 'So, Rosie love, what are your plans for the day? Off back to Jenny's, are you? Or is she resting today? How is the poor little mite, anyway? Her mum holding up, is she?'

I told her all about how Jenny told me that her mum had gone all religious and was always down on her knees praying in her bedroom or at church.

'I suppose it's a big comfort to her. Makes her feel less helpless, I expect.' She spoke in an absentminded sort of way. You could tell that she had half an ear listening to me while the rest of her was wondering what Maltese Joe was talking Uncle Bert into upstairs, well away from her flapping lugs – and mine, come to that.

Finally, Uncle Bert and Maltese Joe came back down to the cafe and headed towards the street door, much to Auntie Maggie's alarm. 'Where are you off to now, Bert?' she demanded.

'Won't be long, Maggie,' was all he would say. Then he was gone, leaving me and my aunt staring at the door.

We were still staring when Luigi arrived, so he didn't have to knock. He just strolled in, whistling quietly through his teeth. 'Wotcha Maggie, Shorty. Bert asked me to pop in, make sure you're all right, but I was on me way here anyway. Do you two girls fancy your dinner round at ours? Mamma says it's been too long since you were at our table. She's been cooking all morning and she's got enough grub to feed the five thousand, and now our Gina's had to cry off because two of her lot have gone down with mumps. Bert's coming later, and so's Betty. So what do you say? One o'clock do you, will it?'

I loved Mamma and Papa Campanini almost as much as I loved Auntie Maggie and Uncle Bert. Mamma was a tiny round woman with the most fetching gold teeth. They flashed and glittered in the light when she smiled, which was often. Papa was bigger and rounder, and he was also given to smiling a lot and pinching my cheeks in what he thought was a playful kind of way. Personally, I didn't like the cheek pinching much but I didn't like to say, because I did like Papa and didn't want to hurt his feelings. He was a lovely man, who looked as much at home bouncing babies on his knee as he did behind his counter at the deli.

Dinner at the Campaninis' always took ages on account of the many courses served, especially on Sundays when Mamma had time to really let rip in her kitchen. It was a tradition that the entire Campanini clan presented themselves straight after eleven o'clock Mass. Mamma and Papa went to the first Mass of the day, which allowed plenty of cooking time afterwards, and Mamma needed every second of it. First of all we had either a soup or cold cuts depending on the season. Then came a pasta dish, followed by fish of some sort, then there was a meat dish, complete with at least half a dozen vegetables and a huge bowl of green salad placed in the middle of the table. Next would come a small water ice, 'to clear the palate' before the sweet course. Then there would be fresh fruit, also in a huge bowl so that everyone could help themselves, and lastly there would be cheese and biscuits, although I was usually far too stuffed by then to bother. All this would be accompanied by wine for the adults and wine with plenty of water for the kids who were able to sit at the table. The tinies had milk or water. Then everyone except us tackers would have tiny little cups of strong coffee that smelled wonderful but tasted bitter and foul the only time I tried it.

That dinner time was no different from any other Sunday at the Campaninis', and the food kept coming and coming. Uncle Bert arrived in time for the meat course, and Auntie Maggie and I heaved sighs of relief as we tucked in with a new enthusiasm. We'd been a bit off our grub with the worry.

Uncle Bert managed to squeeze into a narrow space between me and Luigi and started making up for lost time. He didn't speak until he'd downed the first three courses, then he took enough of a breather to have a slug of wine and a bit of a chat with Papa Campanini about the football. And after that, he turned to Luigi, who had been waiting patiently, and muttered in a low voice that only Luigi and I were able to hear, 'No go with Kid still. He's holed up in that flat of his and hasn't budged since Joe let him go.'

'Anybody tried Ruby yet?' Luigi asked, equally quietly.

Uncle Bert nodded. 'First port of call. Not a sign. Joe's lads turned the place upside down, just to be sure.'

'Kid probably told him about the other houses that service his sort. Checked all those, have you?'

'Even as we speak, Luigi, even as we speak. But I reckon the bugger's left town. I feel it in me water. He ain't stupid; he'll know we'll have a go at Kid. He'll let things settle a bit, then he'll be back. Meanwhile, it's a question of keeping our minces peeled, our ears to the ground and our noses sharpened for the first whiff of smoke. Mark my words, the first hint we'll have that he's back will be another fire. Bleeder can't help himself, just loves setting fires.'

'Christ, Bert, you'd have to be a bloody contortionist to do all that lot, but I get your drift.' Luigi was about to add more when his mother's voice broke in, sounding more shocked than she actually was, for the benefit of the tinies.

'Luigi Campanini, I heard that. In this house, we do not take our Lord's name in vain.' Which shut both men up, much to my relief. Talk of the Widow Ginger and the whiff of smoke had put me right off my afters. Luckily, I rallied when I realized that the Widow was probably miles away by now, which meant I could stop worrying, at least for the rest of the day.

I was hardly through the door the next afternoon after school, when Jenny demanded, 'Guess what?'

'How many guesses do I get?' I've always found that if someone asks you to guess something, it's best to set a limit on the number of tries you get, otherwise it can go on all day and get really boring.

'Three,' Jenny answered promptly. She was obviously in a hurry to tell me, three being a very measly number. So I rattled off my guesses so that we could get down to the big news.

'Pete Douglas has been round to see you.' Pete was one of the fourth year boys and Jenny fancied him like mad, but I don't think he even knew she existed, so I wasn't surprised when she shook her head.

'You've got a television.' But even as I said it, I knew that wasn't it either, because there was no telly in sight. Another shake of the head and a huge grin because she was so sure I wouldn't get it.

For my third guess I wanted to say that the doctor had said she could come back to school the following week, but I didn't have the heart, in case it wasn't that. I tried to think of something else but was struggling. 'You've found a million quid under the floorboards,' was all I could come up with, but somehow that didn't seem likely either.

'No, you daft thing. It's me dad. He's coming home. Seems he caught the Mangy Cow with some wrestler she picked up at Frenchie's, and what's more the bloke's given her "gone ear", or something like that. I couldn't work it out, because when she was here this morning, shouting the odds at Mum and Dad, she had both of her lugs, one each side of her bonce, so the wrestler must've given it back. My mum's ever so pleased. She's been dead sad since Dad went.'

I didn't know what to say. I could tell that Jenny was thrilled to bits because for once she had a bit of colour in her cheeks, but to be honest I didn't think Hissing Sid was much of a bargain, as he should never have left them in the first place. Still, he *was* her dad, I suppose, and I tried hard to look pleased for her. I must have managed it, too, because she prattled happily on.

'It started last week, according to Mum.

He came round one night when I was kipping and asked if she'd have him back and she said she'd think about it. She says she talked it over with the vicar and he said that "to err is human but to forgive divine", whatever that's s'posed to mean. She says she'll take him back as long as he sleeps, in my room until he gets this "gone ear" sorted, which he has because he's got a complete set already. It's OK anyway, with or without his lug, because I'm sleeping in here. So it works out sweet. Gawd, you should've seen the Mangy Cow! You'd've loved it. She was spitting bricks. She tried to scratch me mum's eyes out, but Dad stepped in and forced her to get out of the flat quick. It was ever so exciting. Seeing her being thrown out was better than the pictures, I can tell you.'

On and on she went, hardly stopping for air, until she was so knackered she fell asleep. I never did get to tell her why I'd shot out of her place on Saturday or ask her what it was that Kid had to wear. Still, I did get to tell Auntie Maggie and the others all about the Mangy Cow and Hissing Sid when I got home, which made up for it.

I didn't stay long because Mrs Robbins thought Jenny had had enough excitement for one day. Funnily enough, Jenny's news made me feel that giving her Dingle instead of Eddie Bear hadn't been so bad after all, because she was definitely looking a lot better than she had been. Her luck *had* changed, and she and her mum did feel that the return of Hissing Sid was a jolly good thing, even if I wasn't so sure.

When I got back to the cafe it was so quiet that I thought for a moment that the place was empty. Then I saw a light in the living-room window upstairs and hammered louder on the door. To my surprise, T.C. answered my knock. I hadn't been expecting to see him.

He swung me up in the air and on to his shoulders and carried me upstairs. I was so tall that I had to duck so as not to bang my head on the door frames. Once safely in the living room, I snuggled down on his lap while Auntie Maggie went to make hot drinks, tea for the grown-ups and Ovaltine for me. Then he told me he'd been to see my mum in the clinic and that she was very well and sent lots of hugs and kisses which he dutifully delivered. She also sent a nice, white, crisp fiver for my Post Office Savings book, which was even better. I have to say, I quite liked getting her hugs and kisses secondhand because they didn't come with the smell of gin and three million fags, which was nice. T.C. smelt of Imperial Leather, shaving cream and shampoo instead, and I much preferred that. T.C. didn't get all carried away and start slobbering all over me either, the way my mum sometimes did when she'd been on the bevvy too long. I really hated that and would struggle and squirm to get away from her. That usually made her blub, which made me feel bad. There was none of that sort of thing with T.C.; he seemed to know just how long to keep it up, and I never saw him blubbering. Sometimes his eyes did get all shiny as if he was about to, but he never did, thank goodness.

We had a nice evening. I passed on my hot gossip about Hissing Sid and the Mangy Cow and the trouble they seemed to be having with their lugs, which made everybody roar with laughter. I'm not sure why. On the whole, they thought Hissing Sid's place was at home with his wife and child and that it was a good thing that Mrs Robbins was prepared to overlook his bad behaviour with the Mangy Cow.

Uncle Bert and Auntie Maggie seemed to have got over the last traces of their moodiness with each other and were chatting and laughing with T.C. as if nobody had the hump in the first place, which was a big relief. We all had fun playing dominos, snap and Happy Families before having a bit of supper, poached eggs on toast all round. Once that was over it was my bedtime, and T.C. read me a bit of *The Borrowers*. Before he finally tucked me in and kissed me goodnight I told him I was trying to learn to swim and he promised to take me swimming the following Saturday.

All in all, it was a good day, and I slipped into a deep sleep full of dreams of little tiny people climbing up my bedspread so they could borrow my second-best teddy. When I woke up the next morning, I had poor Eddie Bear in a stranglehold. Nobody, but nobody, was getting my bear if I could help it.

24

School was OK, but I still missed Jenny. The seat next to me seemed ever so empty. Miss Welbeloved must have been missing her as well, because she kept dropping in to see her and she didn't take any school work along while she was at it. She also started getting us to pray for Jenny at the end of every school day. I was giving those prayers some serious wellie, I can tell you. The place just wasn't the same without old Jen.

We were still practising running, jumping, sack racing and the egg and spoon ready for Sports Day at the end of the school year. The weather was cold and we'd even been promised hailstones and pelting rain, so a summer Sports Day felt like months and months away. Shivering in the playground in your PE knickers while you waited for your turn was no joke. I thought a person could overdo the practising bit, but Auntie Maggie said she thought old Welbeloved was probably just sick and tired of thinking up new things for us to do in our PE lessons.

It was all a bit of a yawn until Roger Bannister shoved a boot up our bums by running the four-minute mile. All of a sudden, we were much keener on this running lark than we had been. Every boy in the school fancied himself as another Roger, and at playtime the boys' playground became stiff with red-faced lads, puffing, blowing and sweating despite the cold. It was the boys' clothes that did it. It was still too parky to let go of the thick grey flannel shorts, long grey woolly socks, sturdy white cotton shirts complete with tie and, you've guessed it, grey knitted pullovers that they had to keep on at all times. Grey was a much favoured colour at the time, because it didn't show the dirt when the smoke from winter fires left smuts on everything.

Poor Lardy Lucas, a third year who was definitely not built for running, wound up collapsing in a heap when he tried to copy Roger Bannister. It was more a case of the four-minute yard with poor old Lardy. He wound up like a huge, sweaty tomato being carried by four equally sweaty teachers to what was called 'the medical room'. In fact, it was really a stock cupboard with a chair and a first aid kit in it. Anyone poorly enough to need to lie down had to make do with two chairs pushed together in the staffroom, much to the teachers' disgust. They liked to be shot of us during their breaks, and having a sicko in the corner cramped their style something awful. It didn't do much for the sicko either, especially if they had a rotten cough or were feeling Uncle Dick, because the fag smoke and the stench of old ashtray made a yellow pea-souper smell sweet in comparison.

Anyway, there I was, hanging about in the playground and turning blue in my PE kit, when who should I see walking past but Betty Potts and Johnnie the Horn. I'd've yelled and waved if it had been break, but didn't dare in a proper lesson, so I was forced to just stand and watch them. They didn't see me. They stopped for a moment when they got to the corner and Betty put her hand out and brushed Johnnie's cheek with her fingertips as they parted. She carried on up Wardour Street and he headed towards Shaftesbury Avenue. The whole scene lasted less than a second, but there was something about it that made me feel uneasy.

Before I knew what I'd done, my hand shot up and I asked old Welbeloved if I could go to the medical room please because I was feeling a bit uncle. I wasn't, of course; I just wanted a minute or two in the warmth of that cupboard to think about what I'd just seen and I wanted to be well away from everyone while I did it. I was always able to think better on me tod.

I kept replaying the little scene I'd witnessed over and over again in my head, but whatever way I looked at it, it seemed too friendly by half. I'd never seen Betty touch Luigi like that. Come to think of it, I don't think she'd touched him at all since I'd started going out with them. For once in my life, I decided that the best course of action was to keep my gob firmly shut on the subject, at least until I knew more. It wouldn't do at all for Luigi, Maltese Joe or Johnnie's girlfriend Annie to hear about it, just in case I turned out to be wrong in thinking that it was anything to worry about. I felt in my water that it was; I just didn't know why.

At last Saturday came, and T.C. presented himself with his towel and swimming costume rolled into a sausage and tucked under his arm. Auntie Maggie wouldn't let us go straight away. It was too close to my breakfast and she was very firm about that sort of thing: no baths or swimming straight after food. So we hung about upstairs for a while, chatting and playing hangman, while Auntie Maggie and Uncle Bert dealt with the Saturday morning rush and I digested my grub.

'So, what's new, Rosie? How's school going?' asked T.C. He always took an interest in what was happening in my life.

'Kid's started stinking again, ever since the Widow Ginger went away. I saw him in the street the other day and he was back in his old smelly khaki clobber. He must keep that smart suit for best,' I told him.

'I'm sorry, Rosie, you've lost me. What's this about Kid and the Widow?'

That was the thing about T.C. He was a great listener, and I was a big talker, so we matched up really well. I told him all about being at Jenny's and the binoculars and everything, except about Uncle Bert being around when Maltese Joe and Mick the Tic questioned Kid. I may have been a blabbermouth, but I also knew when to keep it buttoned. It didn't do to tell a copper that my beloved uncle had been running around with a knife, even if he hadn't actually used it on anything livelier than a string of bangers.

'But Kid wouldn't tell anyone where the Widow went, even though the Widow was so horrible to him. I saw him yesterday when he was getting his fags and asked him why he'd got the clout round the head, and he said it was because he'd bought the Widow the wrong sort of cheese. My auntie Maggie and uncle Bert never clout me when I get the shopping wrong, so why did the Widow bash Kid? And why didn't Kid sock him back – that's what I don't understand?'

T.C. said he didn't understand it either. 'But then, there's no accounting for some people, Rosie. If there was, there'd probably be no call for policemen. Well, not as many policemen anyway.' He consulted his watch. 'Righto, my lovely, time to go swimming, I reckon, if your auntie Maggie'll let us out of here, that is.'

We strolled down Old Compton Street in the sunshine chatting about nothing special as we passed Campanini's and the Continental Fruit Stores but I stopped at the French coffee shop and had a good look at the cakes in the window. It looked like fairyland to me, with fluffy meringue castles and chocolate truffle houses. The little cakes were the fairies, with their intricate, cut-out paper doilies or their frilly-edged cake cups made of pastel-coloured paper folded into tiny little pleats. The light caught the towering cream froth and the dusting of caster sugar so that everything sparkled, and every now and then the jewel shades of glazed strawberries, black grapes or frosted raspberries gleamed. The French really knew how to make a body drool all right. In the end, T.C. managed to drag me away with a promise of nipping in on the way back.

When we got to Wardour Street we stopped for a swift chat with Mamma Campanini, who was on her way back from Berwick Street market. She was followed by two daughters-in-law, both so laden to the eyebrows with bags stuffed with vegetables, fruit and long French loaves that it was impossible to tell who they were; so we just said 'Hello' in their general direction and hoped for the best. Mamma seemed happy enough to settle in for a long chat, sunlight catching her gold teeth as she beamed at us and her helpers sagged in her shadow. But T.C. took pity on them and me, and made our apologies for being in a hurry. We promised to drop in for coffee on the way back and carried on.

Without talking about it, we wheeled into Peter Street for a scranny at Maltese Joe's club, to see what progress had been made in getting it back in running order. But it was a disappointment. A new street door was firmly locked and all there was to see were some scorch marks climbing the brick wall around it. Mind you, it was enough to bring back the creeping dread that thoughts of the Widow always set off. I shivered and got a tighter grip on T.C.'s hand.

We carried on into the bustle of Berwick Street, which wasn't strictly necessary, but I wanted to go to Mabel's flower stall. After the quiet of dark little Peter Street, the light, noise and colour of the market was a blessed relief, and the brooding presence of the Widow drew back into the shadows for a while.

Everybody seemed to be yelling at once. 'Come on, ladies, get yer spring greens here. Look at the lovely tops on them, now. Fit for a queen.' Or, 'How about a nice bit of cods' roe for yer tea, ladies? Or potted shrimps, spread on yer toast, luvverly!'

We ignored it all until we got to the flower stall. There were huge buckets of tulips in red or yellow and the last of the spring daffs, looking just a bit sorry for themselves. My purse was deep in my dress pocket. I handed over five large pennies and asked Mabel to wrap up some tulips for my auntie Maggie so we could pick them up on our way back. That done, we turned into Broadwick Street where we didn't stop to talk to a soul, not even outside the cafe belonging to Luigi's cousin Lorenzo, or the pub on the corner. We hurried into Marshall Street and the swimming baths.

I had to go into the women and girls' changing rooms and T.C. had to go into the men and boys', and we didn't meet again until I was up to my chest in warm water at the shallow end. T.C. was ever so patient, and never seemed to get bored with walking from side to side, supporting me under the belly while I tried to get my arms and legs to do what they were supposed to. He never let me slip under the water so I got frightened, either, and unlike Luigi he kept his mind on the job and didn't eye the girls in their bathing costumes.

Backwards and forwards we went, until finally, with a yell of triumph, T.C. told me I had just swum without any support at all.

'You're a swimmer, Rosie! You've done a whole half-width all by yourself. All you need now is a spot of practice and before you know it you'll swim a mile.'

I don't know who was more ecstatic, him or me. We played silly buggers for a bit, whooping and splashing in celebration, then he told me to climb on his back and hang on tight. I did as I was told and then he took off like a dolphin for the deep end.

Which is how I missed them coming in, I expect, because the entrance to the pool was at the shallow end. Of course, they wouldn't have recognized me because I had on my rubber bathing cap, which hid my curls, and all they'd have seen was my back. We were swimming back towards the shallow end when I saw Betty. There was no mistaking those legs that seemed to go on for ever, and that figure that made every bloke in the place – except T.C., who was too busy – stop and stare.

I was just about to wave and shout when I clocked who was with her. It wasn't Luigi who had his hand possessively on her bum, or Maltese Joe either. It was Johnnie the Horn. I was so shocked that I tightened my grip on my dolphin and almost drowned us both. Luckily, it was shallow enough for T.C. to stand up, spluttering and choking, which tipped me into the water. I floundered about for a bit in a panic and swallowed at least half the pool while I was at it. I was just beginning to think I must surely drown when T.C.'s large hands grabbed me in a firm grip and hauled me out of the water and up on to his shoulders. We waded for the side and climbed the steps and only then did he lower me to the cold tiles.

That's when Betty noticed us, and I swear she turned white first, then red. If she hadn't been wearing her bathing hat, her face would have clashed with her barnet.

T.C. was grinning as he waved and yelled. 'Hello there. Guess who has just swum her first half-width alone and unaided? Esther Williams had better watch out. She's got serious competition with my water baby here.'

I was still so shocked at seeing Betty and

Johnnie together again, and wobbly-kneed from almost drowning, that I almost missed it. T.C. had called me *his* water baby. I'd heard him with my own ears. 'My water baby', he'd said. It was all too much, and I burst into tears.

They wouldn't let T.C. into the women's changing room, so it was Betty who led me through the footbath and the showers to the locker with my clothes in it. I couldn't explain what was making me cry in front of T.C. in case he changed his mind about me being his, so I just hiccuped and gulped a lot instead. I would have told Betty, I think, but she was too busy towelling me dry and trying to tell me that she and Johnnie were just good neighbours and friends. I didn't believe a word of it. I wanted to, because I liked Betty, but I had learned a while back that anyone who insisted on explaining something you hadn't even asked about, and wouldn't shut up about it, was almost certainly lying.

Anyway, at that moment, I wasn't too interested in Betty's business. I was far more interested in mine. I kept wondering if T.C. had really meant it: that I was *his* water baby. I found I was hoping that he had. Then I got all confused, because Uncle Bert was like a dad to me, and I loved him dearly, which set me to wondering if I would be allowed to have *two* sort-of dads. And if so, did two sort-of dads equal one whole one? Or not? I found myself wishing that Betty would just shut up. On and on she gabbled, until I finally got out of the changing rooms, and she went back to join Johnnie in the pool.

I was very quiet on the way back to the cafe. T.C. was talked into staying for his dinner, and he had steak and kidney pie, spuds and greens, followed by tinned peaches and vanilla ice cream with two wafers. Nobody noticed how quiet I was, but it was all right because T.C. was busy boasting about my swimming. All the time I kept thinking, *his* water baby, *his* water baby, over and over again. I know that I'd sort of known for ages that he was probably my dad, but it was the first time *he'd* ever said that I was his. Of course, he might not have actually meant that, and the thought worried me, but I couldn't talk it over with Auntie Maggie or Uncle Bert in case their feelings were hurt; in case they thought I wanted to be someone else's little girl, and not theirs. And that would be awful because, true to form, me being a greedy little sod, I wanted all of them.

Come the end, I talked it over with Paulette, who could see why I was worried about hurting Uncle Bert's feelings. 'Don't worry, Rosie love,' she said. 'Your uncle Bert knows you love him to bits, and love ain't a cake, you know. If you give a bit to T.C. that don't mean less for your uncle Bert. It don't work like that. You can have 'em both, sweetheart. Fact is, you've had 'em both for years, so nothing's really changed. It's just a bit of a shock to hear old T.C. come out and say it, that's all. It'll be all right. Meanwhile, keep your gob shut until you feel up to talking to T.C. about it. It'll keep. Now, what's this about Betty and Johnnie the Horn, eh? There's a turn-up for the books.'

Once again, Paulette and I decided that my best course of action was to keep Betty's secret, at least as far as Luigi was concerned. 'If it *is* a secret. After all, she might be telling you the truth; they might just be friends. But it does sound a bit iffy to me, all the same. I can't wait to tell Zelda. It's a right old mess, innit?' And I agreed that it was.

That night, when it was time for bed, I hugged and hugged my uncle Bert until he complained that I'd almost busted his ribs, which was a rotten lie.

25

I think all the excitement at the swimming baths must have made me what my auntie Maggie called 'overwrought' because sleep was slow to come that night and, once it did, it kept coming and going. I was wriggling worse than a tubful of eels – live ones, that is, not the jellied sort that can wobble a bit but don't wriggle. Harry the Haddock sometimes had live eels for sale. The Chinese loved 'em or so he said. When I asked Mrs Wong what she thought of live eels she said she preferred 'em dead with a bit of rice and soy sauce but that they were best sold live. Yuk, yuk and double yuk!

Anyway, what matters was that I wasn't as dead to the world that night as I usually was. Which is how I came to hear the flap of the letterbox rattling. At first I thought it must be the postman with the first delivery of the day and thought nothing of it. I was just drifting off again when it struck me that it was a Sunday and that there was no delivery on Sundays. It was a mystery that I was quite content to think about in that lovely, cosy warm place between waking and sleeping that I loved so much. I had a good grip on Eddie Bear and, happy in the knowledge that there was no school on Sundays, was settling down for a good lie-in.

Then I smelled it. Petrol. Even then I didn't twig that something was wrong. I was just rerunning my time at the swimming baths and me being T.C.'s very own water baby and Johnnie's highly suspicious bum-stroking ways when I thought I smelt smoke. I turned over, ready to ignore the whole thing, when my dopey old brain finally put the pieces together. Rattling letterbox, petrol, smoke: FIRE! I leaped out of bed yelling, 'Uncle Bert, Uncle Bert! Fire, fire! Come quick, FIRE!'

I flung open my bedroom door and charged on to the landing. It was dark and I was groping for the light switch when I looked down the stairs and through the open door into the cafe and saw an eerie orange flickering in the gloom. I forgot the light switch and charged into Auntie Maggie and Uncle Bert's bedroom, hurled myself at the lumps under the gold satin eiderdown and yelled at the top of my lungs, 'UNCLE BERT, FIRE!'

Both lumps reared up, almost tipping me on to the floor. Uncle Bert said 'Wha...? Eh...?' and then *What did you say?*

'Fire, Uncle Bert. Fire.' And that finally did it. He was up and pelting towards the landing like Tom after a mouse.

'Shit! Rosie, get wet towels from the bathroom NOW. Maggie, fill anything you can find with water. MOVE, the pair of you.'

So we moved, me to the bathroom and Auntie Maggie to our little upstairs kitchen. I was back at the landing first with the soggy towels. Uncle Bert took one and wrapped it loosely round my nose and mouth. He wound another towel round his own mush and then Auntie Maggie arrived puffing and panting with a bucket of water in one hand and a sloshing saucepan in the other. Uncle Bert handed her another wet towel. 'Stick this round your kisser, then start passing water down to me and keep it coming'. And then he was gone into the black smoke that was beginning to creep up the stairs, making our eyes stream.

Backwards and forwards we went, filling anything we could find and dumping it as far down the stairs as we could get. I saw the ghostly outline of Uncle Bert beating at the flames with a sodden towel, then rushed to the stairs for more saucepans of water, and charged back upstairs with the empties for Auntie Maggie to fill.

Up and down I went as Uncle Bert ran between the stairs and the front door of the cafe and Auntie Maggie refilled the empties and delivered the dripping pans. My little legs were feeling as if they were just about to drop off when Uncle Bert yelled that it was safe to use the cafe kitchen now. So Auntie Maggie and I went downstairs and into the back and continued filling anything we could find. This time I did the filling and Auntie Maggie did the carrying, catering saucepans being so much bigger than our domestic jobbies upstairs. At last the orange flickering gave way to choking smoke and a weird hissing noise, and Uncle Bert told us that the fire was out.

Then we heard the sound of a fire engine and, for some reason I will never understand, Uncle Bert began to laugh, closely followed by Auntie Maggie and me. I laughed so hard that I wet myself, which would have been embarrassing if I hadn't been soaked anyway. At least the water trickling into my slipper was warm this time.

The next hour was a bit of a blur of firemen and neighbours and people coming and going. Auntie Maggie whisked me upstairs and dried me off with a tea towel – every other towel being soaked and sooty – whipped my nightie over my head and popped me into a dry one. I was wrapped in my winter dressing gown and my slippers disappeared into the rubbish bin and were replaced by socks and sandals. Then she did the same for herself. Finally, she went to the stairs and yelled, 'Bert, get your arse up here

258

for some dry clothes.' Which told me all I needed to know about how serious the situation was, because my beloved auntie Maggie hardly ever used rude words in front of me.

We never did get back to bed that night. Once the firemen left, the police turned up and started asking questions about whether we knew anyone who would want to set fire to the cafe deliberately. We all kept our gobs shut about the Widow Ginger, although we knew it was him. We didn't know another soul who would do such a thing. Looking back, I don't know why we kept schtum. Habit, I suppose. If anyone deserved grassing up, that rotter did.

Friends and neighbours poured through the blackened hole that had once been our front door offering comfort and help. Various male Campaninis followed Luigi in, assessed the situation, and disappeared again. An hour later they were back, toolbags in hand, and our smouldering door was fixed enough to keep the wind, rain and nosy punters out. It was agreed that a better job would be done when the builders' merchants were open to supply the gear for it.

Next came an army of Campanini women and Paulette and Madame Zelda, armed with mops, buckets, scrubbing brushes, huge bars of Sunlight soap and boxes of washing soda. The Campanini children arrived at dinner time, driven by a bustling Mamma, who had given them each a dish of food to carry. She and Papa had decided that we would need feeding and so would our army of willing volunteers.

'Papa thought you wouldn't want to leave the place until you had made it safe and seen what needs doing tomorrow, so Mamma said she'd feed you here. Hope that's all right with you lot,' Luigi explained.

'Of course it's all right. I can't believe everyone's kindness.' Auntie Maggie hiccuped before she burst into tears.

Mamma stood on the bottom stair, flung a comforting arm round my aunt's heaving shoulders and guided her head towards her ample bosom. 'It's the shock, Maggie. You weep your tears and you will feel better. And poof! The kindness is no more than you would do for us, if such a terrible thing should happen. Now weep, cara mia, and then eat, and you will feel better.'

We had just downed the last of the ravioli and green salad and were about to start on the fish when Maltese Joe flew through the door, closely followed by Sugar, still in his hairnet, and Bandy in her scarlet Chinese silk dressing gown with the gold embroidered dragon on the back. They were late risers on account of working all night. Everyone budged up and three more plates were produced and nothing much was said until the final mouthful had been downed. Then Maltese Joe took charge of the situation.

'No need to ask who did this. It's got his mark all over it. Now, Mamma, Papa, can you take the kids out of here? Me and the others need a private chat. No offence meant, but the fewer people who hear what I'm going to say, the less chance of it reaching that toe-rag's harkers.'

'No offence taken, Joe,' Papa assured him, although I'm not sure that Mamma agreed. Her lips looked a bit thin to me as she organized the kids to clear the tables. I was excused hard labour on account of my nasty experience and lack of sleep. Papa ignored Mamma's stern looks. 'I hope you get the man who did this terrible thing, Joe, and if you need any help from our boys, you just tell us. Mamma, bambini, it is time for us to go.' And he led them through the blackened doorway and back to the deli.

'Right. Bert, Maggie, Bandy and Sugar. I want no lip from any of you. I've arranged for you to take over the top two floors of that gaff of mine in St Anne's Court. I want no arguments. Nobody's safe from that bleeding maniac. Don't you worry about your places. They're probably all right while they're heaving with punters; it's when you're kipping you've got the most to worry about. So I want you all to sleep at St Anne's. Got that?' Joe didn't wait for an answer, but ploughed on, voice and expression grim. His eyes sparkled and flashed with rage. 'Your places will be guarded when they're closed for business. Nobby Clark is lending us some of his boys so that we can keep our minces on Kid, the club and the caff. They've been told to try and take the bastard alive if he shows up, but if that ain't possible, then it ain't possible. If he ain't stopped, then someone's going to wind up dead, and I, for one, don't want it to be any of us. Now, get your things and be ready to move out in an hour. I'll be sending cabs to get you, they'll wander about a bit, until we're sure the fucker's not following. Make sure you never take the direct route to or from St Anne's. Is that all clear?'

Nobody said a word, they all just nodded. I'd never seen anything like it. It wasn't like Bandy or my auntie Maggie to allow themselves to be bossed about, or my uncle Bert either, but they took it like lambs. Auntie Maggie didn't even blink at the swear words.

Then Maltese Joe turned to me. 'Come here, Rosie,' he barked, and I went, toot sweet, I can tell you. I almost passed out with shock when he lifted me on to his knee, grabbed my chin in his mitt and looked deep into my eyes. 'I'm relying on you to keep your mouth shut. You can't tell anyone, not your mates, not anyone, where you will be staying. Do you understand me, Rosie? Not a living soul. If you run off at the mouth, then you could get everyone killed, burned to a crisp. I know you don't want that, so keep it zipped. Got it?'

I nodded till I thought my head'd drop off. I'd got it all right. I saw Auntie Maggie's mouth open to complain about him putting the fear of God up me, but Uncle Bert took her hand and muttered, 'The man's right, Maggie love. She's got to understand just how dangerous this is.' She simply nodded and shut her mouth as Maltese Joe spoke.

'I'll arrange for cabs to take you to school and back, so you're not seen on the street,' he said, still looking me right in the eye.

I opened my gob to protest that I had to meet Kathy Moon in St Anne's Churchyard and signal up to Jenny's flat. I still waved my arms about to tell Jenny when I'd be visiting, even though she hadn't been able to answer me for a while. But we'd let Mrs Robbins in on our secret code, so sometimes her mum did it for her. Joe held the look though, so I kept schtum.

'Right then, I think that's that,' he continued. 'Everyone meet here in an hour with all the gear you'll need for the next few days. The decorators'll be here at first cough, tomorrow, Bert. We need to show that toe-rag that it's business as usual and that he can't scare us into cutting and running. That'll drive the sod mad and he might just get careless.'

I knew Maltese Joe was right and we really had to lie low. But even though I was scared to death after such a close shave, another part of me knew that I owed it to my mate to keep her in touch with the world. It cheered her up and made her feel part of things. All the time I was packing, my thoughts were tangled up with fear and knowing my best friend was trapped in bed with my second-best bear. I couldn't let her down. Which meant either defying Maltese Joe, or finding another answer to my problem.

26

It was funny living in St Anne's Court, but interesting too. Lots of professional girls hung about in doorways or strolled up and down muttering, 'Fancy a good time, dearie?' or, 'How about a nice bit of French, sir?' to any likely looking bloke. Some of the girls worked from about eleven in the morning until the early hours, so nobody could call 'em lazy. Brasses came in all shapes, sizes and ages, from their teens to Mavis, who Auntie Maggie said must be sixty if she was a day. Everybody had their own patch, and God help the girl who tried to muscle in. I witnessed more than one fight on that very subject, and often the girls' pimps would get involved as well.

Still, the brasses whose patch it was seemed to get on pretty well together and often helped each other out if they were skint or came across an iffy punter or an irate pimp. Auntie Maggie and Uncle Bert didn't have much time for pimps, because they reckoned that the brasses should keep the money they earned and their pimps ought to do an honest day's graft. I got to know all the regulars pretty well and sometimes got taken out for an ice cream or a trip to the flicks.

The flat that Maltese Joe had lent us took up the top two floors of a narrow house wedged between two identical buildings. On the left of our doorway was the small salt beef bar run by Nosher Cohen and his family. They did a fine line in salt beef sandwiches, to which I had become very partial. Nosher said I must have some Jewish in my ancestry on account of my love of salt beef, chicken soup, latkes and chopped liver, which doesn't sound very nice but was delicious when made by Mrs Nosher. That, along with my habit of answering a question with a question while I waved my hands about, was a sure sign that I was a member of the Tribe, or at least a descendant.

'Rosie,' he'd say, 'if I tied your hands behind your back, you'd be struck dumb. Jewish somewhere, definitely.' And he'd give me a shiny sixpence or even a shilling. Mrs Nosher was just as friendly and said I reminded her of little Rebecca, one of her grandchildren, but I don't know how, because Beccy was as dark as I was fair. She did have curls, I suppose, so maybe it was those that did it.

Everyone in the street knew to keep their gobs shut about our presence there, otherwise they'd have to deal with Maltese Joe or, worse, Bandy with a strop on. Nobody wanted to face *that*, or so Sugar assured us. Certainly, word never got out, which is amazing when you come to think about it.

It was safe to play in the street, too. There was no traffic, and if one of the girls spotted a stranger who showed even the slightest resemblance to either Kid or the description of the Widow, there'd be a piercing whistle. I'd be hustled into a doorway and hidden behind a gaggle of girls, smoking and chatting amongst themselves, until the danger had passed. I'd almost suffocate in a cloud of Evening in Paris, Woodbines or those posh new tipped fags like Bachelor. There were all sorts of jokes among the working girls about their Bachelor's tips, but I didn't get them and Auntie Maggie said I didn't need to because they were smutty. I'd finally be released into the air, to carry on with my two balls, hopscotch, jacks or skipping. Sometimes the younger girls would join in, playground games being more recent for them, and it was funny to see them trying to hop in high heels and tight skirts with their bosoms bouncing up and down.

To the right of our door was a theatrical costumiers that had the most fabulous clothes for hire. This was run by a good friend of Sugar, Freddie the Frock, and his friend Antony. I spent hours and hours in that shop, draped in feather boas, Egyptian headdresses, beads, bangles, sparkling, jewelled hats and Elizabethan ruffles. I learned a lot about the history of clothes and about the theatre while I was at it. The following Christmas, when we did the school play, Freddie, Antony and Sugar pulled out all the stops and dressed us. Everyone agreed they'd never seen a school play anywhere near as gorgeous, splendid and well turned out as ours. I didn't half earn some Brownie points for that lot, I can tell you. Miss Welbeloved said all the other schools were dead jealous and we were in the newspaper too. My chest was pigeon-puffed with pride.

Living with Bandy and Sugar was interesting as well. I was able to tell Jenny that they shared a bedroom but not a bed, there being two singles crammed in there. But Madame Zelda pointed out that might just be the case at St Anne's Court; it might be different in their flat above the club. Which was true.

I didn't see a lot of them on weekdays because Uncle Bert, Auntie Maggie and I left really early in the mornings to go round the houses to get to the cafe by six. It was practical for me to go with them, because if I left later I'd be hanging about on my own, waiting for the right time to go to school. It also meant I could keep my date at St Anne's each morning, so I needn't have worried after all. Uncle Bert and Auntie Maggie had understood straight away why it was so important. Uncle Bert told Maltese Joe the new plan and it was sorted. I was escorted to the churchyard by a whole variety of people. Nobody had forgotten I'd been kidnapped only the year before, and although it was unlikely to happen again I was 'better safe than missing' according to Uncle Bert. My favourite escort was Luigi because he was a good laugh and joined in my frantic signalling with messages of his own that made no sense.

Bandy and Sugar used to stagger in in the early hours and were soundo by the time we got up. It made sense to eat breakfast at the cafe, so as not to wake the sleeping beauties, as Uncle Bert insisted on calling them. We'd tiptoe about getting washed and dressed and try and keep our legs crossed until we got to the cafe, so that the sound of the flush being pulled in the thunderbox didn't wake them – although we didn't always manage that. Still, Sugar said they appreciated the effort, so they didn't mind when the khazi did wake them, knowing that we'd tried.

What Maltese Joe had forgotten to tell us was that he'd relocated four working girls so that we could have the flat. This meant that the first couple of weeks was spent 'repelling randy punters' as Sugar put it, but luckily Uncle Bert and Bandy were 'just the men for the job'. And they were, too. Bandy was amazing. They only had to see her beaky fizzog glowering at them from the top window and hear her roar, 'Piss off, you degenerate little wanker, or I'll tell your better half,' for them to leg it, toot sweet. Of course, Auntie Maggie wasn't entirely happy having me exposed to such awful swearing but as she said, it'd take a braver woman than her to tell Bandy to watch her language.

Sundays were the best days because we all

stayed at home. Auntie Maggie, Uncle Bert and I still had to creep around until about dinner time, when Bandy and Sugar would rise and slop about in their dressing gowns until after they'd eaten. I loved those dressing gowns. Bandy's was red with a gold dragon, as I already knew, and Sugar's was black with a large gold embroidered lotus flower. Sugar even wore slippers to match, but Bandy didn't. The dinner table would be a happy place, with Bandy, Sugar, Uncle Bert and Auntie Maggie chatting, laughing and joking, pleased to be free of work for the day, or night, depending. And of course, it helped that we knew that no one was going to set fire to us – well, not deliberately anyway.

We often heard the most beautiful music coming up between the floorboards, which was a bit of a mystery until we realized that old Mr Rabinowitz had moved into the little flat below. He'd told Maltese Joe that the fire that T.C. and I had seen at the Peter Street club had reminded him of something he called the pogroms in the Old Country, so Joe had moved him so he felt better. Having Nosher Cohen's salt beef bar next door was something of a bonus for him as well, so he was content. And so were we, because he could play the violin beautifully. So, incredibly, could Maltese Joe. Even Uncle Bert was amazed. Of course, we'd all heard about his violin lessons, but nobody had realized that he was really, really good at it.

'You think you know a bloke through and through and then he chucks in a complete bombshell,' said Uncle Bert.

Once, Bandy managed to persuade the two of them to give us a little concert after Sunday dinner and I saw a Maltese Joe I never would have guessed existed. Not only was he a completely different bloke with a violin under his chin, but he was shy about it too. Now, who would have thought that?

So, all in all, those weeks of early summer were wonderful in their way and really educational too. It was during that time that I took up playing a little cello lent to me by Mr Rabinowitz. Maltese Joe insisted on paying for my lessons; I'm not sure why. Mr Rabinowitz said it was because he was a genuine music lover and wanted to encourage me to be the same. That seemed a bit far-fetched when you realized that it was Maltese Joe he was talking about, but neither Uncle Bert nor I could think of a better reason for it. What's more, when it became clear that I wasn't going to get fed up with it, Maltese Joe bought me the cello and presented it to me for my birthday. You could've knocked mc down with a violin string, honest you could.

27

I went to visit Jenny more often once the days began to draw out a bit. I'd nip in just for half an hour or so because she got tired easily. We had some good chats, and I passed on any hot gossip I heard on the street or at school. She was always interested in what Luigi and Betty were up to, and was as disgusted as I was when I told her about Johnnie the Horn. I explained why I'd rushed out after spotting the Widow at Kid's flat and she started watching for me, being ideally placed. And it gave her something to do. But she had nothing much to report. Kid was letting himself and the washing up go, and that was about it. He never had any visitors and he did nothing much but slop about in growing piles of dirty plates and clothes. The man was a terrible slob.

Everyone in the little brown flat seemed a bit happier since Hissing Sid had come home. The Mangy Cow had stopped calling round, which probably meant she had a new bloke, according to Jenny. It made sense to me. As long as she stayed away, who cared? Mrs Robbins looked years younger, although she still looked at Jenny with sad eyes. And no wonder. Poor old Jen was ever so pale and skinny. Her panda eyes had grown bigger and sunk deeper and her hand was so thin you could see all her veins sticking out clear as anything. She was proud of those blue, snaking veins, and said they looked like the picture in the encyclopedia at school. I had a look and they did too.

Sometimes she went to hospital for some sort of treatment. She'd be gone a day or two, and once it was a whole week, but she always came home again and I'd carry on popping in. She was fascinated by my life with Sugar and Bandy, even though the news mostly happened on Sundays on account of their sleeping habits. She found the idea of Sugar in a hairnet really funny and almost wet herself laughing, but I couldn't see the funny side myself. Sugar was Sugar, and that meant painted toenails and lashings of cologne. As he said, he demanded the right to wear what he chose in the privacy of his own socks, trousers and, indeed, living room. And if he wished to smell like a 'whore's boudoir', that was entirely up to him. Bandy said she didn't know about the boudoir. 'More like the whole bloody brothel,' she wheezed, and let out a loud cackle that was husky with about three million Passing Clouds. You rarely caught Bandy without a cloud of smoke round her. If I was ever so good I got to fit the cigarettes into her long black cigarette holder. Jen was thrilled to bits when I gave her one of Bandy's cast-off holders. She'd pretend to be all lah-de-dah as she waved it about like Ginger Rogers.

As the days went on, my visits got shorter and I got more worried. I told my auntie Maggie how peaky Jenny was looking.

'Ah, sweetie, try not to worry too much,' Auntie Maggie said. 'People often look like two penn'orth of Gawd help us just before they take a turn for the better.'

And Hissing Sid and Mrs Robbins kept saying that it was a bad patch, nothing more. So I did try not to worry, but sometimes Jenny would really scare me by not making any sense at all when I visited. Soon she'd be her old self again, though, and I would breathe a sigh of relief.

It was a bright Monday morning a week or so later and the sun was pouring through the hall window, making the dust dance and swirl about in the air, and the headmistress was droning on about Sports Day and then about 'the rough male kiss of blankets', a line from a poem that had always made me and Jen snigger. What did our headmistress know about rough male kisses? Not a lot, we were sure of that. Miss Smith was about a hundred and eight and she even had a large wart on her chin, with a single hair growing out of it; proof that she was a witch when she wasn't being boring in assembly. The poem made it a Monday, definitely. On Mondays we got told what we had to look forward to in the coming week, followed by 'All Things Bright and Beautiful' a long prayer from Miss Smith and an 'Amen' from us when the droning stopped, followed by 'These Things I Have Loved' I think the poem was called but, to be honest, by then I wasn't listening. I was hanging on for the Lord's Prayer and 'Rock of Ages', then we would be free.

Not on this Monday, though. Miss Smith asked us to wait a moment, and she had to get pretty sharp about it because we were already pushing towards the door, keen to get out of there. The hall was airless and it ponged a bit of loads of kids and the rubber feet on the legs of the chairs piled up around the hall. That rubber really stank; it reminded me of the gas mask at the dentist and I hated it. She finally got us to stop and shuffle back to our places. Then she asked us to kneel and join her in a prayer for Jenny Robbins who was very poorly indeed. She said if we prayed hard enough, maybe the good Lord would hear us and spare her.

It took me a minute to catch on. 'Spare her'? What did that mean? Then I twigged.

The next thing I knew I was in the staff-room, laid out on the chairs, choking on fag smoke and looking around for the dog that was howling. It sounded pitiful, as if it had been locked out. It was only when the howling turned to hiccups that I realized it was me.

28

I was sent home from school that day so that I could pull myself together, as suggested by Miss Smith.

I spent the day in the cafe and I was very quiet as I sat at the corner table. Everyone tried to be comforting in their own way. Auntie Maggie gave me a hug along with a rich tea biscuit and a glass of milk.

'I'm sorry, love, I really am,' she said as she stroked my curls. 'I want to tell you that everything's going to be all right but, truth to tell, no one's sure. We just have to hope for a miracle, sweetheart. It's been known to happen.' My auntie Maggie always liked to hang on to her silver linings for as long as possible. As she said, 'If bad news is coming, it'll find me soon enough. Meanwhile I might as well look on the bright side until proved wrong.'

I know it sounds daft, but it had never crossed my mind that Jenny wouldn't get over her yard of Latin and be bouncing around in the playground again before too long. Miss Smith's announcement changed all that. It made it official. My eyes weren't deceiving me; Jenny really was fading away.

Madame Zelda was cuddly and kind when I told her why I wasn't at school. I even told her the shameful bit about howling like a dog in front of everybody. She was bracing about that. 'Don't worry, petal. I expect you do a very good dog and the little 'uns were well impressed. How many people do you know who can do dog impressions in assembly and get away with it? Not only get away with it, but get a day off and all? Takes real talent, that. I'm sorry about little Jenny, though. We'll just have to wait and see, love. That's all anyone can do.' And I was enveloped in a very soothing cuddle. Madame Zelda had a smell all of her own; maple brazils always seemed to linger on her breath, Ponds Cream clung to her face and neck, and wintergreen floated up from her feet.

Uncle Bert took one look at my face as I came into the cafe and scooped me up on to his lap. He listened to my worries about not coughing up Eddie Bear when I should have, and thought about it carefully before he answered. If he'd been too quick to tell me it was all right and that I was being daft, I wouldn't have believed him. But as it was, seeing he was giving the matter really serious thought, I knew I'd get the truth according to Uncle Bert, which was usually good enough for me. 'I'm sorry to hear about young Jenny. She's a good kid. But Rosie, love, life *ain't* fair and people don't always get what they deserve. Any fool can see that Jenny deserves a better shout, but that don't mean to say she's going to get it. Life just ain't like that. As to the question of the bear,' and he gave me a squeeze here, 'I reckon that the number one bear wouldn't have swung it. God don't work like that. It's as simple as that. Bribes is for mortal men. God's above that kind of thing. More to the point, was Jenny pleased with the bear she got?' He paused while I nodded. 'Well then, there's your answer. Jenny's happy, you're happy, Eddie Bear's bound to be happy, so I expect the Almighty's happy too. Can't see where you've gone wrong there.' Which made me feel a whole lot better, I can tell you. The bear question had been worrying me a great deal.

I was back at school the next day. The week followed its usual routine of lessons, playtimes and dinner and tea at the cafe. It was familiar and it made me feel that I was on safer ground. Understanding that Jenny might die had changed my view of the world for ever. Children were supposed to grow into grown-ups, it was as simple as that. Puppies grew into dogs, foals into horses, kittens into cats and children into grown-ups. It changed things when I could no longer take all that for granted. It changed things a lot.

I was very quiet at school and found myself concentrating hard on history, geography, English and even arithmetic, though the last always seemed to make my brain go numb with fright. I was running my heart out in PE ready for Sports Day, and I even sewed some place mats with chunky cross-stitch for the table at the new flat. We all had one with our name on. Sugar was particularly impressed and said he'd have me on the gold braid and seed pearls before I could blink.

'I'm sure that Jenny will buck up, the way tackers do,' Bandy assured me vaguely, before urging me to 'Scoff another chocolate thingy, do.' So I did, and it was delicious. Every Sunday, around eleven, Bandy would produce a large bag of pain au chocolat from the French bakers round the corner from her club. She'd stop off in the early hours and 'quaff a cognac or two with Jean-Paul and purchase a large bag of warm, chocolate thingies, sorrows for the sweetening of. That's if you're too young for booze, which, of course, you are.'

Sugar was different. He didn't try to change the subject and he didn't try to pretend things were better than they were. He was very much like Uncle Bert in that way. 'Well, Rosie love, life can be tough, you know,' he told me. 'You lose people; it happens to us all. But the thing to remember is that you had to have 'em in the first place, otherwise you couldn't lose 'em, now could you? So, in time, you remember when they were here more often than you remember that they're not, and that makes up for it a bit. It's just a question of time.' This too was comforting in a way, I suppose, but not straight away. He was also reassuring about bears, saying that Uncle Bert was right: everyone was happy, so there was no blame to attach to anyone.

T.C. was a regular visitor at the cafe. He'd heard about our fire and he hadn't forgotten what Uncle Bert had told him about the Widow and fire insurance. He was worried, but like everyone else he had to wait for the Widow to reappear, like an evil genie in a puff of smoke. Until someone got wind of him, there was nothing anyone could do.

He was sympathetic about Jenny. 'It's rotten for everyone, Rosie, especially Jenny's parents and friends. It's hard, realizing that people can leave us too soon.' His crinkly eyes took on a faraway look. 'They seem as if they must be there for ever and then they're gone. There doesn't seem to be any logic to it sometimes, and it's like that with Jenny.' I like a firm squeeze and he squeezed me good and hard. 'But don't go thinking anyone's to blame, because they're not. I agree with your uncle Bert. God's above bribes and bargains.'

Lately, T.C. had seemed to spend all his spare time at the cafe, or nearly all of it. Uncle Bert wondered what his boss thought of that. 'Let's face it,' he told Auntie Maggie one afternoon, 'the men in blue are not that keen on their officers hob-nobbing with villains or those hanging about on the fringes of villainy neither. Fires – plural – in Soho spells villainy. We know it, and sure as eggs is eggs those buggers know it. What's more, you can bet your life some sod who has recently had his collar felt will have told the men in blue all about T.C. being here morning, noon and bleeding night.'

Auntie Maggie nodded and looked sad. 'And there's Pat. Don't forget her. Gawd knows what she thinks! He's got her sister down to look after her. He says she understands. But what does she understand, that's what I'd like to know?' Nobody seemed to have an answer to that one.

Still, I found it comforting to have T.C. on our side, even if it was causing trouble at his work and his home. I often caught him in a huddle with Uncle Bert, talking about safety precautions. A fire extinguisher appeared in the corner of the cafe and another at the top of the stairs. An old stirrup pump, from Uncle Bert's firewatching days during the war, was hauled out from the cupboard under the stairs, ready for use. Pots and pans were left handy, I noticed. Most exciting of all, a black telephone appeared in the hall upstairs and another sat on Uncle Bert's dresser at the back of the kitchen. Next to it, tacked to the wall, was a list of important telephone numbers: Sharky Finn's, the cop shop, several for Maltese Joe and one for the bookie, Tic-Tac. I loved those telephones and longed for one of them to ring, but they didn't, not for ages and ages.

Around this time, Luigi was on the quiet side as well. He took my news about Jenny with sad-eyed calm. 'Ah, Shorty, I'm sorry to hear that. That's a swine, that is. Makes you wonder what the Man Upstairs reckons He's up to. It was like that in the war, perfectly fit and healthy blokes, here today and gone tomorrow. It's a bugger all right.' And he patted my arm for a bit while I wondered what on earth he was talking about. Jenny hadn't been perfectly fit and healthy for ages, but I didn't like to ask because he seemed so sad.

I hadn't seen Betty Potts for a long while,

not since she had been at the Marshall Street baths with Johnnie's hand on her bum. It seemed to me that that might have been why Luigi was so unlike his normal self. Paulette agreed that Betty probably had something to do with it. 'She's gone all scarce on us for quite a while now. According to the girls at the club, she just comes in, does her shift and leaves again. Nobody's seen her and Johnnie together, but rumour has it that him and Annie ain't been hitting it off too well lately. They've been seen having words; worse, they've been 'eard. Sally says they was screaming good and proper between shows the other day. Annie's had the hump all week and Johnnie's stamping around biting everyone's heads off. Sally says you daren't even breathe around 'em any more.'

We agreed that things did not look good for Luigi's love-life.

'Still, one thing to be grateful for,' Madame Zelda said, 'Maltese Joe's lost interest, so he and Luigi ain't on the outs no more. I think the club almost going up in flames showed Joe there was more in life to worry about than who gets Betty Potts. She'd made it pretty plain that he didn't stand a snowflake's chance in hell anyway. It's no good for Joe's reputation to be seen to be trying too hard and getting nowhere fast; best to concentrate on more pressing stuff. In a way, the Widow's been a real face-saver for Joe. Of course, in another way, the man's a right royal liability on all fronts, and the sooner he's dealt with the better for everyone.'

Which was true. We were still living in St Anne's Court with Bandy and Sugar, which was lovely in some ways, but inconvenient in others. All the creeping about in the mornings was tricky, and it was virtually impossible to find room above the bath for anyone's knickers because the little line was always full of Sugar's stockings. In the end, we took our washing home and dried it in our own bathroom, which was easier.

Although I loved Sugar and Bandy, and living with them was interesting and fun, I did miss my own bedroom. I missed being able to pick up a toy or a book when I felt like it and not having to wait for the next day to collect it from the cafe. And if I brought in anything new to the little flat, then something had to go back because of shortage of space. It was a nuisance all right.

Another thing: you don't really feel free to wander about in your knickers when there are strangers in the house. So, if I noticed yesterday's dinner on the front of my school blouse, I couldn't just charge out to the airing cupboard for a fresh one; I had to find my dressing gown, and that wasn't always easy, given that tidying wasn't one of my natural talents. Or so Auntie Maggie was always saying.

It was during this time that I discovered just how hard waiting is. Everyone was waiting for something and it made it seem as if nothing was going on in the most maddening way. Luigi and Betty had stalled; Bandy, Sugar and our little family were waiting to go home. What made it harder was that absolutely nothing had happened since our fire, so our homes appeared all the more inviting. My toys and books were still there, waiting for me. At home, we could listen to the radio whenever we felt like it and not have to wait until everyone was up and about. Everyone was waiting for the Widow Ginger to resurface and, of course, we were all waiting to see what was in store for Jenny, Mrs Robbins and Hissing Sid.

We were just talking about moving ourselves back home when the Widow Ginger delivered a double blow. He set fire to our cafe and Bandy's place in the very early hours of a weekday morning. Bandy and Sugar closed up around one, half-past, on weekday mornings, punters being scarce mid-week. So he struck around two, when both of Joe's boys, left as watchmen, were sparko. The first they knew of the fire was 'toasting toes and a hooter full of smoke', according to Sugar. Luckily, they were on hand to use the new, red, shiny fire extinguishers and Uncle Bert's stirrup pump, and they put the fires out before they did much harm. But they didn't get a hand on the Widow, which set Maltese Joe on the warpath.

'What were the bloody fools doing?' I heard him saying. 'Kipping, that's what. Counting bleeding sheep when they should've been feeling that sod's collar, or at least grabbing him by the testicles. I'm surrounded by bleeding half-wits. They couldn't find their *own* bloody wedding tackle without a sodding map.'

'He was clever, Joe. Left it just long enough so that we were all off our guard.' Sugar's tone was reassuring. 'We were even thinking of moving back home, the lot of us. We was all lulled into a false sense of security. Don't blame your boys too much. We were all caught snoozing.'

I don't think it made Maltese Joe feel any better about it, though, judging by the black eyes and fat lips the watchmen were wearing next time they turned up for guard duty. As Sugar said, 'He can be a tetchy little bundle, that Joe, very tetchy.' It was agreed that the watchmen were unlikely to be caught nodding off again, but then it probably wouldn't matter if they did; the Widow had made his point. We all knew he was still there, waiting.

29

I continued to visit Jenny after school, sometimes for just a few minutes and sometimes for a little longer. We all seemed to creep about, Hissing Sid, Mrs Robbins and me, and we talked a lot in whispers as if we were afraid any sudden noise would blow Jenny into the next world. She no longer seemed to be part of ours, which is how I knew for sure that Miss Smith was right.

It was during what was to be my very last visit, although I didn't know it at the time. Jenny rarely made sense any more. That's when she was awake, which wasn't often. I was just staring out of the window, wondering if Jenny would notice that I was there, when I realized something was missing from the view. Then I snuffled under the couch, searching for the binoculars, which had been abandoned when Jenny ran out of interest in them. I blew the dust off and adjusted the lenses, focusing on Kid's flat. There was no teetering pile of washing up cluttering up the kitchen window. And in the living room, there was acres of clean carpet and there was Kid, just letting himself out of the flat and wearing his *suit!*

Jenny was still asleep, so I whispered to Mrs Robbins that I had to go and I got out of there quicker than a dog with a stolen bone. I knew what it meant when Kid started taking a pride; it meant someone was making him do it, and the only person I knew who had managed that was the Widow.

I tore down the road to the cafe and arrived just in time to find Maltese Joe supervising Mick the Tic as he was trying to replace the door after the latest fire. Mick's eyes were swollen and he looked as if his ribs hurt. Bearing in mind Maltese Joe's mood, I was careful to keep schtum until I was alone with my uncle Bert in the kitchen.

'Uncle Bert,' I whispered.

'Yes, flower?'

'I've just been to Jenny's.'

'I thought as much, when you was a bit late home from school. How is the poor little mite?'

'Very poorly, Uncle Bert. She didn't really wake up today.' I took a deep breath, then said in a rush, 'Guess what I saw, over at Kid's place?'

Uncle Bert stopped ladling stock through a sieve and waited for me to carry on. He stood very still, ladle in mid-air.

'I saw Kid, all clean and in his suit and all the washing up had gone. His place looked tidy and everything. Last time it was like

that, Uncle Bert, was when the Widow
Ginger was staying there. He won't let Kid
be messy. He makes him tidy up and take
baths all the time. I reckon he must be
around, keeping an eye on things. What do
you think?'

He dropped his ladle. 'Bloody hell! You're
right, Rosie. I'd better tell Joe toot bleeding
sweet. Did you actually see Stanley, in the
flat?'

I shook my head. 'No. I didn't see anyone
except Kid and he was on his way out.'

Uncle Bert had already whipped off his
apron, and now he ran through the cafe,
yelling, 'Joe, come with me.' And he was
gone.

I wasn't surprised when the Widow wasn't
found at Kid's. But after what Uncle Bert
called 'a swift bit of illegal entry' it was clear
he had been there and was expected back;
his luggage was in the bedroom, neatly
packed. This meant he'd either just arrived
or was expecting to leave in a hurry. Maltese
Joe set his men to watch and to wait, yet
again.

The Widow was a real expert at disappearing. The first time I clapped eyes on
him, I blinked and he disappeared. Outside
the church, I turned my head for just a
second and he was gone. And he'd been
disappearing ever since. Usually in a cloud
of petrol fumes and smoke. I was beginning

to think he wasn't human. Perhaps he really was the Devil's spawn, like Auntie Maggie said he was. Especially if Maltese Joe couldn't get a hold on him. I shivered and wondered where the Widow was and what he was planning to do to us next.

It's strange the things you remember. It was 'the rough male kiss of blankets', which made it another Monday. Miss Smith announced that Jenny had been taken to hospital at the weekend and had died in the early hours of Sunday morning.

Madame Zelda said it was funny how people nearly always died in the early hours, 'when the 'uman spirit's at its lowest ebb'. Auntie Maggie gave me a long cuddle and said how sad it all was. And I suppose it was, but I didn't cry this time, or howl like a dog. I took it very quietly, mostly because I didn't know what it meant, not really. I didn't know what came next.

'Well, there'll be a funeral, probably at the church, and then she'll either be buried in the churchyard, or she'll be cremated at the crematorium,' T.C. explained.

That's when I found out that being cremated was the same as being burned, and I didn't fancy it, not at all, not after the fires. I became quite obsessed with the question of whether Jenny was to be burned or not. I found it crept into my dreams and

I'd wake up sweating and crying. Sometimes I felt suffocated, as if I was buried alive. I'd wake up so convinced that my mouth would be all gritty as if it was full of dirt or the ashes they talked about at funerals. Dust to dust, ashes to ashes; the whole thing was awful. So I took to sleeping with Auntie Maggie and Uncle Bert again. Uncle Bert said I still had a hundred and ninety-three elbows, all working on his ribs.

30

I had seen Jenny for the last time. It felt as if it couldn't be possible because I hadn't said goodbye. There should have been time to say goodbye. If only I'd thought before rushing off like that, things might be different. I'm not sure what I thought would have happened, but I just knew that I hadn't done things properly. One glimpse of a clean and tidy Kid and I'd shot out of that little flat without a backward glance.

Auntie Maggie said that all the visits I had made more than made up for forgetting to say goodbye. She said I wasn't to know that I was seeing Jenny for the last time. This was true, but it felt as if I ought to have known, to which she replied, rather sharply I thought, that I wasn't God and that things like timing were up to Him.

There was some disagreement among our nearest and dearest about whether I should attend Jenny's funeral or not. People were worried about my nerves.

'I think Rosie should be excused funerals, on the general principle that tackers have to learn about death soon enough, so why rub it in now? I say let her skive off.' That was Bandy's two penn'orth on the subject.

Sugar wasn't so sure. 'I remember being left out of my Nan's funeral. I loved that old duck and I never really forgave 'em for leaving me with mad Maureen and her snot-nosed kids. I just sat at the window and watched 'em all leave and I was still there two hours later when they got back without her. It took me a long time to accept my Nan'd gone. I reckon you should leave it up to Rosie. She'll know what she wants to do.'

When I talked it over with Madame Zelda, I realized that I did want to go to Jen's funeral. It was that final goodbye that was bothering me. 'Well, there's your answer then,' she said. 'You'll get the chance to finish things up proper if you go to the funeral. It'll be trickier if you stay here. Your classmates from school are going, ain't they? They wouldn't be letting 'em go if they thought they'd be scarred for life or something. I reckon you'll be OK, love. If I was you, I'd go.'

My auntie Maggie swung into action. The funeral tea was to take place at the cafe. It had the room and enough chairs and tables for everyone who wanted to pay their respects to have a sit down with their sandwiches and cups of tea. Madame Zelda, Paulette and Mamma Campanini helped with the organization. An army of shoppers scoured Berwick Street market and the roads around it for sound tomatoes, juicy green cucumbers, watercress, lettuces, spring onions, radishes, cold cuts, eggs – Scotch and fresh – and cheeses. Enough bread, cakes and biscuits were ordered to feed the five thousand. Nobody was going to go short at Jenny's 'do'.

I had to be dressed for the occasion. All the grown-ups had black, on account of the war and the Blitz and everything, but I didn't. My clobber had to be chosen with care because it had to be useful afterwards. Kids didn't wear a lot of black; grey, yes, and brown, but not black. In the end I wound up with a black pinafore dress in needlecord, with a little pocket in the bib for a hanky, a white blouse with lace collar and cuffs, a black cardigan and black patent leather T-bar shoes with white ankle socks. I was told I could wear my school mac if it rained and white gloves either way. The white gloves were a mistake. By the time I got in from the rain, the bible I was carrying had leaked dye all over them. They were all dark blue, black and grey blobs and streaks come the end. The dye even leaked right through and made my fingers murky too, so you'd never believe the scrubbing I'd had before we left for the church.

The funeral was to take place on Thursday afternoon, straight after dinner. Auntie Maggie, Madame Zelda, Paulette and Mamma Campanini spent the morning buttering bridge rolls, cutting up bread and assembling mountains of sandwiches. They chatted quietly among themselves, saying how awful it must be to lose a child. All the while, butter knives flashed in expert hands. Once the food was laid out on plates on the counter, the helpers, Uncle Bert and me had our dinner: chicken and mushroom pie with spuds, peas and cabbage, followed by stewed rhubarb and custard. Only then was I dressed, when there was no possibility of dribbling gravy or custard on my new clothes.

The road was packed outside Jenny's flat. Two huge black horses, complete with waving black plumes and black harnesses, pulled the glass-sided carriage that carried the small white coffin and a mountain of flowers. Jenny loved horses. Behind the hearse were Jenny's mum and dad, ready to walk behind their daughter to the church. I hardly recognized Hissing Sid, he looked so smart and dignified. He kept shaking people's hands and laughing a lot, although I couldn't see a lot to laugh about myself. Auntie Maggie said he was nervous and some people do laugh and joke when they're nervous.

Mrs Robbins wasn't laughing or joking. She didn't seem to notice anyone at all. She was dressed in black and carried a black-trimmed hanky to bury her face into. I noticed that her shoulders were shaking and heaving. She looked so little and lonely standing there. Every now and then, she'd have to lean on Hissing Sid, when he stopped still long enough, that is. Mrs Robbins looked a lot like Jenny standing there, only older. My eyes went all blurry, but I didn't cry.

Behind Hissing Sid and Mrs Robbins came Jenny's grandparents and aunts, uncles and cousins. I'd never seen any of them before, not even the cousins. According to Jenny, Mrs Robbins's lot never could stomach Hissing Sid and his lot, so there wasn't a great deal of love lost there. It showed, too. Each group kept to itself, exchanging no more than slight nods. As Madame Zelda said, it wasn't hard to pick out who was whose. Mrs Robbins's family were very respectable in their dark felt headgear, black gloves and armbands. They wore the kinds of hats that Uncle Bert said looked as if they had been turned on a lathe; all stiff and unyielding like the perms underneath and the corsets lower down. It's true, too; they did look ever so stiff, like over-starched Queen Mums. Which is why it was funny when one of the horses decided to drop a large, steaming pile right next to the most starchy of them all. I wanted to giggle and ached for Jenny to share the joke. You can always rely on a horse to lower the tone. They just don't care.

The men wore dark suits, black ties and shoes that shone with spit and polish, army fashion. The women stood quietly, clutching the arms of their silent husbands or, if they didn't have husbands, their large, black handbags.

Hissing Sid's mob were a lot looser in style. Draped jackets, heavy on the black velvet trim, narrow trousers and thick-soled suede brothel creepers were the order of the day for the younger men. The younger women and girls wore full-skirted shirt-waisters, high heels, lots of petticoats and wide plastic belts, white or black depending on the outfit. I was dead jealous of the heels. I loved the click, click, click as they hit the pavement. Some of the older women wore daring pencil skirts that made them walk funny, in teetering little steps that tipped them forward as if they were about to fall on their noses. None of them did, thank goodness. They were held up by the older men, uncomfortable in their demob suits and stiff collars. All the women were chattering twenty to the dozen, and the men were slapping each other and Hissing Sid on the back whenever things got too quiet.

Then came the rest of us. We'd formed groups that depended on how well we knew the Robbinses. Mrs Robbins's ex-workmates had come as one group. Hissing Sid's punters and associates formed a couple of others. Kid joined one of these. He was looking very well turned out and clean to his fingertips. Our cafe formed a large, untidy straggle of people made up of all of our family members, official and unofficial, and a mob of punters too. The school sent Miss Welbeloved, with our class, but I stuck with Auntie Maggie, Uncle Bert, T.C., Luigi and Betty because I felt happier with them. Mamma and Papa Campanini joined us, along with Madame Zelda, Paulette, Sharky Finn, Bandy, Sugar and Mrs Wong.

The procession finally took off and made its slow way through the little streets to the church. We twisted and turned and went back on ourselves so much I lost all sense of direction. Everywhere we went, shops had their blinds down, flats had drawn their curtains and people stopped by the kerb.

The men removed their hats and looked sombrely down at the gutters. After the whole of Soho had had their chance to pay their respects, we finally wound up at St Anne's where the vicar was waiting for us.

Jenny's coffin was carried to a platform covered in a gold and red cloth, where it rested for the whole service. It glowed very white in the gloom, and candlelight flickered back off the silver bowls and candlesticks that stood on the altar.

The vicar said stuff about it being difficult to understand God's plan when he took a child to His bosom. And I thought he was right there; it was hard to understand. I was certainly having a lot of trouble with it. How Jenny could be screaming around the playground with the rest of us one day and then the next day she wasn't, and she never would be again, I simply couldn't grasp. Of course, it wasn't that sudden, she'd been ill for ages, but it felt sudden and shocking all the same. And I didn't believe for *one minute* that Jesus wanted Jenny for a sunbeam because He had loads and loads already.

I kept saying my goodbyes to her in my head, all the way through the vicar's talk, but I can't say I felt any better for it. I wasn't convinced that Jenny could hear me anyway, which brought me to the realization that she hadn't really been in a position to hear me when I'd last seen her either. She'd been sparko at the time, I remembered, out like a light, so it wouldn't have been so very different if I had managed to say goodbye on that last afternoon after all. For some reason, that idea seemed to take a huge weight off my shoulders and I was able to sit up and take notice properly for the first time that day.

The vicar was very nice about Jenny, but I still didn't cry. None of it felt that real to me. At last we sang 'All Things Bright and Beautiful' and then we filed past her coffin, which someone had opened. I almost fainted. There was Jen, looking like a nasty plastic doll, all pink and white and scary, surrounded by white satin. She even had lace on her pillow. She'd have loved all that satin and lace. She'd made up her mind to have white satin for her wedding: white satin, lace and tons of seed pearls for the trim. The last time we'd talked about it, bridesmaids were getting ghastly pastel blues and pinks. Yuk! Jenny had loved planning weddings. Me, I found it sort of boring, although I liked talking about the clothes.

Clutched in her little white hands was a bald bear – my bald bear – with his silver bell tied round his neck with a ribbon. Dingle wasn't anything like the bridal posy of white and pink rosebuds that Jenny had set her heart on during all those planning sessions. It was then, when I realized there never would be a wedding for Jenny, that I felt hot tears overflow from my brimming eyes and trickle down my cheeks. The trickle turned into a torrent and I sobbed and sobbed so that I thought I must surely drown. Uncle Bert got to me first and scooped me up and cuddled me close to his chest.

As I flew through the air on my way to Uncle Bert's best waistcoat I caught a flash of the congregation behind us. Everyone was there. Soho must have come to an absolute standstill, with nothing being bought or sold, because everyone was at church. And right at the back, near the doors, almost hidden behind a pillar, I thought I caught a glimpse of the neat, pale head of the Widow Ginger. It might have been a trick of the light through salty tears, I couldn't tell for sure, but as I strained for another look he was gone. Surely it couldn't be? He didn't even know Jenny.

I decided that there was no reason for the Widow to be at the church. Then something struck me. He didn't know Jenny, but Kid did. The Widow would know that everyone would be at Jenny's funeral. Everyone: Uncle Bert, Auntie Maggie, Sugar, Bandy, Maltese Joe and me to name only six of us. Who knew how many others he had the needle to? It was a golden opportunity to get us all in one place. I was so busy trying to catch another glimpse of the man who might or might not have been the Widow that I forgot about crying.

Uncle Bert put me down but kept a firm grip on my mitt. I kept trying to attract his attention by squeezing his hand, talking in church not being allowed, but he thought I was being friendly and just squeezed back.

It had been decided that the cafe mob would give the crematorium a miss so that they could put the finishing touches to the grub, so I went straight home. Nobody thought the crematorium was the place for me, and I must admit I agreed with them. I didn't want to see any more fires.

Paulette told me later that no one saw any actual flames at the crematorium, that it was all ever so tasteful with organ music, sliding coffins and thick curtains, but I'm glad I missed it anyway. My class didn't go either. They went back to school and even missed the food, poor things. I was kept close to Auntie Maggie, Uncle Bert and the others, I'm glad to say.

At last, I finally managed to whisper to my uncle Bert that I thought I'd seen the Widow, but now the bloke in question had disappeared. He said he'd keep his eyes open and spread the word to a few others to do the same.

Auntie Maggie and Mamma Campanini

decided that action would help sort me out, me being all twitchy and damp. They had me dashing about with plates of this and bowls of that until every table was well stocked and my legs and arms ached.

As I ran backwards and forwards with loaded plates and cups and glasses, I kept getting a flash of that pale head at the back of the church and my stomach would lurch. The trouble was I wasn't allowed to stop still long enough to have a good butcher's, but I did notice Uncle Bert, Luigi and a variety of Campanini men floating in and out of the cafe and looking up and down the road in a casual manner. Sometimes they'd stop on the pavement for a fag and a natter, but all the while their eyes would be moving restlessly over the crowd gathering around the cafe, or sliding over the passers-by and watching their backs hurrying away. I got the really comforting feeling that here was a bunch of blokes who were not in the business of allowing a flutter to ruin an important thing like a funeral. There was a time and a place for everything, and this time and place was for Jenny and the Robbinses and their friends and families. Italians, their restless eyes said, know about these things.

31

The men were not the only watchers, however. Madame Zelda, Paulette, Auntie Maggie, Sugar, Bandy and I were all watching Luigi and Betty. They were holed up in the opposite corner, trying to talk as an endless stream of men swaggered up to eye Betty and natter with Luigi. You could tell, even from the other side of the room, that things were not going well. Luigi seemed to be asking Betty something and she was shaking her head and looking sad.

Hissing Sid was drunk and so were the rest of his family – except Mrs Robbins. She sat on the table next to ours with Mamma Campanini and Mamma's daughters and daughters-in-law. She wasn't saying much, but she was watching Hissing Sid with great sad eyes. Her own relatives hadn't stayed long. They'd had a sandwich, a cup of tea and a word with Mrs Robbins and then they were gone. That's when she'd been scooped up by the Campanini women, who would pass her their hankies when she cried and tut gently as they squeezed her arm or patted her hand. Nobody knew what to say, except that they were sorry, and that didn't even come close to covering it.

Meanwhile, Uncle Bert, Maltese Joe, T.C. and Joe's boys were wandering about the cafe, the street and the alleyway behind, watching all the time. Occasionally they'd stop by a group of men for a chat, but their eyes would be looking over their shoulders, watching the crowd, the windows of the buildings opposite and the street corners. Normally, T.C. didn't mingle with Maltese Joe or his boys if he could help it, but Uncle Bert said there was a truce in operation, there being a common enemy to watch out for. Soon, I began to wonder if I'd imagined the whole thing, and felt bad for getting everybody on the alert. Mick the Tic said they'd have to keep their minces open anyway, everybody being together like we were, and it being a perfect opportunity for the Widow to do some real damage. That made me feel worse, so I made my way back to our table to join in the Luigi and Betty watching.

Just as I arrived on Auntie Maggie's lap, Luigi grabbed Betty's arm. She shook him off angrily and got to her feet. Her voice was loud, sharp and as clear as anything. 'It's not what I want, Luigi. I'm sorry, but there it is. I don't want any more upset and aggravation. There was enough of that at the farm and during the damned war. I want a quiet life, kids, husband, that sort of boring stuff. You'd never be right in Surbiton or Tunbridge Wells; you know you wouldn't. You'd never even manage in Camden Town – it'd be too far out in the sticks for you. You'd be back here every day, visiting your family, seeing your mates. You'd never settle. And before you say you'd try, I don't want you to try.'

Luigi was standing now and running his hand through his hair as if he wanted to tear it out by the roots in his frustration. 'But Johnnie the Horn, Betty. Can't you do better than that? He'll never stay in sodding Surbiton either, a month, maybe two. He's a musician, for Christ's sake. They travel all the time.'

I noticed that Mamma Campanini didn't say anything about blasphemy this time when her baby was in trouble. You could tell she was just itching to barge in and tell that nasty girl to stop upsetting her boy. But as Madame Zelda said, Mamma had brought too many kids up not to know when to keep her opinions to herself. That's why her children still adored her. She simply sat among her women folk, arms folded across her belly, dark eyes glinting dangerously, lips pressed tight shut, with no sign of flashing gold teeth to brighten things up a bit.

'He's said he'll change, Luigi. Settle down, get a job with his dad at the Co-op. It's been decided.' Betty didn't sound as sure as she tried to look. I couldn't imagine Johnnie the Horn at the Co-op, not even to stock up on Spam, let alone to work in one.

I was afraid that Luigi'd be bald any minute, with that hand raking away at his lovely, glossy barnet. 'Don't you realize he's a bastard, Betty? He'll shag anything between nine and ninety, that one. All that about the Co-op is to get into your drawers girl, and when he's done that, he'll be off. He always is.'

But Betty wouldn't listen. 'You're just jealous, Luigi, and I'm sorry about that, but Johnnie's who I want and that's that. I don't want to be mixed up in all this business with that mad American and neither does Johnnie. He was due to play in that club in Peter Street and I was working there. We could wind up dead in a fight that's nothing to do with us, and why?' She didn't wait for an answer. 'We're leaving next week.' She leaned over, pecked Luigi on the cheek and headed for the door. She was in such a hurry to get out that she didn't even stop to say goodbye to us.

Poor Luigi slumped back in his chair as if he was a long balloon that someone had just stuck with a ruddy great hatpin. I had never seen him look so miserable.

Nobody moved for ages, we just stared at the door. Once again, Mamma kept her

306

distance. Later, when I asked why – because if I'd been his mum I'd've rushed over to him – Paulette explained it to me. 'He'd look a right noddle in front of his mates and the other blokes if his mum went all mumsy on him, now wouldn't he? He's nearly a grown man, Rosie, he'd look stupid and, worse, he'd be a mummy's boy. No, she'll save it for private. Pity that bloody Betty didn't do the same.' We all agreed with that.

After what felt like a week in which Luigi continued to stare at the floor and the rest of us stared at the empty doorway, while sliding our eyes sideways to see how he was doing, Maltese Joe ambled over to Luigi's table with a bottle and a glass. He put the glass on the table, poured a generous slug of brandy into it, patted Luigi's shoulder for a second, then, without saying a word, ambled away again, puffing gently on his cheroot. As Luigi picked up the glass and took a hefty swallow, the whole room seemed to let out the breath I hadn't realized we'd been holding.

As Madame Zelda said later, 'Round our way, you can't just have a simple funeral. Oh no! You have to have the bloody floor show as well.' And how right she was.

After Betty stormed out things went very quiet for a bit. Then the women got busy and started clearing the dirty crocks, washing them up and then refilling them with more food and drink. As Paulette said, it was handy being a girl because there was always something to do. There was always someone to feed at the difficult times, like funerals and when there's just been a socking great public domestic, leaving everyone staring at their toes in embarrassment.

The men set up barrels of pale and brown ale in the kitchen. The Coach and Horses had supplied pint glasses and smaller ones for the shorts. Most of the women and children went home, leaving Hissing Sid and the blokes to carry on with the wake. Get-togethers were a serious business.

Still Luigi sat on his own, staring at the floor and looking up only when someone refilled his glass. It was ever so sad to see him like that, but everyone said it was best to leave him to it, so we did.

Mrs Robbins looked as if she'd been set in concrete. Only her eyes moved as they followed Hissing Sid around the room. Every now and then Madame Zelda, Auntie Maggie or Paulette would offer her something to eat or drink, but she'd just shake her head slightly and carry on watching Sid. It was eerie.

Auntie Maggie was just talking to Uncle Bert about what to do with me, on account of the fact that I was knackered and about to fall asleep on the floor if we didn't watch out, when I heard a peculiar high-pitched wail and the crash of a chair hitting the floor. My eyes flew open to see Mrs Robbins hurtling across the room, hat tilted across one eye, as she made for the cafe door in a terrific burst of speed. There was no sign of concrete now. I followed the direction of her mad charge and saw, framed in the doorway, the Mangy Cow. She was looking around as if trying to spot someone. She caught Kid's eye and jerked her head sharply towards the door. He was about to get to his feet, had his bum off the chair, when Mrs Robbins hit the Mangy Cow on her blind side and at speed. The Mangy Cow went flying sideways, knocking over a table and several chairs before she hit the deck in a glittering shower of breaking glasses and plates. The words 'Cat fight!' flew around the room quicker than a startled sparrow and a crowd gathered in seconds. I managed to crawl under a table and had a clear view through a pair of dark drainpipe trousers. Mrs Robbins had taken the Mangy Cow completely by surprise and it took her a moment to get her wind back. Mrs Robbins put those few seconds to good use and was gouging any exposed flesh she could reach with one hand, tearing out blond hair by its dark roots with the other and sinking her gnashers into the Mangy Cow's arm. I could see her face clearly from under my table, and it had a glazed, crazed look only made human by the black hat that was still hanging on with the aid of a hatpin. I almost felt sorry for the Mangy Cow, but then I remembered how hurt Jenny had been when her dad left, and I found myself cheering on Mrs Robbins along with the rest of the crowd. You get sort of caught up in it somehow, especially if you're on someone's side. And there was no question whose side we were on. Not a single, solitary voice was raised for the Mangy Cow, not one.

Still, she didn't seem to need any encouragement once she got her breath back. She let out an ear-piercing scream, heaved Mrs Robbins off her and flipped her on to her back. She was astride her chest before you could spit, and her fists were pounding away at Mrs Robbins's head and shoulders. I couldn't bear to watch that bit, and before I knew it, I'd squirmed out of my hiding place, through the drainpipes and was hauling at the Mangy Cow's arm. Then, when that didn't work, I kicked her really hard in the side and managed to knock her off Mrs Robbins.

Suddenly, the forest of legs surrounding us parted to reveal an elegant pair of narrow Italian shoes and a smart pair of trouser legs, accompanied by a solid set of brogues and rumpled tweed. One Italian arm reached down and tenderly moved me aside and a tweedy set picked me up and carried me away, stroking my hair and shushing as we went. The smell of T.C. was the final straw. I cried my heart out.

Luigi set about untangling Mrs Robbins from the Mangy Cow.

Unfortunately, Mrs Robbins had got her second wind and was busy trying to gouge out the Mangy Cow's left eye. She squirmed and wriggled like mad, but Luigi hung on, talking quietly into her left ear as he did so. At last she began to quieten down and Luigi was finally able to lift her up to her feet. Harsh, howling sobs seemed to be wrenched out from deep, deep down inside Mrs Robbins. Luigi simply held her against his chest very tightly and muttered soothing noises into her hair.

The party broke up soon after that. Hissing Sid was found cowering at the back of the kitchen and a rather tattered Mrs Robbins was delivered into his care. Although, as Madame Zelda said, 'How the hell he's going to be any use is beyond me. He can barely stand by himself. Still, I s'pose he's got to try. He can hardly leave poor old Luigi holding her up for ever, can he? She is his wife after all, poor woman.'

While everyone was milling about, trying to find Hissing Sid, I saw Kid help the

Mangy Cow to her feet and try to brush her down a bit. She was covered in shattered glass and bits of fish paste sandwich. She slapped his hand away hard, and if looks could've killed, the entire roomful of people would've been flat on their backs, legs in the air and as stiff as boards. Everyone else was busy with Mrs Robbins and I don't think anyone saw them leave.

'You don't normally encourage violence at a funeral, even round our way,' Auntie Maggie said later, 'but what do you do if one of the fighters is also the chief mourner? I ask you. I mean, you can't sling the chief mourner out of their own do, now can you?' And of course it was agreed that you couldn't.

'Young Rosie did well, trying to break it up like that. That fight lowered the tone something awful.' Paulette, like everybody else, didn't know what to say. People were not supposed to fight at a funeral, everyone knew that, but what *were* you supposed to do if the chief mourner forgot the rules and socked her husband's ex-girlfriend?

'I shouldn't think that eventuality is covered in the official handbook. Luigi was a brick, especially as he had just got a public drubbing. That Betty is a fool, but then it was ever thus with women and their ruddy hormones.' Bandy was sitting at the counter, cigarette holder waving about in one hand

and a gin and tonic steady as a rock in the other. Silk and gin didn't mix, so it didn't do to splash the precious stuff about, according to Bandy.

'It was everyone's nerves,' Sugar said sadly. 'Poor Jenny was only a little girl. She should have had a life. If you think about it like that, you can see why it all got too much for that poor woman. Seeing that Cowley creature must have been the last straw. Did you notice that not a single bloody soul from her family did the honours? Sid was too busy getting pissed with the lads and her mother and mob couldn't wait to get away; practically had sparks flying from their heels. We'll have to be good to her and hope she dumps that wretched Sid somewhere along the way, when she feels up to it.'

'Bert, Rosie here's almost gone. Time we got to our beds, I reckon.' Auntie Maggie waved her hand at the dirty crocks, over-flowing ashtrays and trampled sandwiches covering every available surface of the cafe. 'Best leave this lot for tomorrow.'

There was a chorus of 'We'll help' from the remaining mourners and everyone went their separate ways, agreeing that it had been one hell of a funeral.

T.C. was talked into stopping the night on the settee in the little living room round at St Anne's Court, so he and Uncle Bert took it in turns to carry me home. I was far too sleepy to walk, ungluing my eyes only when Uncle Bert passed me over to T.C. As I flopped over his shoulder in what he assured me was a fireman's lift, I could have sworn I saw someone flitting in and out of the shadows. I stared harder at the last spot where I'd seen movement. Surely the shadows were darker in Frenchie's doorway, and was that a brief flash of a white hand?

My eyes were sore from staring into the darkness all the way home, but nothing else moved.

32

I was excused school the next day and got to loll about in bed until Sugar and Bandy were up. I loved spending mornings with those two. Their starts were always so leisurely, like something out of a Hollywood film and just as shiny. Sugar would be first up, and would float into the kitchen in a cloud of cologne and silk pyjamas. On cool mornings he wore his lotus blossom dressing gown. He favoured Chinese silk slippers, black with a gold pattern. He'd stand at the little gas stove, chatting to me as he spooned coffee into the pot, added water and set it on the ring.

'God, I'm cream crackered today. Give me a solid night's work with a bunch of squabbling actors any day over a do like yesterday's. All that naked emotion, dear; so tiring. Bandy's snoring like a warthog. Do warthogs snore, do you think?' He didn't want my opinion, so he didn't wait for it. 'You know, I think they might. Imagine a warthog with a cold, or a ninety a day fag habit like Bandy's. It's enough to make anyone's sinuses kick up, I should think.'

When the coffee was perked, little spurts of hot water bubbled into the little glass dome in the lid. I loved waiting for that first spurt. Meanwhile, Sugar would be laying a tray with a linen tray cloth, embroidered with hollyhocks, delphiniums and other flowers all growing round a lady in a large crinoline frock and what Sugar called a 'poke' hat, whatever that was. I'd never heard of poke hats before. Sugar had done the embroidery during the air raids in the war. He never said how he got the linen and silks. He'd point out little blips in the running stitches and say, 'That was when Park Lane copped it, and that one there was Bond Street. You could feel the ground shake it was that close. Look at that stitch there – shot straight out it did, like a dog's leg at a lamp-post. I used to put 'em right. Then I thought, no, I won't; if I leave 'em that way, I'll remember. And I do too.'

Sugar would carefully pour the coffee into a warmed pot made of fine white china decorated with a thin gold trim, then he'd add a white and gold cup and saucer and a small plate to the tray. A matching jug of milk and a bowl of sugar lumps followed. Silver sugar tongs, in the shape of twined lizards, their feet clawed to grab the sugar, were buffed up and added to the sugar bowl. A silver spoon was placed in the saucer. A linen napkin, in a ring also made of silver lizards, came next. A slightly warmed croissant, wrapped in a fresh napkin, with butter and strawberry conserve in little glass bowls was the finishing touch. Bandy's breakfast was ready to be served. That over he'd be back, ready for a small cup of bitter black coffee and a chinwag.

'So, Rosie, what about that Betty, eh? I wonder if Annie knows her Johnnie's been swiped. She's not the kind to allow such an insult to go unremarked, you take my word for it. If Annie didn't know yesterday, she does today, after Betty's little announcement. The fur's about to fly. Betty had better watch herself. Now, poppet, how's yourself today?'

Sugar could certainly talk a lot. 'Sugar?' Bandy would say. 'Sugar doesn't confine himself to talking the hind legs off a donkey. No, the whole of bloody Derby Day's legless by the time he's finished with 'em. Finest bloodstock in the land and not a bloody limb between 'em!'

The good thing about him, though, was that he could listen, too. He did it very well. He said it was part of the job of being a barman. Anyway, he listened to me when I told him how I felt about Jenny and how badly I was going to miss her. He gave me a little squeeze, but he didn't tell me not to be sad. He knew that when you miss someone, you miss them, and it's never quite all right that they've gone.

Once everyone was up and able to take notice, we made our way round to the cafe to clear up. Pretty soon, a small army of volunteers had the place up and running again and we were able to open for business. Naturally, all the talk was about the funeral, the fight and Betty's announcement that she was leaving with Johnnie the Horn.

'You mark my words,' Sugar told us, 'there'll be some unpleasantness. I can't imagine Annie letting Betty walk off with her bloke without showing that she's just a tad narked.'

Bandy summed up the general opinion. 'A spot of vengeance is likely, I'm afraid. Annie's never been one to balk at inflicting a few conspicuous bruises, possibly even the odd broken bone; just a small one, to alert the breakee to the depths of her displeasure. Let's hope it's Johnnie who cops it. Betty's just an innocent, really. She isn't the first young gal to have the drawers charmed off her and she won't be the last.'

'True, O wise one,' Sugar cooed. 'Now, are you going to get your bony arse off that chair and lend a hand with this broom?'

I asked T.C. to slap Johnnie in irons, on Luigi's behalf, but T.C. wasn't hopeful. 'Unhappily, there's no law against snaffling a chap's lady friend, Rosie. Otherwise I'd be delighted to rid you of the fellow. Luigi may be able to go the breach of promise route, of course, but a chap'd have to be a prize wally to follow that line. Blokes are supposed to take it on the chin, not snivel like a disappointed girl. Anyway, there was no formal promise, was there? No promise, no breach. Sorry, little 'un.' I was sorry too. I didn't want Luigi to wind up in a fight, and although she'd dumped him I didn't think Betty would like it either – and I was certain his mum wouldn't.

A few days later, I glimpsed Johnnie wearing a socking great black eye and a large bald patch where a clump of hair had been wrenched out by the roots, and wondered. Rumour had it that Betty's beautiful ivory skin sported areas of purple, red and yellow. Sugar had seen them together at Bandy's and he said that they didn't look good.

'Seems that Annie did register her

objections to Johnnie's new liaison on his and Betty's persons. She really made her feelings felt, thank you very much. We *are* having more than our fair share of fisticuffs lately, and from the gentle sex too.'

As the days rolled past and Luigi moped a lot and drooped about but still didn't explode, the tension began to tell on me, so that in the end I asked him straight out what he intended to do. He looked bewildered.

'Do? What am I supposed to do? A girl's entitled to take up with who she likes if she's a free agent. Betty didn't promise me anything. I was just hoping, that's all. You can't slap a girl around because you had your hopes poured down the pan, now can you?'

I agreed you couldn't, but that didn't necessarily stop you from slapping the sneaky toe-rag who stole her away.

'Blokes are blokes, Shorty. You can't stop 'em from chasing girls, even if you fancy one of the girls for yourself. The best you can hope for is that the girl will fancy you enough not to let herself get caught. In this case, Betty didn't. It's my hard cheese. I'll get over it. I'm a big lad now.'

Which was not what I was expecting at all. I didn't know what to make of it. Most of the men I knew seemed to think that Luigi's honour depended on clouting somebody – anybody – and the sooner the better. Auntie

Maggie seemed surprised but pleased when I told her that Luigi didn't agree.

'Well, who'd have thought Luigi would take it so quietly?' She beamed. 'Still, his mum must be proud; she's brought up a good lad there. He really did like that girl; pity she hasn't got the sense to grab him while she's got the chance. Never mind. Some other girl will be grateful for the opportunity, doubtless.'

Mrs Robbins was a bit scarce in the days after Jenny's funeral but she did still wave at me from her kitchen window when I went to feed the churchyard pigeons. I would always look up and there she'd be, feeding Peter and his pals.

At school, Enie Smales got an A for a story she wrote and Miss Welbeloved decided to move her up a few desks so that she was in the top group. The trouble was, this meant that I came in after playtime one day to find Enie Smales moving her gear from her desk over to Jenny's desk next to me. I just about put up with that, but when she took Jenny's stuff out of the desk and slung it in the bin, I chinned her.

Miss Welbeloved's voice was like a whip-lash. 'Rosa Featherby, what in God's name do you think you're doing?'

And I was blowed if I could tell her. Not only did I not know, but the blood pouring from Smales's hooter was making me feel a bit sick.

Next thing I knew, I was choking my heart out on the staffroom chairs and Enie Smales was sitting next to me with a wet tea towel pressed firmly to her nose by a grim-faced Miss Welbeloved. 'Ah, I see you have rejoined us, Miss Featherby. Perhaps in future you will take into account that you're squeamish and not cause your classmate's nose to bleed all over the place.' She lifted the wet towel from Smales's kisser, inspected it carefully and said, 'You'll do, Enie. Go and sit in the medical room while I have a word with Slugger Featherby here.'

And have a word she did, and the less said about it the better. She left me to understand that, although clearing out my friend's desk was probably a little tactless, she expected me none the less to behave like a lady and not clock my classmates. I opened my gob to tell her that Smelly Smales was not my mate, class or otherwise, but she gave me the Glare and I kept it buttoned. I was also told that she, Miss Welbeloved, decided who sat where in her classrooms and that was final.

'Last, but not least, Rosa, what do you think we should do with Jenny's books?'

I thought about it for a bit. 'Give them to her mum, Miss,' I said.

'Good idea. We'll do that then,' Miss Welbeloved said. 'I expect you back in the classroom in ten minutes, Rosa.'

When I finally got back to the classroom, Kathy Moon had moved over on to the other half of my desk and Enie Smales had taken Kathy's place. Although the new arrangement was better, much better, it still felt wrong. It should have been Jenny with her bum parked at the other end of the bench and it wasn't.

33

That afternoon, soon after I'd got in from school and been given my milk and biscuits, a slightly battered Betty came to the cafe to say goodbye. We all liked Betty, but we liked Luigi better and nobody cared much one way or the other about Johnnie the Horn – except Betty and Annie, of course, and possibly Johnnie's mum – so it was a bit tricky.

Auntie Maggie was tight-lipped and her large arms were folded, a sure sign that she didn't approve. She was brief but not unkind to Betty. 'Well, dear, it's been a pleasure, I'm sure. Good luck with your new life; I hope it works out for you. Now, I must get on.'

Uncle Bert stuck his head out of the

kitchen where he was making scrambled eggs on toast for a punter. 'Off now, are you, Betty? Well, I wish you luck. You're going to need it with that one. Blast! Me eggs are sticking. Hope we see you round here again sometime.' And his head popped back like a tortoise into its shell.

'Personally, I think you're a dozy twollop,' Madame Zelda chipped in. 'No offence, Betty. I'm speaking as your mystical advisor, that's all. Johnnie will bring you very little joy, but he will leave you with plenty of trouble. Luigi's the better bet, but I can tell that you'll not listen. It's your destiny, as we mystic types say. Try all you like, you can't talk a girl out of making a fool of herself if it's her destiny. Remember to keep a sixpence between your knees, gel, that's my advice, but I don't s'pose you'll take that either.' She gave Betty a big hug, then headed for the cafe door. 'Got to go. I've got a half past four dying to be told he'll be a star and that his boyfriend's faithful. All bollocks, of course.'

Betty called out to her retreating back, 'Tell Paulette I'm sorry I missed her.' Madame Zelda waved to show she'd heard, but didn't turn.

That left me. To be honest, I was choked, and finding the biscuits hard to swallow. I liked Betty. We'd been friends, and I was fed up to the back teeth with losing my friends.

I liked things to stay pretty much the same and people to stay where they belonged, but nobody ever takes into account what kids want, or not often anyway. Kids were supposed to put up and shut up when it came to big decisions like coming or going, staying or leaving. I was also very cheesy about Betty upsetting poor Luigi the way she had. I was sulking, there was no doubt about it.

'Well, Rosie dear, this is cheerio then.' Betty's voice sounded hearty but I couldn't tell what she looked like because I'd turned my back on her. I didn't answer. Auntie Maggie frowned and jerked her head at me but I ignored her too. Betty had another stab at it, louder this time. 'I said that it's time to say cheerio, Rosie.'

Still I munched that dry digestive that wouldn't get past the lump in my throat and kept my back to her. She could bugger off if she liked, but she couldn't make me watch her go. I'd had just about enough of that.

Auntie Maggie was sharp. She liked good manners, did my auntie Maggie, and anyway kids were not supposed to be rude to their elders; it was a *rule*. There weren't that many rules in our house, compared with some, but children not being bad-mannered to grown-ups was one of them. I was breaking that rule and right under Auntie Maggie's hooter too. I must've been feeling brave, or stupid, but the funny thing was I didn't care.

Now, my beloved auntie Maggie never hit me, or physically bullied me in any way and neither did my uncle Bert, but she came very, very close to it the day that Betty left.

'Betty's speaking to you, Rosa! Rosa!' Her voice could have sliced bacon; bricks even. I was in big, big trouble, but I'd started sulking and didn't know how to back down gracefully, so I stuck my heels in.

'I said, Betty is speaking to you. Now turn round and behave yourself like a decent human being and not a spoilt brat.'

Spoilt brat! Things were heading downhill fast and I had no brakes.

Still I didn't turn round. Then I heard Betty's voice. 'Don't force her, Maggie. I expect she's upset. She's already lost one mate recently, and perhaps she's miserable about losing another. I'll be back to see you, Rosie, I promise.' I felt a hand brush my curls briefly and then a little squeeze of my shoulder.

Suddenly it was all too much. I turned round and hurled myself at Betty's legs, sobbing my heart out. She had a big damp patch on her skirt by the time Auntie Maggie was able to prise me loose. Uncle Bert had appeared and picked me up and I got a whiff of pipe tobaco and fry-up. A few minutes later, all three of us stood in the cafe doorway, waving as Betty walked down the street towards Cambridge Circus, her head bowed into her hanky.

What with Jenny's funeral, and Betty leaving, there had been a lot of changes in my life, but one terrifying thing stayed the same: the Widow was still on the loose. It was a Sunday morning, and our little living room at St Anne's Court was full. Auntie Maggie, Uncle Bert, Maltese Joe and I were dressed. Maltese Joe was smart in a suit, having just got back from taking his ma and his missus to Mass. Sugar was still in his hairnet and Bandy was in her dressing gown. The room was littered with coffee cups, plates full of pain au chocolat crumbs and brimming ashtrays that reeked of dead Passing Clouds and pipe cleanings.

Maltese Joe prowled around as there was nowhere to sit. His left leg was slightly shorter than his right, which gave him a limp but didn't seem to slow him down any. Auntie Maggie said he always reminded her of a terrier: small, but powerful, aggressive and dogged. Maltese Joe never gave up on anything, unless he wanted to, and right now he obviously didn't want to. 'Rita told me she saw the bloke who set fire to Peter Street dodging out of that spieler down Brewer Street yesterday. I don't think we need use our loaves too hard to work out who that was. That backs up Rosie's feeling that the Widow's close by, at least some of the time. So I'm going to have to free up some of the boys from watching our various business enterprises and set 'em to doing the rounds of the clubs again.' Maltese Joe's eyes bulged a little more than usual as he shoved a lock of dark hair back over his high forehead. 'Some fuckers know he's here and are keeping it to themselves. I think it's time we handed out some reminders.' He thwacked his fist into the palm of his other hand with a dull thud, then added, 'Any chance of a coffee in this bleeding desert?'

Sugar got to his feet. 'Righto. I'll knock up another pot and get into something less comfortable. I was due at Freddie's half an hour ago to help them with some costumes. Boring stuff. Nun's habits – ghastly! Why do they call 'em habits, does anyone know?'

Nobody did, but I gave it some thought and piped up, 'Could it be that nuns always wear the same thing, so it's like a boring habit instead of a bad one?' Everyone laughed, but I couldn't see why.

Once coffee had been served, Sugar drifted off to get dressed and the rest of us settled down for a natter. Bandy was sprawled across an armchair, her slender feet hanging over the arm, cigarette holder loaded and smouldering. 'I suppose Maggie and I could swan around to Lizzie Robbins and see if she'll let us in. Hissing Sid says she'll hardly see anybody and she hasn't been out since the funeral.' She didn't sound keen, though, and made no move to get up and get dressed.

'I'll go on my own,' my aunt said. 'No need to get dressed if you don't want to, Band. I've got poor little Jenny's school stuff that Rosie brought home. I ought to take it round. I've got to drop in on Mrs Williams anyway, to remind her she's coming here for her tea. I've got the cucumber specially.'

So it was agreed: Bandy'd look after me, Uncle Bert and Maltese Joe would go for a Sunday drink and try to track down information while they were at it, Sugar'd be next door with Freddie the Frock and Auntie Maggie would pop round to see Mrs Robbins on her way to old Mrs Williams at the grocer's shop.

My heart sank at the thought of cucumber sandwiches for tea and having to be seen and not heard. On the bright side, though, I was being babysat by Bandy, and she was always good fun. Apart from anything else, she told the most amazing stories right off the top of her head.

'Right, Rosa, my blossom, I'm off back to my pit. Find me my cigarettes, there's a honey. Then you can snuggle up next to me and I'll see if I can think of a story I haven't told you yet.' And Bandy wandered off back to her room, while I turned over the chair cushions looking for a pink packet of Passing Clouds.

I loved Bandy's room. She had managed to make it her own by bringing stuff from her flat. There was a thick silk bedspread on the bed, all rich reds, deep purples and dark greens, with just the odd touch of gold, and a huge mound of cushions and pillows, so it was like settling back into a feather throne. Once we were both comfortable, she was off.

'Once upon a time' – you have to start stories like that, it's the rule, Bandy told me, and anyway it's in all the books – 'there was a princess, and she lived in a funny sort of castle.' Bandy spun a tale that involved dragons, genies – 'only a puff of smoke, you know' – and a wilful flying carpet that took you where it felt like taking you and not necessarily where you wanted to go, *and* expected a tip. It was given to much sulking, folding its fringe in a huff and refusing to move if the tip was not up to expectations. 'Not unlike one of our cab drivers, really,' Bandy remarked. That carpet took us all over the place in Bandy's imagination and it was a good hour and a half later that I surfaced.

'And what do you think happened then?'

I knew what this meant. 'Oh no, not tomorrow, Bandy,' I wailed.

But she was firm, as she always was. 'I'll tell you tomorrow. Now run along and play or something, and let me grab a little more shut-eye.'

I knew when I was being dismissed. I dutifully left the bedroom and went to the kitchen for a glass of milk and a biscuit, if I could find one. Travelling on an imaginary flying carpet, with just a puff of smoke for company, was very thirsty work. I had just wiped up the pool of milk on the kitchen table when I heard the front door open. I would have sung out to Auntie Maggie to tell her where I was, but I remembered that Bandy was trying to sleep. I tiptoed to the kitchen door, milk in hand, and was about to step out into the hall when I realized that my auntie Maggie was not alone.

When she moved to one side, I saw the neat, pale head of the Widow Ginger, and in his hand, pointing at my beloved aunt, was a socking great gun.

34

For what felt like a year, I stood there, hidden behind the kitchen door.

Rooted to the spot, unable either to move or to breathe, I prayed and prayed that they wouldn't come into the kitchen. It was in those long, long moments that I realized just how terrified I was of coming face to face again with the strange American. Soho had more than its fair share of villains, toe-rags and nutters, let's face it. I would be mad to say that we were all decent people in our own way, because some of us were seriously nasty bits of work. But without doubt, the Widow Ginger was far and away the nastiest I had ever come across. And he was just outside in the hallway, holding a big, black, ugly gun on my lovely aunt.

I heard movement, and a glance through the crack in the door showed me that they were going towards the living room. Then I heard his voice. 'What is it with you English? Don't you ever clear your dishes? Kid's the same way. He thinks that letting the faucet drip on the platter is enough to shift eggs and all kinds of shit.'

I'll say this for my auntie Maggie, if she felt afraid of the madman, she wasn't showing it. Her voice was strong and sharp as she answered him. 'I don't remember asking you to come in, so if you don't like what you see, then piss off somewhere else.' I realized then that Auntie Maggie had no idea that she and the Widow were not alone. She'd never have said 'piss off' if she'd thought I could hear. She must have thought that Bandy and I had gone out somewhere.

'Temper, temper, Margaret. We don't want Albert to come back to find that you have displeased me, now do we? You never know, he could stumble across all kinds of ... what's the word now? Unpleasantness! Yes, that'll do, unpleasantness. It has that pleasing sense of understatement that you guys are so big on. Do you think "unpleasantness" covers blood on the walls and brains on the rug, Margaret?'

'You can threaten all you like, Stanley. I ain't telling you where they went and I've got no idea when they'll be back. What do you hope to gain by trying to scare the living daylights out of us, that's what I'd like to know? You've never said; just slunk around setting your fires and putting the frighteners on poor sods like Kid. You're a sad man, Stanley, a very sad man.' Auntie Maggie's voice really did sound sad as she said it.

'Spare me the pity, Margaret. The day I need pity from a fat, ugly pile of trash like you is the day I might as well chuck myself off the Brooklyn Bridge. I'll tell you what I want. I want what's coming to me. I want what's mine. You guys cheated me out of my dues and I've come to claim my share, with interest. I figure I'm owed quite a chunk of change from all the business I missed out on when I was in the penitentiary.

'Then there's the matter of exacting a little vengeance. There I am trying for some of your famous English understatement right there. I don't want a little vengeance, Margaret, I want a lot. I suffered for years in that shithole, and as it was Albert, Joseph and Bandy who put me there I figured it was time they suffered too.'

'I don't remember my Bert or anyone else having anything to do with that,' said Auntie Maggie sharply, like she'd caught him out in a whopping great porkie. 'The way I remember it, you tried to kill one of your own, a bloke from your barracks – just shoved him under a night bus from Waterloo in the blackout. All over a crate of booze you tried to cheat him on. He was paralyzed and you was court-martialled. That's what I heard. How you've managed to work any of our lot into it I don't know.'

I heard a hissing sound like something heavy flying through the air and a muffled whump as it landed. I risked another peek through the crack and to my horror Auntie Maggie was holding her face and a trickle of blood was oozing through her fingers.

'Not one of those bastards spoke for me, Margaret. All they had to say was that I was with them. Friends stick together when they're jammed up, but they refused to my face. Said I had it coming. For that, they suffer.' I heard another sickening blow and looked again, but the Widow's back blocked my view. His pale hair glimmered in the dim light. His voice went very quiet. 'Now, would you like to know how I'm going to make them suffer, Margaret?'

Both the Widow and I waited for her answer, but Auntie Maggie kept schtum.

'No? Well, I reckon I'll tell you anyway. I'm going to get them through their loved ones, Margaret. They have all allowed themselves to get emotionally tied up, and people with emotional ties, Margaret, are weak people. Take my word for it: I've been studying that fact of life for many years. By the time I've finished with you, that faggot of Bandy's and Joe's mom, they'll be begging me to take anything, everything, just so I leave you alone.'

You know when people talk about getting a red mist in front of their eyes? When they do something that wouldn't have crossed their minds in a million years? Well, that's what the sound of the Widow's threats and the sight of my aunt's blood did to me. I really did see a red mist, and before I knew it I'd grabbed the nearest object from the table and was out of that kitchen and behind the Widow before my brains had caught up with me.

I heard a voice from miles away saying, 'You leave her alone, or I'll kill you.' And it took me a moment to realize that the voice was mine. I shoved what I had thought was the carving knife into the middle of his back before I realized that, instead of several inches of cold steel threatening his liver and lights, I was armed with a foot of fresh, but very blunt, cucumber. I was just about to panic; I knew that what might work in the Westerns on Saturday mornings was less likely to come off in real life. The Widow only had to turn round and Auntie Maggie and I were both goners.

All this was just dawning on me when a cool hand covered mine and moved the cucumber up to the back of the Widow's head so that I had to stand on tiptoes, making me wish I'd had ballet lessons like some of the girls in my class at school. Then I heard Bandy's posh tones. 'Rosie, my sweet, if you wish to make sure that your protagonist is in no position to argue, hold the gun to his *head*. That way, if you do have to shoot him, he won't be in any condition to walk away. We don't want him to cause any *unpleasantness* on another day, now do we? Oh, and while you're at it, do release the safety catch, there's a good girl. Now, you hold that steady, squeeze the trigger gently if he moves, and don't jerk. I'll just relieve him of this nasty Luger. There, that's much better.'

Bandy stepped well back, out of the Widow's reach. She fiddled with his gun for a moment and then carried on speaking. 'OK, Rosie dear, you can stand easy now.

This is loaded, and I for one would quite enjoy shooting this sod. Perhaps you'd like to help your auntie out of here, clean her up, try to stop the bleeding, that sort of thing.'

We didn't need telling twice. Without speaking Auntie Maggie and I went into the kitchen. I was just wetting a tea towel for her face when there was a commotion in the living room. Auntie Maggie swept the carving knife from the table and headed back in, with me right behind her. The Widow had obviously made a grab for Bandy, and they were struggling over the gun. Round and round the room they went, knocking over furniture, smashing a lamp and finally landing in a writhing heap on the settee. Bandy's arm, waving the gun, managed to escape the scrum and I darted in to grab it.

The heap heaved again and the Widow came out on top for a moment. Auntie Maggie stepped forward, carving knife flashing dangerously. She looked as if she was going to plunge it into his back but she spoke first. 'Let her go, Stanley, or I swear to God I'll stick you with this.'

Then the Widow did something that none of us expected. He let go of Bandy suddenly, leaped to his feet, and lunged for me before we could blink, let alone move. Of course, I was standing there like a lemon, still holding that rotten gun. Without thinking, I hurled it away as hard as I could, out of the door and into the hallway, where it bounced off the wall with a terrible explosion and then slid along the lino and came to rest against a huge pair of feet that had just walked in the front door. My eyes travelled up from the gun and the feet to see a nun standing there, with two more crowding the doorway behind her.

We all froze for a moment: Auntie Maggie with the carving knife poised in a stabbing motion. Bandy sprawled on the settee, the Widow looming over me – and the three nuns who stood stunned in the hall.

One of the nuns was the first to find her voice. 'What the bloody hell is going on here?' she barked.

The Widow, who was looking even paler than usual, muttered 'Nothing, Sister' as he stumbled out of the living room, barging past the nuns and scattering them like skittles as he rushed down the stairs to the street. Nobody followed him.

Once again, it was the nun who broke the silence. 'Would somebody *please* tell me what is going on? Bandy, what *were* you doing grappling with that bloke on the sofa?'

Bandy sat up, still breathing hard. 'It is you, Sugar, isn't it?' Her voice sounded just a tiny bit shaky. 'What are you doing kitted out like a damned nun?'

'Is anybody hurt?' asked Auntie Maggie. 'You, Rosie, are you all right, love? That explosion – it must've been the gun going off. Is anybody hurt?'

We all checked ourselves over carefully, then we checked each other, finding nothing except a few bumps and scratches on Bandy and a large swollen nose on Auntie Maggie. She was a bit gory, when you stopped to look at her, but the blood from her nose was dry and there was nothing fresh anywhere else.

'No? Then if we're all right, whose blood is that?' Auntie Maggie pointed to a brownish smear on the door jamb, a couple of spots on the top step and a steady drip that disappeared into the murk of the lower hallway.

We stared down the stairs and then we all jumped as a dark figure appeared out of the gloom and spoke. 'Is there shooting here? Are the authorities taking us? Please, are there soldiers?'

Sugar was the first to react. 'Oh, Mr Rabinowitz. No, there are no soldiers and no authorities. It's only us.'

'You bloody fool, Sugar. How is Mr Rabinowitz going to find you, Freddie and Antony dressed as bloody nuns reassuring? Leave this to me.' Bandy swept Sugar aside and stood at the top of the stairs, hair flying in all directions, her bruises already showing

338

blue. 'Don't worry, Mr Rabinowitz. Rosie's just shot a madman. There's nothing at all for you to worry about. The only Nazi has left, dripping claret.'

'Rosie's shot a madman? Which madman? How did she shoot him when we don't own a gun? What the hell's going on?' Uncle Bert appeared behind Mr Rabinowitz at the turn of the stairs, followed by Maltese Joe and T.C. My heart sank.

The last person you want to see if you've just shot someone is a policeman, even if he is your dad.

35

Uncle Bert was firm and got everyone to stop milling about and sit down. Even T.C. didn't try to take over, although he must have been dying to, being a copper.

'Right, three things. Who got shot? What condition are they in? And why are you lot dressed as bleeding currants?' Uncle Bert asked finally.

Me, Auntie Maggie, Bandy and Sugar all started to speak at once. Freddie and Antony looked warily at T.C. and started towards the door. 'We'll be leaving you now,' said Freddie. 'Sugar'll tell you about the ensembles. P'raps you'll explain this lot later, Sugar. Ta ta for now.' And with little waves, they were gone.

It took a while to restore order. 'You, Maggie, you tell me. And while you're at it, what happened to your hooter?' demanded Uncle Bert.

'It was Stanley, Bert. I'd just nipped in to see Mrs Williams about tea and had another go at raising Lizzie Robbins, to give her Jenny's books, but still no luck. She just ain't answering. Then I thought I'd make sure everything was all right at the cafe. It was quiet, so I did a bit of sorting for tomorrow, checked the stores and made a list. Then I came back here.' Auntie Maggie paused for a moment to steady her voice and carried on.

'I'd passed Nosher's and had my key in the lock when I felt something slam into my back and it was Stanley. He had a bloody great gun.' Her voice shook dangerously, but held on. 'He shoved me in the door and forced me up the stairs. All the time he was asking where you and Joe were. I kept telling him that I didn't know. That you'd gone out together. I was trying to keep him out of the flat, you see, but he wasn't having it. He clouted me in the nose with his shooter. It's nothing much.' Auntie Maggie touched her poor nose with fingers that trembled slightly and then her eyes filled up with tears as she continued her story.

'Next thing I knew, Rosie had rushed out of the kitchen and shoved Mrs Williams's cucumber in his back and said he was to leave me alone or she'd kill him.' She turned to me. 'I want you to know, Rosie, that that was a very brave but stupid thing to do. Saturday morning pictures, I suppose, filling your head with dangerous nonsense. Still, there's no denying it worked for long enough for Bandy to come to the rescue. I am grateful, Rosie, honest I am, but a *cucumber?* Really! Whatever next? You silly, silly girl.' And with that she burst into tears and scooped me up into a soggy hug; it was some considerable time before I could surface to grab a couple of lungfuls of air.

'Can anyone tell me exactly *why* this madman seems to want to inflict so much damage on you?' T.C. asked in a quiet, mild voice. 'I realize it doesn't take a lot to set off your bona fide nutcase, but surely there must be something at the back of it?'

Once again everyone spoke at once, but it was Auntie Maggie who was heard. 'I think we should tell T.C. everything. He can be trusted, Bert, you know he can. He's not going to do anything to hurt Rosie or her set-up, now are you, T.C.?'

T.C. shook his head and Uncle Bert, Maltese Joe and Bandy exchanged long looks. Finally, Sugar piped up, 'Oh, sod it!

For Christ's sake tell him, someone. All that stuff in the war's a long time ago and what's happening now is just too bloody much for body and soul to stand. For starters, I don't know about you lot, but I wouldn't mind sleeping in my own bed for a change. Get it over with, that's what I say.'

So they told him everything. As time was of the essence, or so Bandy said, they kept it as brief as possible.

As ever, T.C. was a good listener and didn't interrupt at all. Then he summed up. 'So, we know the Widow's wounded, though probably not badly, judging by the blood trail. But he'll need a place to get it washed and dressed and to get his wind back. His known associate is Kid. Kid and Mary Cowley seem to have some sort of connection as well. It's reasonable to assume, then, that she knows the Widow and could be aiding and abetting his mysterious disappearances, along with Kid.' We all looked at T.C. in wonder as he continued. 'Let's find the whereabouts of Kid and Mary Cowley. They're key. Joe, I think you're more likely to get cooperation from their associates than I am. Can we leave that to you?'

'Right.' Maltese Joe made for the door. 'I'll get the boys' arses into gear. Bert, you might as well come with me. You'll want to get your mitts on the bastard.'

'I'll catch you up, Joe. I want a word with Maggie first.' Maltese Joe nodded and left.

'Maggie, my love, will you promise me that you'll stick with the others until I get back?'

Auntie Maggie opened her mouth to speak, but Uncle Bert's expression told her that she couldn't talk him out of hunting the Widow down, so she didn't even try. She just shrugged and looked away.

'Right, I'm off. T.C., can you keep our Rosie out of trouble? Either throw her in clink or keep a beady eye on her. Loaded cucumbers and shooting villains; whatever next? I bet Princess Anne doesn't kick up like that.' He swept me into a giant hug, put me down, and was almost out of the door when T.C.'s voice stopped him in his tracks.

'If you find the Widow, Bert, or his whereabouts, make sure that he stays alive long enough to face a judge and jury, won't you? I won't be able to cover for a murder.' He paused. 'And I wouldn't want to. Insane or not, the man deserves a fair trial. It's his right. He's a human being.' T.C. and Uncle Bert held a long, long look, then Uncle Bert left.

T.C. was all business. 'Right, you lot. The cafe's the best place for you to be. Safer than here or at the club because the club's in a basement and either way the stairs are the only way out in case of trouble. I'll escort you all round there.'

It was quite a relief to be back at our corner table in the cafe. I sat close to Auntie Maggie and Sugar and Bandy sat opposite us. T.C. stayed standing. 'Can I borrow Rosie for half an hour, Maggie?' he asked. 'It occurs to me that Hissing Sid or Lizzie Robbins might know where the Cowley woman lives. We can deliver Jenny's books – that'll explain why we're there – and report back on Mrs Robbins. I know you've been worried about her.'

We had to ring the bell several times before Mrs Robbins's head popped out of the upstairs window. 'Oh, er ... hello' was all she managed to say before her head disappeared. A few moments passed and we were just debating whether we ought to lean on the bell when she reappeared. 'Can I help you?'

T.C. beamed his best crinkly smile and held up the bundle of Jenny's school books, all neatly tied up with string, that he was carrying. Each one was carefully covered in bits of wallpaper scrounged from pattern books. It brought a bit of colour and it protected the flimsy exercise books from tears and grime. The war had taught us that it didn't do to waste paper. 'We've brought these for you, Mrs Robbins. May we come up?'

'Oh no! I'll come d–' Once again her head disappeared, a bit sharpish I thought, as if she'd been yanked. It was probably Hissing Sid giving her instructions. This time, T.C.'s finger was actually hovering over the bell when her head reappeared. 'Yes, all right. I'll throw down the street door key. Watch it doesn't land on your head.'

We trudged up the dimly lit stairs, past the little landings with their brown doors, one to each landing. The stairs themselves hugged the other wall. At last we reached the top floor and Jenny's flat. It'd always be Jenny's flat to me.

The door opened a crack and Mrs Robbins's head appeared. I was beginning to wonder if she still had a body and legs to go with it, when they followed it out, a bit reluctantly. She had a large brown paper bag in her hand and she was trying to smile, but you could see it was a strain.

'Hello, T.C. Hello, Rosie love. Thanks for bringing Jenny's books.'

'That's all right, Lizzie.' T.C. crinkled again. 'How are you getting along? Everyone is asking.'

'Oh. You know,' Mrs Robbins said vaguely. She kept trying not to look behind her, but her eyes were darting this way and that. I was just thinking that she reminded me of a jittery bird trying to feed when there's a cat about, when she made me jump by saying,

'Rosie, I've got Jenny's bird food here. I thought you and T.C. might like to go and feed the pigeons in the churchyard.' And she thrust the paper bag at me so hard, it split a little and spilled seed on to the lino. She looked straight at me. Her eyes were frantic, but the rest of her was rigid.

T.C. answered for me. 'Righto, Lizzie. Thank you. Shall we go now, Rosie?' And he took my hand.

I had my gob open to say it was the wrong time of day, and that the birds might not come to us, when T.C. stepped gently on my foot. Mrs Robbins looked relieved and her eyes settled down for a second. We were just turning to go when T.C. turned back. 'Silly of me. Here's Jenny's books; we almost took them away again.' He laughed reassuringly. 'Oh. And one other thing – I nearly forgot. I wanted to ask you if you knew where that Cowley woman lives? I know it's an awful cheek, and I'm sorry to have to open an obviously painful wound, but it would help a great deal if you could tell me.'

Mrs Robbins didn't say a word. She was trying to – I could tell by the way her eyes filled up with tears and her mouth opened and closed – but no sound came except a little whimper. T.C. dropped my mitt, shoved me behind him, a bit roughly I thought, and gently put his arms around Mrs Robbins. He squeezed her tenderly and whispered in her right ear, so quietly I almost missed it. 'You hang on there, Lizzie. Just hang on.'

I thought she would shatter like dropped china but she took a few deep breaths, nodded once and stepped back into the doorway of her flat. She stood there, holding the bundle of books close to her chest, her arms crossed over them as if her life depended on it. Her knuckles were white and sharp as she clutched the tops of her arms. She looked at me, her eyes enormous, with exhausted panda rings like Jenny's, and mouthed, 'Feed the pigeons, Rosie. Please.' And she was gone.

We shot down those stairs and round the corner and stopped by the wall, topped with railings, that separated the little cemetery from Wardour Street. 'What was she trying to tell us, Rosie?' I explained about the signals. 'Right,' he said. 'We can't just barge into the yard, then, in case someone's watching. Do you think you can hunker down and creep along the wall until you can get a good view of the window?'

I nodded and set off. It didn't take long. I crept back again. 'The red scarf's out,' I told him. 'That means "Help".' I was swept off my feet almost as soon as the words were out of my mouth and we charged back to the cafe past a blur of astonished passers-by.

Once through the door I was dumped un-ceremoniously on Auntie Maggie's waiting lap as T.C. panted, 'Telephone?'

'In the kitchen,' Auntie Maggie answered. 'What's the matter?' But he was gone, so I told her, Bandy and Sugar what had happened.

'Time to rally the troops, I think.' Bandy was on her feet and it was only then that I realized she was still wearing her pyjamas and dressing gown. 'Sugar, let's get back to the club. We can call around on our phone and track Joe and Bert down. We have to tell them to stop wasting their time; we've found him.'

I felt a stab of shirtiness at the 'we'. It was T.C. and me that found him! With Mrs Robbins's help, of course.

Everything happened very quickly after that.

'I've got some of the chaps from work turning up outside the Robbinses' place in a few minutes. I'm off to meet them there,' T.C. informed us. 'Maggie, I'm afraid I'm going to have to leave you. A couple of men should be with you for protection very shortly. Meanwhile, don't let anyone in unless you know them and trust them. Can you call some friends?'

We called Sharky, but got no answer.

'Keep trying, Maggie. I must go. Be good, poppet, help your Auntie Maggie. Lock the door behind me.' And with that, T.C. was gone.

Auntie Maggie bolted the door top and bottom. 'Right, little 'un, how about a bite of something to eat while we wait?' She believed in keeping busy and full in times of trouble, so we went into the kitchen and got to work.

36

By the time we were dishing up bacon and eggs on toast in the kitchen, T.C.'s coppers still hadn't come. When we heard a hammering on the front door, we stopped dead and looked at each other. In the end, Auntie Maggie whispered, 'You stand by the telephone, Rosie, just in case it ain't who we're expecting. If I shout NOW, you ask the operator for 999 as quick as you can. Get help. Remember to tell them where we are. Got that?'

I was awestruck. I had never been asked to make a call before. I nodded at her and went to stand by Uncle Bert's chair at the back of the kitchen, right next to the telephone. When I was ready, Auntie Maggie stepped out into the cafe and yelled, 'All right, hold your horses, I'm coming. No need to bash the door down.' There was a bit of a pause and then she shouted back to me, 'It's all right, Rosie, it's Mr Rabinowitz.' And I relaxed. I heard the bolts on the cafe door being drawn and then shot home again, and realized my knees had turned to jelly. I'd thought it was the Widow Ginger! I collapsed into Uncle Bert's chair. Even my hair had been clenched.

Mr Rabinowitz held out a fag packet. 'Mr Bert, I saw him. He sent this.'

Auntie Maggie took the scruffy bit of cardboard. There was a note scribbled on it and she read it out loud. 'With T.C. Don't worry, old girl. No monkey business, I promise.'

She stood quiet for a moment, then started sobbing into her pinny, and fled upstairs. 'I'll be back in a minute. Rosie, eat your grub,' she called out over her shoulder. 'Please sit down, Mr Rabinowitz. I won't be long.'

So I tucked in. What else could I do? Mr Rabinowitz and I found conversation dried up quite quickly between us. He didn't know a lot of English and I only knew the odd work like 'schlep', 'schtum' and, of course, 'nosh' in Yiddish, which didn't take us far. Nobody round our way spoke German. Or if they did, they didn't let on. People were still a bit touchy about German.

I couldn't even offer Mr Rabinowitz

Auntie Maggie's bacon and egg, which was getting colder and yukkier by the minute. Eating anything at all in our place wasn't really kosher for someone as holy as Mr Rabinowitz, so we sat there in silence, listening to me eating and to the ticking of the big clock over the piano.

After what felt like years, but was probably only a minute or two, Mr Rabinowitz excused himself and went into the kitchen for a glass of water. I carried on eating. I'd moved on to Auntie Maggie's plate by then, knowing just how much she hated waste. I'd just finished and was moving behind the counter, empty plates in hand, on my way to the kitchen, when I heard banging and rattling at the cafe door.

I turned and there, to my horror, stood the Widow Ginger. He pressed his face up against the glass in the door and peered in. His hair gleamed and his terrible eyes seemed to linger on me for a moment, but I don't think he really saw me.

His mouth split into a crazed grin, with tiny flecks of froth at the corners. I saw his right hand reach up, and with one thump of his fist the glass in the door shattered near the lock. He reached through the jagged hole and turned the key. Once again, he tried to push the door open, but still it wouldn't give. Thank God for the bolts, I thought, a fraction of a second before I saw him stumble back into the street, then shoulder-charge the door like an all-in wrestler. He came crashing through it and stopped in the middle of the cafe floor, shards of broken glass and splinters of wood from the door frame showered all around him. A sudden hush followed the awful noise.

The Widow Ginger stood absolutely still for a moment. His neat, pale head was cocked to one side as if he was listening. The grin was still fixed to his face, as if nailed there. His quiet suit and shiny shoes looked out of place in the wreckage around him. Into the silence came a steady drip, drip, dripping sound as blood from a cut on the Widow's wrist flowed down his fingers and splashed on to the lino.

His head lifted and turned suddenly, like an animal that had had a whiff of prey on the wind. He saw me, and was across the room and wrenching my arm out of its socket. The plates and cutlery I was carrying crashed to the floor.

I struggled and clawed at his hand as hard as I could. Cursing, he changed his grip to the back of my neck and held me up by the collar. His breath rasped in my ear. My feet were dangling inches from the lino, and I thought my head and lungs would burst if I didn't get my feet on the ground and some air very soon.

Then I heard a terrible, heart-breaking scream, and out of the corner of my eye I saw a skinny black figure scuttle out of the kitchen and launch itself at the Widow's back. The shock made the American drop me. I heard Mr Rabinowitz wail, 'Not the children, no! Not the children. Not this time.' And he hurled himself at the Widow once more like a maddened dog.

The American crashed on to his back among the broken crockery, with the black, spider-like figure on top of him, banging his head on the floor over and over again and wailing pitifully.

I looked round to see Auntie Maggie rooted in the doorway to the stairs, staring blankly at the scene before her, mouth set in a large O.

A pair of gentle arms lifted Mr Rabinowitz off the still and bleeding figure on the lino and deposited him carefully on a chair. 'Get him a drink of water, Shorty,' said Luigi. I did as I was told. When I got back with it, Luigi was checking the Widow over to see if he was still alive. He was.

'Call 999, Shorty. Get them to send the coppers quick and to bring an ambulance with them.' I didn't need telling twice. I wanted the Widow a long way away from me and quickly.

I screeched to a halt at the telephone, all too aware that I was a learner. I'd watched others do it, though, so with a shaking hand I picked up the receiver and waited for someone to talk to me. Once the nice lady at the other end had heard about a bleeding Widow and poor Mr Rabinowitz she put me through to the nick and Smiley Riley.

'Sergeant Riley,' I wailed. 'I want my dad.'

Poor Mr Rabinowitz rocked backwards and forwards moaning gently to himself. His black, unblinking eyes stared at some horror a long way away from our cafe and Old Compton Street, and his skinny black arms hugged himself as he rocked. My eyes filled up with tears as I watched him. Not knowing what to do, I found myself patting his thin shoulder gently and whispering, 'There, there. It will be all right.'

It didn't take long for the cafe to be heaving with people. The police arrived swiftly and in force. Sharky, Madame Zelda and Paulette came from next door and just about the whole world's supply of Campaninis turned up. Uncle Bert, T.C. and Maltese Joe piled in just in time to see the ambulance cart the bloody and still groggy Widow Ginger away. When I saw him lying on that stretcher, between two burly policemen, it struck me that it seemed all wrong that such a neat, slight man could cause so much trouble and fear.

I noticed the Widow's shoes as they poked

out from beneath the grey blanket. They were all bright and shiny with spit and polish as usual, apart from one toecap that had a splodge of blood smeared on it. I took my hanky out of my pocket, spat on it and very carefully rubbed the smear away.

Once I was satisfied, I looked up into the cold eyes of the Widow Ginger, and for a long moment it seemed as if there was just the two of us. And then the spell was broken and they took him away.

37

We were going home! There was a party atmosphere in the little flat in St Anne's Court as we all packed our clothes for the short trip back to our gaffs. It was over! We could have our lives back. Then it hit me how much I was going to miss Sugar and Bandy. Sugar was, as usual, comforting.

'Don't you fret, honey bundles, we'll come to you for breakfasts at weekends and you can come to us,' he assured me as I grabbed a bit of lap time and a cuddle. Being a big man, Sugar was good at cuddles, like a large teddy bear.

Bandy was less cuddly, but just as reassuring, 'Do you think we could *live* without our regular doses of Rosie?' As usual, she didn't wait for an answer. 'Of course not, of course not, you daft gel. The pain au chocolat are on us on Saturday morning. Crack of eleven thirty; don't be late.'

The Widow Ginger was in hospital for a week, closely guarded by policemen day and night. 'Better choose non-smokers,' Bandy said, blowing Passing Cloud smoke rings into the air. 'We don't want that deranged fucker to get his hands on any matches.' I could tell things were getting back to normal because Auntie Maggie tutted and asked Bandy to watch her language. She hadn't done that for ages. Bandy's face split into a huge grin, and she winked a long, slow wink at me and laughed like a drain.

Once it was decided that the Widow was fit enough for prison, he was taken from the hospital to court to be committed for trial. T.C. took me to see him in handcuffs in the dock and to hear the judge telling him that the charges against him were so serious that there would be no bail. Then we stood outside the court to see the Widow bundled into a Black Maria and driven away. Seeing him taken into custody like that did a lot to calm my nerves, as T.C. had hoped it would. I'd had some awful nightmares about the Widow coming back to get us, but they stopped once I'd seen the handcuffs and heard the doors of the Black Maria clang shut behind him.

Later, a lot later, the Widow Ginger was certified insane and committed to Broadmoor, to be held at Her Majesty's pleasure. Which, according to T.C., could mean that he would never be allowed out, not until he died and probably not even then.

Hissing Sid was in big trouble too. It turned out that he had let the Mangy Cow talk him into harbouring the Widow when Kid's place became too hot for comfort. Not only that, but when T.C., his copper friends, Maltese Joe and Uncle Bert had burst into the little brown flat, Hissing Sid had made it his business to get in the way of a swift arrest. That's how come the Widow was in a position to crash through the cafe door. The police didn't like that. They charged him with aiding and abetting and with obstructing the police, and while they were at it they popped him for his dirty books as well.

'Where he's going,' Uncle Bert explained, 'he won't be in a position to pay his usual backhanders to carry on trading, so they might as well get their Brownie points for ridding Soho of one of its grubbier booksellers. It's not as if we're short of 'em.'

Mrs Robbins took a long time to recover. 'After all,' Auntie Maggie told Madame Zelda, Paulette and me, 'the poor woman's lost almost everything. Her child, her marriage. It's really terrible all right.'

It seemed to comfort both me and Mrs Robbins if we met up regularly. She came to the cafe or we went out to the park or the pictures, or to St Anne's Churchyard to feed the pigeons. Once we'd got used to the idea that Jenny was gone and was never coming back, we could think about her without breaking our hearts. Well, not as much, anyway. We began to talk about her a lot as time went on. We enjoyed that more and more because it kept her alive for us, in a way. Funny thing, though, she always stayed a little girl in our conversations, as I grew older and she didn't.

Once things finally settled down again, Mrs Robbins surprised us all by divorcing Hissing Sid and taking a job with Freddie the Frock and Antony. They said she was fabulous behind their counter, and a real asset to their business. You could have knocked me over with a sequin when they told us what a wonderful eye she had for colour. I thought she only knew about brown. It was lovely to see her surrounded by rainbows and sparkles. She bloomed and went from strength to strength. Freddie and Antony simply adored her and wondered how they had ever managed without her. I think she felt pretty much the same about them.

Kid and the Mangy Cow were both

charged along with Hissing Sid, and like him they did a bit of porridge. We never saw either of them again.

Poor Luigi missed Betty for ages and was very quiet by his standards. However, he did finally leave home, and move into Kid's old flat. He amazed everybody by being very good at cooking and cleaning up after himself. Mamma kept sending daughters in to give his place a once-over and they kept reporting back that there was no need. Mamma thought it was against nature, but Auntie Maggie thought it was a jolly good thing.

'Everybody should be able to shift for themselves, even men,' she said firmly and nobody liked to disagree.

If Bandy hadn't told us, we would never have known that T.C. wound up in quite serious trouble with his bosses over his dealings with us during those terrifying weeks. She heard from his guvnor that the powers that be took a dim view of his and Sharky's scheme to ensure that Hissing Sid and the Mangy Cow were made to pay maintenance to Mrs Robbins. Their view was even dimmer when it came to his dealings with Maltese Joe and his associates.

'In fact, the swine are positively blind on that subject,' Bandy told us. 'Bloody nerve, I say, being one of those "associates" myself.'

However, the authorities were unable to

prove anything, because everybody concerned kept their gobs very firmly shut; T.C. was now considered one of our own. He was warned, though, and his prospects for promotion got very slim.

Auntie Maggie taxed him about it during a Saturday morning visit a few weeks after the Widow Ginger finally disappeared behind the walls of Broadmoor. 'Why didn't you tell us you'd landed in the muck at work?'

'Now what would be the point of that, Maggie, my dear?' T.C. replied, giving her the full crinkle. 'You're in no position to talk them round and, anyway, I'm guilty and we all know it. There's no point in whining, because given the same circumstances, I'd do it all again.'

Still, somewhere in the middle of the whole thing, I couldn't help feeling that somehow T.C.'s trouble was all my fault. If he didn't think he was my dad, he probably would have stayed on the right side of the law.

38

T.C. and I were splashing about at the Oasis. We liked the open air swimming bath much better than Marshall Street when the weather was hot and stuffy. We took it in turns to throw the large beach ball as far as we could, then to race after it through the water. T.C. would tell anyone who would listen that I swam like a seal and would stick out his chest with pride and grin like a loony.

When we were finally too puffed to play any more we settled down on our towels in the sunshine. Uncle Bert had packed us a picnic of Spam sandwiches, hard-boiled eggs and fairy cakes. We had a flask of orange juice, and a peach each for afters.

For a while we were too busy munching to say much, but as the drowsy afternoon wore on and we digested our picnic we fell to chatting about this and that. It seemed like the right moment to ask a few questions that had long been troubling me. I took a deep breath.

'T.C.,' I said, looking down at him as he lay with his eyes closed against the glare of the sun.

'Mmm?'

'T.C.' Another pause. I was scared. I wasn't sure I was going to like the answers I might get. Still, it was time I found out for sure. 'T.C., are you my dad?' There, it was out!

I thought he was asleep, he lay so still and so quiet for so long with my question hanging in the air between us. Then he pushed himself up on one elbow and looked at me with a funny sort of smile on his face. He nodded slowly. 'Nobody can be absolutely sure, Rosie, but I think I probably am. Do you mind the idea?'

My heart leaped so hard, I thought it'd choke me. But I was cautious; I had to make sure. 'Do *you* mind?' I asked, hardly daring to breathe.

His face lit up like a box of fireworks all going off at once. 'Mind? Of course I don't mind. I'm as pleased as Punch and as proud as anything, you daft ha'porth, you.'

I landed on him so hard I knocked him flat, and all the puff went out of him. We rolled around and giggled for a bit and then he lifted me off, held me at arm's length and looked at me for a long time. 'But how do you feel about the prospect, poppet? You haven't told me.'

This was the tricky bit, but it had to be said. 'Well. I'm ever so glad, honest, but there is my uncle Bert. I love him like my dad, too, and I could never give him up. Not even for you. Is it all right to love two dads?'

I swear tears oozed into the crinkles around T.C.'s blue eyes. He took me in his arms and pressed his nose into my curls for so long, I was a bit worried he'd gone to sleep, but then he whispered in my ear. 'Of course it's all right to love two dads, as long as one of them is me.'

The publishers hope that this book has given you enjoyable reading. Large Print Books are especially designed to be as easy to see and hold as possible. If you wish a complete list of our books please ask at your local library or write directly to:

Magna Large Print Books
Magna House, Long Preston,
Skipton, North Yorkshire.
BD23 4ND

This Large Print Book, for people
who cannot read normal print,
is published under the auspices of

THE ULVERSCROFT FOUNDATION